PRIDE AND PREMEDITATION

NEVERMORE BOOKSHOP MYSTERIES, BOOK 3

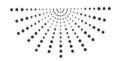

STEFFANIE HOLMES

BACCHANALIA HOUSE

Cover design: Amanda Rose

ISBN: 978-0-9951222-2-2

❀ Created with Vellum

To all the book boyfriends
who keep me up at night.

"The person, be it gentleman or lady, who has not pleasure in a good novel, must be intolerably stupid."
– Jane Austen, *Northanger Abbey*

CHAPTER ONE

"$\mathcal{I}$ have my doubts about the sagacity of this plan," Morrie said as he hitched a pile of pillows under his arm.

"If your sagacity is so offended, you don't have to come with us," I reminded him, tying back my hair and smoothing down the front of my Snoopy pajamas. "You could go back downstairs and finish off that display I started for the Argleton Jane Austen Festival."

"Don't joke, gorgeous. This room has confounded me since I arrived in your world. I won't be tying ribbons around frivolous books while the rest of you discern its secrets." Morrie reached under my shirt and rolled my nipple between his fingers. "Besides which, the opportunity to spend the night with you should never be overlooked."

"Jane Austen isn't frivolous," I shot back, grabbing his wrist and twisting it, so his hand slid off my nipple and I could think straight again. "You shouldn't say things like that around Argleton right now. The whole village has gone Austen-mad."

It was true. Ten years ago, a famous local scholar by the name of Julius Hathaway discovered a record of Jane Austen spending a

1

Christmas at Baddesley Hall, the grandest of the grand stately homes overlooking Argleton, now owned by the Lachlans. Ever since the discovery of their famous temporary resident, the village has celebrated with an annual Regency Christmas festival that has grown ever more elaborate over the years. There were tea parties, dramatic readings, a costume promenade, and a Regency-style dance at the community hall, as well as a book drive where villagers donated reading materials to poor children.

This year, the Lachlans were even hosting the Jane Austen Experience – an academic conference and immersive event where guests paid hundreds of pounds to stay at Baddesley Hall for a weekend, dress up in silly costumes, attend fancy balls and tea parties, and go about proposing marriage to each other. This year, the famous scholar Professor Hathaway himself was the guest of honor.

Of course, Heathcliff wanted nothing to do with the Jane Austen Festival. He rebuffed all my clever ideas – hosting Professor Hathaway for a free public lecture in the World History room, putting together a Pride & Prejudice quiz night, dressing Quoth up in a tiny bird-sized bonnet (actually, Quoth was the one who vetoed that one). Heathcliff's blatant lack of mercantile interest was probably why he'd suggested the eve of the festival to make good on my idea to spend the night in the magical room and attempt to discern its secrets.

"I'll say what I please," Morrie winked at me as he affected a posh accent. His hand slid beneath my shirt again. "You haven't minded before."

No, I don't mind at all. Morrie's lips fluttered along the edge of my neck. His hand cupped my breast, the fingers pinching and teasing my nipple. *If this is any indication of what tonight might offer, the past better watch out—*

"Out of the way, lovebirds," Heathcliff bellowed from his bedroom. A moment later, an enormous brown duvet sailed through his doorway and slammed into the wall above our heads.

I tore myself from Morrie's embrace and leaped away as it slid to the floor to join the large pile of Heathcliff's stuff already piled against the door.

He's hoping we don't emerge again until next week.

"We'd better take this elsewhere, in case Sir Pricklyton starts throwing his whisky bottles." Morrie led me aside, his hand skimming the small of my back in a possessive way that made my heart flutter.

Morrie's lips had barely grazed mine when we were interrupted again. Quoth clattered down from his attic room with his gear. As usual, he wore the minimum amount of clothes – in this case, a pair of black boxers that left nothing to the imagination. I wet my bottom lip. How was I going to survive the night with all three of them without things devolving into a Bacchanalian orgy?

Why did the thought of a Bacchanalian orgy with the three of them make heat pool between my legs?

Remember why we're doing this. Don't get distracted by Quoth's beautiful eyes or Heathcliff's strong hands or Morrie's wandering tongue—

"This is all I need." Quoth handed me a bag of berries. I tucked it into my emergency snacks.

"You sure we should bring along all this gear?" Morrie frowned at the tote bags I'd stuffed with dehydrated food, a camping stove, water bottles, emergency flares, and boxes of tampons. Heathcliff wasn't the only one in Girl Scout mode. "It's not very conspicuous, or very historical."

"There's no telling what we're going to encounter on the other side and how long it's going to take us to get the door open again into the present day. I want to be prepared for anything."

"Agreed." Heathcliff stumbled out of his room. Under one arm, he carried three bottles of whisky and a package of Wagon Wheels. Under the other, a long, pointed sword with an elaborate hilt.

"What are you going to do with that thing?" Morrie frowned

at the sword.

"Roast marshmallows," Heathcliff grunted. He shoved his bottles into my bag, tucked the sword into a scabbard on his belt, and pulled out his key. "Are we doing this or not?"

I nodded. We needed answers, and the only way to find them was to unravel the secrets of Nevermore Bookshop, starting with the room that traveled through time... or something.

Morrie smoothed down the collar of his Armani pajamas. "Which room do you think we'll see on the other side? I propose a wager – the loser has to clean the bathroom. I'm hoping for a Regency boudoir, complete with Edward VII's infamous Le Chabanais sex chair."

"I vote the empty attic," Heathcliff said.

"Of course you do."

"I want Herman Strepel's offices," I added. "But I'm not participating in this bet, because there is no way in Hades you're getting me to even step foot in that bathroom."

"I'm hoping for dinosaurs," Quoth added.

"You're *hoping* for dinosaurs? You're an idiot. Good thing Heathcliff has his sword." Morrie grabbed the key from Heathcliff and shoved it in the lock. I blanched at his insult, although Quoth didn't seem to care. The last couple of weeks, Morrie's comments to all of us – usually friendly teasing – had become more barbed. It was as if he wanted to keep reassuring all of us he didn't really care about us, that he thought himself superior in every way. It was starting to wear me down a little, especially when he did it to Quoth, who never snapped back and seemed to internalize every comment.

The door turned with an ominous click. Morrie stepped back and gestured to the door. "After you, gorgeous. This was your *clever* idea."

Yes, it was. And if it gets us closer to figuring out what's happening in this shop, you'll be thanking me.

I sucked in a breath and pushed the door open.

CHAPTER TWO

*T*he door swung open, revealing an elegant four-poster bed bedecked in rich fabrics and a lounge suite covered in white dropcloths, like ghosts lounging in the window. Heavy velvet drapes hung from every curtain rod, and through an open door on the other side of the bed I made out the edge of the claw-foot bath in the center of the octagonal bathroom. It was the bedroom I'd seen when I first entered this room over a month ago, before I knew what the room really did.

"Phew," I let out my breath. "At least we got a decent bed."

"And no dinosaurs." Heathcliff stalked around the room, using the tip of his sword to lift the drapes and check under the chairs.

"It doesn't look as though robot overlords have taken over the world yet," Morrie said, peeling back the velvet drapes to peer out the window.

"The windows still give us a view of the present day, remember?" Satisfied no velociraptors were hiding under the bed, Heathcliff leant his sword up against the wall. "It's only inside this room where we exist out of time."

"I knew that. I'm not stupid," Morrie snapped. "I judge us to be in the late Victorian era, based on the weave of these drapes."

"Well, aren't we an expert on soft furnishings," I smirked as I went to help Quoth drag our supplies through the door. Morrie was already on my nerves, and the good sensations he'd created in my body while we were waiting for the others had faded completely.

"Meeeow!" As I lifted Heathcliff's duvet, a bundle of black fur bolted out from underneath and dashed between my legs.

"No, kitty!' I spun around in time to see Grimalkin throw herself at Heathcliff's trousers, sinking her claws into his thigh. He roared and grabbed her by the scruff of her neck, hauling her off. *RIIIIP.* Ribbons of his trousers came away with Grimalkin's claws, and probably a not insignificant amount of flesh as well.

I raced across the room and grabbed Grimalkin. She swung her paws in the air, trying to fight me. "We're not putting you in danger. Out you go." I turned to place her back outside, but as I took a step toward the door, it slammed shut.

'Meow!" Grimalkin exclaimed in triumph.

Quoth grabbed the knob and tugged. "It's stuck fast. We're not getting out of here."

"All our emergency dinosaur supplies are still on the other side," Morrie pointed out helpfully.

"And my Scotch," Heathcliff grunted.

I cradled Grimalkin to my chest. "You silly cat. We put out several days of food for you downstairs. I didn't even pack so much as a morsel of fish for you."

Grimalkin purred and nuzzled my cheek, apparently unconcerned about the lack of cat food in our immediate vicinity.

I set Grimalkin down on the windowsill. Outside, the village in the present day wound down for the night. The only people in the streets were stumbling home from the pub. The pale orb of the waxing moon glowed like a streetlight over the thatched roofs and Tudor buildings. Across the street, I could make out a square of light at Mrs. Ellis' window. I hoped she was doing okay. It had been only a few weeks since her close friend Gladys Scarlett had been killed, and her cousin Brenda Winstone was now awaiting trial for murder. Given Brenda's state-of-mind, I suspected she'd end up in psychiatric care rather than prison.

When I turned from the light of the window, my vision blackened. It was as though someone had thrown a blindfold over my eyes. Curiosity gnawed at my stomach. I wanted to search every corner of the room and figure out this mystery. But I could barely see my own fingers wiggling in front of me. I could hear the boys shuffling around, but I couldn't see any of them.

I hate this. I hate being so useless.

From my pocket, I drew a lighter. I lit one of the candles I'd brought with me. I fumbled along the wall to locate the sconce I remembered from last time. The candle slotted in easily, but beyond the faint circle of its light I could barely make out the shapes in the room. I lit another candle and shoved it into a silver holder. I held it up near my face and navigated my way to the bed, listening to the boys as they explored the room from top-to-bottom, searching for clues. *If we'd come in the daytime, I could have searched, too.* But we'd thought it less likely someone from the past would catch us if we stayed the night.

"I found some more candles," Quoth announced from somewhere in the shadows. He came over and lit the candles from my flame, then placed them in sconces about the room. It still wasn't light enough for me to search, but at least now I could make out the figures of my boys and some of the basic furniture shapes. At the small desk, Heathcliff held up a letter to a nearby candle. "You guessed correctly about the period," he told Morrie. "This letter is dated 1896. Do you have another candle, Mina? I'll read through this correspondence. Perhaps it might offer an identity to our room's current occupant."

I fumbled through my bag and found a second candle, which Heathcliff set on the desk beside him. I lit it from my flame, leaning against the edge of the desk to observe him at work. The light illuminated the edges of Heathcliff's face, flickering over his wild beard and dancing eyes. My heart skipped as he bent his head to read, arrested for a moment by his feral beauty.

What answers might we find in this room? All of my boys had been plucked from their novels and thrust into the world, and we still had no idea why. If this room could tell us that, if it could give them answers, then maybe Heathcliff would be able to forgive himself for who he was in his book, Morrie would be able to let go of his need to control everything, and Quoth... maybe Quoth would find the freedom he truly craved.

As I watched my boys, a base hunger rising inside me, another question crowded out the last. *What might happen while the four of us are together and there was only the one bed?*

I know what I wanted to have happen, and also what I was terrified of happening. *If we cross that line together, we can't go back.* And as much as I told myself it was just sex, and it was perfectly fine for me to sleep with whoever I wanted while I mourned the loss of my eyesight, a niggling sensation at the back of my neck and an ache in my chest when I wasn't near the guys suggested my feelings for them were deeper than that. If I had to make deductions, I'd conclude that maybe, possibly...

... maybe I was falling hard. For all three of them.

A grunt from the bathroom distracted me from my thoughts. I stood and thrust my candle into the room. Morrie's shoulders strained as he held up the bath while Quoth fiddled around with the primitive Victorian plumbing. "I'm curious as to where the ancient stops and the modern begins," Morrie explained when he saw me watching.

"I can't see a thing." Quoth set aside the mobile phone flashlight app he'd been using, transformed into his raven, and poked his head down the pipe. "Crooooooak!" he called into the darkness below.

"Hurry up, bird, this bath ain't light," Morrie complained.

Quoth hopped away. He transformed back into a human, clamping his hands over his nose. "It reeks down there."

"What did you see?"

"Not much. It all looks pretty ancient. And disgusting. Whoever owns these rooms has never cleaned out the drain." Quoth went to the jug of water at the wash basin to splash his face.

Leaving them to investigate the rest of the bathroom, I wandered into the closet, running my hands through the racks. Luxurious silk, chiffon, velvet, and linen slid through my fingers. Fine lace and sumptuous trims adorned collars, sleeves, and hems. Bustle pads and fashionable hats adorned with lace, mesh veils, silk flowers and strings of pearls hung from a rack by the window. Victorian fashion was so sensual, so *extra*. I could enjoy the tactile impact of the clothes, even though I couldn't see the colors or shapes.

I pulled a particularly fine silk and damask dress from the racks and held it up against my body. Corset ribs rubbed against my skin. Morrie watched me from the doorway with an evil grin on his face as I twirled around, admiring the way the heavy skirts fanned around my legs. "Isn't it odd that the desk is full of letters and this closet bursting with clothes, yet the chairs by the window are covered up, as though they're not to be used?" I asked.

"Not necessarily," Morrie replied. "This might be a room reserved for guests. Covering the furniture would help to keep it free of dust."

"That's not it," Heathcliff called from the office.

I dropped the dress back into the rack. Morrie offered me his arm. I hesitated. *I can make out the door on my own.* But it was dark and a headache flickered across my temples, the start of one of the migraines that plagued me more and more these days. Biting my lip in frustration, I looped my arm in his, and he led me back into the main room. We passed Quoth at the window, splashing water from my drink bottle over his hands, in a further attempt to wash away lingering drain gunk. I sat down on the bed while Heathcliff read passages from the letters aloud.

"'Dear Madam,'" he intoned, his deep voice reverberating through my body, right down to my toes. "'I hope this letter finds you well. I have enclosed the Works of Francis Bacon, ten volumes in large octavo, bound by J. Johnson of London in calf, gilt titles, and tooling, as you requested. The second has a slight imperfection on the cover, and I have adjusted my price accordingly. If you are compiling a collection of occult materials, I have enclosed a list of additional titles I hold in my possession. I draw your attention in particular to the *Sphere Cabalistice Fatidicis numeris contexte* I have recently acquired – this attractive Cabalist manuscript contains twenty-six leaves of divination tables and lists of animals and birds for augury. If you wish to possess this, please return my letter with haste, for I have two other interested buyers...'" Heathcliff set down the letter. "Most of the letters are of a similar vein, relating to the buying and selling of occult books. This particular missive was addressed to the infamous French clairvoyant, Madame de Thèbes. There are similar such missives between other noted occultists of the era. The woman who lived in this house – one Victoria Bainbridge – was a book dealer. She specialized in buying and selling rare antiquarian occult volumes."

"A basic assessment judged solely through surface details, as to be expected from your savage, lazy mind," Morrie sulked. "Give me the letter. I'll be able to tell you her hair color, sister's middle name, and views on colonialism."

Heathcliff bristled at the word *savage* but didn't rise to Morrie's jab. Instead, he slotted the letter back into the desk. "The Victorian book trade was dominated by men, but Ms. Bainbridge made a name for herself by courting her clientele at the spiritualist gatherings in fine houses and amongst the intellectually curious of the upper classes. It seemed she had to keep a certain standard of living, as she frequently entertained clients at her home. However, from the looks of the ledger here, as she fell on hard times she had to dismiss staff. Likely, she also closed off rooms to lower heating and cleaning costs."

I loved the idea that an enterprising woman lived here in Nevermore Bookshop, making a life for herself using her wit and intelligence.

"According to her latest letter, she's visiting the continent for the winter to peruse the latest volumes of the French spiritualists and escape the inclement weather." Heathcliff set the paper down. "Clever woman. She won't be returning until after Christmas. Hence, I believe, the drop cloths over the furniture, to avoid an excess of dust when she returns."

"Another bookseller," Morrie noted. He shifted beside me, his body twitching with excitement. "This can't be a coincidence."

Heathcliff rubbed his eyes. "Likely not, but I'm too tired to consider it now."

Tired? I was anything but tired. I wanted to know more about this woman. I wanted to pull out every drawer in that desk and try on every fine outfit in her closet. My skin tingled with anticipation. *We're on the cusp of figuring out Nevermore's secrets, I can feel it.*

A hand brushed my leg, and I realized that Heathcliff might have been thinking about bed, but not sleep.

"Yes," I said, my voice catching as my heart pounded in my chest. "We've conducted our search, and it's getting late. I think we should all go to bed."

I pulled back the covers. Heathcliff held up the candle and inspected the bed to make sure it was clean. We had no idea what kind of woman Victoria Bainbridge was and what she did between these sheets. Heathcliff declared the bed safe and I slid in between the covers. Grimalkin bounded across the duvet and nuzzled into my hair.

"Not right now, kitty," I whispered as I untangled her and

dumped her on the floor. She meowed in complaint before scurrying off into the gloom.

"Wise move, gorgeous." Morrie slid in beside me, slipping his arm beneath my head. "We wouldn't want Grimalkin to see what was about to happen."

"What's about to happen?" I demanded, still not sure I wanted him right now, after the rude things he'd said. "You going to insult your friends some more?"

"Only if they get in the way."

Morrie's lips met mine. The kiss seared me inside and out, packed with all the promises he'd been teasing me with all day. I sank into the soft linens as Morrie's hands explored my body, and all his niggling insults and barbed comments faded from memory as his touch lit me up.

I should be stronger... I should make him open up to me... but maybe later...

The bed creaked as Heathcliff climbed in behind Morrie. He'd snuffed all the candles bar one beside the bed, so all I could see was the corner of his head, the flickering light dancing against his wild hair. "Get your feet off my side," he complained to Morrie.

"Sleep on the couch if you're worried about our feet touching," Morrie warned. "Mina and I have plans."

"Don't listen to Morrie. He's being a wanker." I reached behind Morrie and grabbed Heathcliff's wrist, holding him in place. Morrie didn't get to be in charge tonight. I did. And I wanted all of them in the bed with me, even if that meant...

Stop. Don't think about it, or you'll talk yourself out of it.

Quoth's wings fluttered as he flew up to find a perch. His talons scraped about the chamber door. With my free hand, I patted the bed behind me. "Quoth, why don't you come here?"

"Croak!"

"Yes, I'm sure." I flashed him my brightest smile. "I'm *sure*."

Heathcliff tugged at his arm, trying to free himself, but I held fast.

"Turn the light out, will you?" Morrie muttered, his lips trailing along my collarbone.

After checking his sword was within arms' reach should any marauding dinosaur surprise us, Heathcliff blew out the nearest candle, plunging the room into darkness. Quoth fluttered down and landed on the pillow behind me. The bed creaked again as he forced his change, sliding his warm, naked body between the sheets. Between him and Morrie, my skin hummed with heat. I listened hard as Morrie laid trails of kisses along my neck, searching the silence for some sign from the other guys, some clue as to what they were thinking.

Morrie didn't waste time. He clamped his lips over mine, and his hand reached under the waistband of my pajama bottoms, seeking the warmth between my legs. "What are you doing?" I whispered. "Take it slow. Quoth and Heathcliff are right here."

"I know." His voice rumbled in my chest. "Isn't it delicious?"

A hand slid around my torso, pushing up my shirt. Lips pressed into my collarbone. *Quoth.* "Mina," he murmured against my skin.

I still hadn't released Heathcliff's arm. He leaned his elbow into the pillow to bring his face closer to mine. "If this is how it's going to be, Morrie better shuffle his fat arse over."

Morrie swept me beneath him, pinning me to the bed with his body. "Better?"

"Much." Heathcliff tipped my head toward his and claimed my mouth in his. His savage kiss threw me into the tumult of his mind. When Heathcliff kissed, there was no forgetting who he was or the ferocity with which he felt and acted.

My chest constricted. The intensity of the three of them with me, the heat rising from their bodies as they touched me and kissed me and claimed my body, pulled me deeper into their hearts. The room, the bookshop, the unanswered questions, my frustration with my broken eyes and with Morrie's behavior... it all disappeared as they teased and stroked my body.

Heathcliff kicked back the sheets as Quoth gently lifted off my pajama top. Morrie, in a rare display of uncontrolled haste, tore my pants from my legs with such force I heard a seam tear. The air crackled against my bare skin, as though a magic spell weaved us four together.

How is any of this real? I gripped Heathcliff's bicep, certain that at any moment I'd fall through the floor and wake up in my bed back at my mum's flat, and they would no longer be living, breathing men but characters from books, and I never would have been kissed by three beautiful souls who lit my heart on fire.

Heathcliff's kisses drew me back to the present. Of course they were real. Only something real could feel this good. Quoth's fingers danced over my chest – his featherlight touch shooting sparks through my body. His lips pressed against the small of my neck, and his hardness slid between the cheeks of my ass.

Morrie moved down my body, parting my legs. He pressed his lips between my thighs, right on the spot that buzzed with urgent desire. I moaned between Heathcliff's lips as Morrie licked slowly along my slit. He paused over my clit, making me wait, waiting for me to beg. Quoth moved his mouth to my chest, tightening around my nipple.

Three sets of lips on me, kissing, pleasuring, pleading for more. Three sets of lips to drive out my fears.

I tightened my hips around Morrie's head. He took the hint, his tongue lapping at my clit in his slow, gentle strokes, drawing out the ache inside me until it became a fire. Heathcliff deepened the kiss, pouring fire and brimstone straight down my throat and into my chest. My fingers reached down to curl in Quoth's hair. He moaned and scraped his teeth against my nipple.

I came with a shudder that became a wave rippling through my body, pulling me under before dashing my body against the shore of their bodies. Heathcliff's lips slipped from mine as I sank back into the cushions, riding that wave until it crashed over me and ebbed away into a steady, warm hum.

"What do you say, boys?" Morrie asked. "Should we try for one more?"

"I say it's my turn down there," Heathcliff shot back. A wild grin spread across my face. *How is this my life?*

Heathcliff and Morrie swapped places. Morrie pushed my face toward Quoth. "Give the little birdie some love," he whispered, his fingers trailing down my back.

Eagerly, I took Quoth's face in my hands, seeking the solace of his mouth. Quoth's lips on mine were soft, tender, promising that he'd always look out for me. But then Heathcliff's mouth met my clit, his tongue attacking me with all his pent-up aggression, and my back arched and I held Quoth to me, tightening my body against his and mirroring Heathcliff's relentless onslaught.

Behind me, Morrie kissed and stroked my back. Under his fingers, the hairs on my skin stood upright, and warm shivers trickled through my skin. He angled me on my side, and his hands kneaded my thighs and ass. His hardness pressed between my ass cheeks, and his muscles tightened against me, as though he were very close to losing that tight grip on control.

What is Morrie up to?

I didn't have time to ponder, because Heathcliff's nails dug into my thighs and his tongue did this *thing* and Quoth's lips opened and Morrie's grapefruit-and-vanilla scent filled my nostrils and my body exploded. I floated in the dark space between waking and sleep, living in the pleasure until it released my body and I could sink back to earth.

"That's two," I could hear the satisfied smirk in Morrie's voice. "Do you think she'll come again if two of us are inside her at once?"

Excuse me, what?

"I think you'd better discuss that with Mina first," Heathcliff said, a hint of warning in his voice.

"Obviously she's down for it, or she wouldn't have begged all three of us to be in bed with her." Morrie's fingers stroked my ass cheek. "I've been *dying* to be inside her arse ever since she sashayed that pretty thing into the shop."

Oh no, he didn't.

Quoth's arms tightened around me. "Don't let Morrie push you," he whispered.

"Don't worry. Morrie won't be not pushing me into anything, or putting *anything* inside me, the way he's acting right now." I scrambled up in the bed to face Morrie. Quoth's arms still held me tight. "As the owner of said arse, I'm weighing in. You don't get to—"

"What the hell do you think you're doing?"

A sharp voice broke through the darkness. Heathcliff sprung off me. Quoth's arms tightened around me, pressing me into himself as though his body would shield me. Morrie, of course, rolled over as though he had all the time in the world.

"I sleep in that bed," the voice snapped. A match flickered in the gloom. A moment later, a candle revealed a stern woman with a face like boiled cabbage. Behind her, Heathcliff lunged for his sword.

"Heathcliff, don't!" I cried, just as his hand slid around the hilt and he swung the weapon at her head. The woman ducked under the blow, grabbed Heathcliff's arm and twisted it around herself, applying pressure to his elbow until his fingers unlocked and he dropped the sword. Quoth yelped in fright. Feathers exploded across the bed as he shifted, swooping up to perch above the door.

"I learned that particular trick from Algernon Blackwood," she said, a note of triumph in her voice.

Morrie clapped. "Brava!"

The woman straightened up, dropping Heathcliff to the floor, where he landed with a *THUD*. She picked up the weapon and swung it through the air. "This is a fine blade. Under the circumstances, I think I shall keep it. If he had told me you would use my boudoir for bacchanalian rituals and try to cut my head off, I wouldn't have delayed my trip to Paris to meet you."

Paris trip? I gasped as I made the connection. "You're Victoria Bainbridge, the occult bookseller."

She swept the candle over the bed, no doubt taking in our state of undress. "I am a *dealer*, thank you very much. A dealer who shall now have to burn her bedsheets and hire my dear friend Mr. Crowley to cleanse this space," she declared. "I've half a mind to send you a bill to replace the sheets. What on earth possessed you to carry on in such a manner, given the gravity of the situation?"

"What situation? Who told you to come back for us?" Heathcliff demanded. "Who knew we would be here?"

"Is your friend *Aleister* Crowley? Did he tell you we'd be here?" Morrie said. "I've always been interested in meeting him."

"Heavens no. Aleister would never get mixed up in this. He'd not wish to risk leaving his disciples in another century. I cannot tell you who forewarned me of your visit. The names of my clients are strictly confidential. You will not learn the time-traveler's name from me. You are the girl Wilhelmina, correct?"

"How do you know my name?" I scrambled around for my Snoopy top and pulled it on.

Victoria went over to the desk. I heard her slide out a drawer and pop something open.

"Heathcliff, you missed a hidden drawer," Morrie said. "I wouldn't have missed the hidden drawer."

"Go to hell, Morrie."

Victoria leaned across the bed and waved something in front of my face. A small, white envelope. "Take it. He left it for you."

"Who?" I demanded.

"Your father, of course."

17

CHAPTER THREE

I snorted. "I think you have me mixed up with someone else. My father was a useless waste-of-space petty criminal in *my* century who walked out on my mum right after I was born. He left me nothing except bitterness and deteriorating retinas."

"You believe I have mistaken you for some other time-traveling girl named Wilhelmina with two rude men and a raven as companions?" Victoria smirked. "Take the letter. Perhaps there is more to your past then you have been led to believe."

The paper slid between my fingers. *Am I really holding something from my father?* This didn't make any sense. We'd entered this room looking for answers, but I never anticipated *this*.

"Now." Victoria smoothed down the front of her corset. "Since I see you've ransacked my desk and upended my bath, I can assure you there are no further clues to be found in my boudoir. If you could vacate my home at the earliest opportunity, I'd be most grateful. My client explained to me something called the ontological paradox. I'd hate for you to accidentally squash a spider and start the great spider/human war of your time."

"Just in case, I'd like my sword back." Heathcliff held out his hand, but Victoria dangled the blade out of his reach.

"How do we get back to our own time?" Morrie asked. "We can't get the door open."

"Wait until morning." Victoria sighed and slunk into the darkness. "When he visited me, he always had to wait until morning. At one time I believed he meant it merely as an excuse to stay with me, but he assured me it was part of the room's magic. I guess I shall have to sleep in my chair."

"Meeeoorrww!" Grimalkin cried.

Victoria leaped to her feet. "I see my chair is already occupied."

I tried to slide out of bed, but Morrie's body weighed me down. "We shouldn't steal your bed. The guys and I will take the chairs—"

"Meeerrw!" Grimalkin sounded indignant.

"I insist," Victoria said. "After what you've been doing between those sheets, I do not wish to touch it. You may as well enjoy it for the rest of the night. However, your feline friend will have to join you."

Grimalkin meowed as Victoria deposited her on my feet. The candlelight bobbed across the room. A sofa creaked as she threw back the covers and settled herself in. A moment later, the light flickered out.

"You heard the lady." Morrie's hand snaked around my chest again.

I threw him off. "You can't seriously be thinking about that now?"

"Yes, yes I can."

"Morrie, get off me. Aside from the fact that I'm holding a letter from my father and a Victorian book dealer is sleeping on the sofa three feet from the bed, so I have *other shit on my mind*, I'm angry with you."

"Have I done something to offend?"

20

I snorted. "I'm not talking about this now. But when we get back, I'll write you a list."

"I look forward to it," Morrie snapped in a hurt tone. He turned over and yanked the blanket around him, leaving me with a tiny corner and Quoth with nothing at all.

Quoth leaned over the bed, back in his human form. His hand settled over mine. "Mina, if we light the candle, I could read the letter for you."

My heart pounded. My fingers itched to hand it over. I desperately needed to know what it said. But I drew my hand back and shook my head. "I appreciate that, but I think I need to read it for myself. Which means there's nothing else to do but wait for morning."

"I can think of plenty to do," Morrie pouted. But he didn't turn back around or throw himself at me. He did, however, relinquish another foot of blanket.

I slid back down under the covers, all thoughts of sexy times fleeing my mind. Quoth slunk away into the gloom, and I heard the flutter of feathers as he shifted back. Heathcliff slid in the other side of me, draping his arm across my chest, steadying and protecting me with his bulk. My fingers traced the edges of the envelope. What did it contain? How was *my father* connected to Nevermore Bookshop?

Beside me, Heathcliff snored, his beard tickling my shoulder. The steady rhythm of Morrie's breath caressed my skin. Only Quoth remained awake, high on his perch above the door. His eyes captured moonlight, piercing the gloom as they fixed on mine. We regarded each other.

Sleep, Mina, he said. *I'll watch over you.*

But I couldn't sleep. Not with Victoria Bainbridge whistling through her nose on the couch, Grimalkin's tiny body purring against my foot, the strange-but-familiar house creaking and groaning, and the edges of the envelope resting against my fingers. I stared at the ceiling, my eyes grasping for some visual clue that never came. I went over the information we'd uncovered so far. But all it brought was more questions than answers.

My father came back in time to purchase books from Victoria and leave a note for me. But how did he know I would come here one day? Mr. Simson told the guys to watch out for me and that I was in danger. Was he trying to protect me from my father? Were they working together somehow? This building has been related to the book industry for a thousand years. Why? What about before Herman Strepel's time? What was Nevermore Bookshop then? And how did it come to have these magical abilities? How long have fictional characters been appearing? How long has this very room been a portal through time? Is Mr. Simson a fictional character? Is he my father?

Outside, the sun rose over the village. Shop bells jingled. Lorries rumbled around the village green on their early morning deliveries. I rubbed my eyes, wishing the gloom would lift so I could see. But I would need the sun to be full in the sky and several more bright lamps before I could make out much of this room. The church bells tolled the hour. The door creaked open, revealing the hallway in the flat with all the lights still blaring, and our emergency equipment piled against the wall.

Grimalkin stood up, stretched out her body in a cat-yoga pose, then trotted back through the door.

I flung myself out of bed. "Let's go!"

On the couch, Victoria startled. "Young lady, you might attire yourself properly before you leap about in fits of excitement!"

My cheeks burning, I grabbed my pajama bottoms from the floor, picking up a handful of the guys' clothes and tossing them at the bed. Morrie yawned and slid out of bed, completely naked, his cock bouncing in front of Victoria's face. "It's been a pleasure."

"Indeed." Victoria's lips curled back into a sneer so terrifying, Morrie's cock grew soft under its power. He winced as he ducked his head under the door. Ancient builders never made doorways for someone of Morrie's height.

Heathcliff pulled his clothes on under the covers and slid out of bed. Quoth fluttered down and perched on my shoulder as I stepped over the bags. "Thank you for my letter, Victoria," I said. "I really appreciate—"

"Sword." Heathcliff held out his hand.

"Goodbye, Wilhelmina." Victoria gripped the hilt close to her and grinned back at us. Heathcliff looked ready to fight her for it. I shoved him toward the door. "Next time we meet, you'll be covered in blood."

"Wait, what do you mean by—" I didn't get to finish my sentence before the door slammed in my face.

"Hey." I banged my fist on the door. "Hey, Victoria? What did you just say? Why am I covered in blood? *Whose blood is it?*"

"Relax, gorgeous. As long as it's not your blood, or my blood, who cares? I need coffee," Morrie yawned.

"You'll have to buy it yourself." I shoved him toward the living room. "Because I'm going to read this letter and I don't want your shitty attitude anywhere near me while I do it—"

My words died in my throat.

In the middle of the hallway stood a teenage girl, tall and slim with a fair complexion and brown hair curled into luscious locks around her face. But what was unusual about her – apart from the fact she was standing in the flat, which was supposed to be locked and empty – was what she wore: a white muslin dress with an empire waist that stretched to the floor, white gloves extending above her elbows, and a lace-edge bonnet hanging askance around her neck. I hadn't been following the latest fashion trends since I left New York City, but I wasn't aware that empire gowns and bonnets were back in style.

"Pardon me, handsome sirs." The girl rushed toward us, picking up the hem of her dress as she stepped over our belongings. She elbowed me in the side as she rushed to Morrie and grabbed his arm. "I was on my way to London with a most delicious paramour. He has declared his undying love for me, and everything's just wonderful! Our coach stopped in the town for lunch, and I seem to have taken a wrong turn. A rather wrong turn, judging by the shabby nature of your establishment."

"If you're looking for the rest of the Jane Austen fruitcakes, they're on the town green or up at Baddesley Hall," Heathcliff muttered. "Now, get out."

Of course. This was probably one of the festival guests, unable to find the country lane that led up to Baddesley Hall. "Let's not be rude. I'm sorry you got lost. If you tell us what event you're supposed to be at, Morrie will take you where you need to go. Do you need a cup of tea first? It's awfully cold outside." Snow and wind hit the windows in icy sheets, although I noticed the girl's dress was dry.

"Thank you, but I've already made myself quite at home." The girl gestured to the living room, where the coffee table was buried under a stack of empty teacups and a half-eaten box of Wagon Wheels. Sticky chocolate fingerprints covered the arm of Heathcliff's chair.

Heathcliff shoved his way past her and launched himself at his chair. "Your bloody arse has ruined it. It took me years to get this chair just the way I liked it. Didn't you read the sign?" He glowered at our visitor. "No customers upstairs."

I turned to Heathcliff. "If you'd let me hang that illustrated map of the festival in the shop window, this wouldn't be a problem."

"It's unbecoming for a lady to gloat over her perceived victories, especially when they are at the expense of such a worthy gentleman." The girl batted her eyelashes at Heathcliff. When he scowled and looked away, she turned her attention to Morrie. "Ah, I see you are the gentleman of this group."

"Yeah, Mina. No gloating. We can't turn away a damsel in distress. We'll call you a rideshare as soon as we get downstairs, ma'am." Morrie clasped his hand over hers, flashing her his brilliant smile. His eyes darted to mine, daring me to protest.

What's he doing? Why is he acting so childish?

"Pardon? I don't understand. What is this rideshare? Is it the name of your horse? How are you rich enough to afford to keep a carriage? Are you foreigners? Your clothes are frightfully odd." She inclined her head. "My name is Lydia Bennet, soon to be Lydia Wickham. I'm looking for my fiancé. Have you seen him?"

CHAPTER FOUR

"*L*ydia Bennet?" My words dried on my tongue. I rubbed my side where her sharp elbow had caught me. "As in, Lydia from *Pride and Prejudice?*"

She squinted at me. "Did your mother drop you on your head? I said my name was Lydia Bennet, and I had no reason to lie about such things. As to your other insult, I have neither excessive pride, unless it be upon the handsomeness of my Wickham or the bonniness of my curls, nor unwanted prejudice! Since I have no reputation to speak of in this backward county, it could not have proceeded me. Yet you speak as if you know my name."

"Ssssh," Heathcliff snapped. "She doesn't know who she is yet."

Of course. This truly was Lydia Bennet, just as Heathcliff *was* the swoon-worthy hero of Wuthering Heights and Morrie *was* the Napoleon of Crime and Quoth *was* the bird who beguiled Poe's sad fancy into smiling. The bookshop's other power – apart from the room that traveled in time – was to occasionally bring characters from novels into the real world. That was how I ended up with my three guys. Until now, I'd only heard about the others

– this was the first time I'd actually been present while it happened.

And for that fictional character to be Lydia Bennet, *the* Lydia Bennet – perhaps the most famous spoiled brat ever to grace the pages of literature – and for her to arrive during the Jane Austen Christmas festival just after we exited the bedroom… like Morrie always said, I didn't believe in coincidences.

If I was being honest, I wasn't that fussed with Jane Austen. Sure, her skill with witty conversation and satirical lampooning of the concerns of the upper class was second-to-none, but there weren't nearly enough dead bodies, exciting mysteries, or – Darcy aside – swoon-worthy passionate heroes for my liking.

But that didn't mean the prospect of getting to know Lydia wasn't exciting. Provided she didn't keep clinging to Morrie and shooting me that possessive look.

If Morrie was in the least bit as shocked as I was, he didn't show it. He swept up Lydia's hand in his and gestured toward the living room. "If you'd like to come with us, Miss Bennet, my friend and I shall explain everything."

She giggled. "I'll come with you to the ends of the earth, sir, if your friend consents to accompany us. Oh, what fun we shall have!"

I smiled as Lydia slipped her other hand through Heathcliff's arm and led them boldly down the hallway. How quickly she'd forgotten her 'dear Wickham'!

"Croak!" Quoth said, his tone disapproving.

"Exactly," I agreed.

At least Lydia's presence got Morrie out of my hair for the moment. As soon as they were out of sight, my mind flew again to the letter. I collapsed into Heathcliff's chair, fortified by the smoke-and-spice scent of his body that had been woven into the fabric. Quoth fluttered down to rest on the chair arm. He used his beak to push over the arm of the reading lamp.

I turned on the lamp to light a circle across my lap and tossed aside a stack of books and yesterday's *Argleton Gazette* with the sensational headline ARGLETON JEWEL THIEF STRIKES AGAIN! on the front page. I held the envelope close to my face, studying it from every angle. It was square, made of a thick card-stock that felt rough to the touch – homemade or recycled paper. On the front, my name was written in a cursive font with flicked ends that looked oddly familiar, although I couldn't place the writing now. It was sealed with wax.

My hand trembled. I stared at my name for what felt like an age, my heart fluttering. I couldn't reconcile this fine envelope and fancy handwriting with the sperm-donor who'd run out on my mother. For my entire life, I'd thought my father was a lowlife criminal who abandoned us. Mum never spoke of him, and she'd evaded every question I ever asked. I only knew the bare details of their relationship – she didn't want me to grow up surrounded by criminals, so she and my Dad ran away to Argleton. When he couldn't find honest work, he left us, and he'd never bothered to try and contact us. Mum had never even shown me a picture of him. To me, he was a ghost.

This letter made him real.

Quoth tapped the seal with his beak, twisting his head so his brown eyes regarded mine. Fire flared at the edges.

Whatever that letter contains, you can handle it, he spoke inside my head.

"I guess we'll find out," I said, slipping my finger under the wax and breaking the seal.

I pulled out a single sheet of paper, thinner than the envelope but of the same rough, handmade quality. It was folded into quarters, the edges neatly trimmed and filled with a hand-drawn ink border of leaping animals and tiny men carrying swords and shields. A few of the animals ran over the edges of the border, as though they were too wild to be contained. A date in the top corner set the letter about a year after I was born. That date had been crossed out, and another date written beside it. But that had been so rigorously scrawled through that I had no hope of reading it.

I sucked in a breath, and began to read:

My dear Wilhelmina,

I have left this message with Victoria for you to uncover on your visit. I have placed copies with Mary (in 1741) and Henrietta (in 1220), in case I was mistaken about the date you stepped through the bedroom door. When one is talking about time travel, it pays to be thorough.

This done, I will be leaving you.

It is not my wish to abandon you, but it is a father's duty to keep his daughter safe. My enemy has made his move, and in the great game of chess we two play, it is now my turn. As long as he knows nothing of your existence, you remain safe.

Know that I will always love you, and you and your mother are forever in my heart. For as long as you remain in the protection of Nevermore Bookshop, he cannot harm you. But you must be careful. You are, after all, my daughter.

All my love,

H

I stared at the words until they lost all meaning, until they were just scratches of ink on the page. Even then, scratches made more sense. Quoth nuzzled my hand. I stroked the frill of feathers around his neck with trembling fingers.

My father was somehow connected to Nevermore Bookshop. Before he left my mother, he'd gone into the room upstairs and left a note for me in three different time periods.

But why?

A million questions danced around in my head. *Who is this enemy? What does he want with my father, and why would he go after me?*

Is he somehow connected to what Victoria said, about me being covered in blood the next time she sees me?

Why did this letter read like an intelligent, articulate man on the run from some kind of trouble? That didn't at all match the image of my father as a drug-addled small-time criminal who ran out on his family because he didn't want the responsibility.

What do you need? Quoth asked me.

I folded the letter and shoved it in my pocket. My head spun and pain throbbed across my temples. A lime-green neon light flicked across my vision. *Please, no fireworks right now.*

I didn't know what I needed. Right now, Lydia Bennet was downstairs, Morrie was being a wanker, my eyes were getting worse, I hadn't figured out how I felt about the guys and what *almost* happened last night, and the village was overrun with Jane Austen fans. I needed to not think about *this*.

I rose from the chair, steadying myself with the arm of the lamp and holding out my elbow so Quoth could hop on. I picked up the newspaper, showing him the headline about the jewel thief. I skimmed the text. According to the article, five stately homes in the area had been burgled in the last month. In each burglary, the only thing taken was jewelry. There were no signs of forced entry, and many believed the jewelry may have been missing for weeks or months before the thefts were noticed. *Imagine being so rich you didn't know when some of your priceless gems went missing.*

The police asked anyone with information to come forward and warned residents to report any jewelry theft. *Interesting.* Immediately, my mind whirred through possibilities. *It has to be someone who had access to the houses, like cleaning staff or a corgi groomer...*

Mina, if we could return to the letter of the moment... Quoth hopped along my arm. *What do you need?*

I grinned. "I need to solve a mystery, one that doesn't involve my life. What do you say, Quoth? It's no murder, but catching a jewel thief might be just what I need."

Inside my head, a raven sighed.

CHAPTER FIVE

"Oh dear. It's all very strange." Lydia sat in the window seat opposite the Classics shelves where she had first appeared. She waved a fan in her face. It was difficult to tell under her makeup, but she looked pale and frightened, although she hid it well with her pouting expression. "I don't much enjoy books, and to discover I am a character in one is a horrible tragedy!"

"You'll get used to it," Morrie cooed. "You'll also find many things about this world to be an improvement over Longbourn. For one thing, the takeout food is infinitely better. Have you ever had a rogan josh? It's *divine* – the food of the gods."

"You mean to tell me I won't see my Wickham again? Or my parents or sisters? I admit that Mary's a frightful bore, but I will probably miss Kitty. And how am I to keep myself? I have no money with me, no fortune of my own." She cast a critical eye between Morrie and Heathcliff. "I see no wedding bands. You are both bachelors, and handsome enough. One of you must do the honorable thing and marry me. I demand it!"

Yup, Lydia's really cut up about losing her beloved paramour.

"You don't need a husband in this world," I said. "This thing called feminism happened, and now women are able to make their own living and choose their own future. We can have a career and make our own money, so we don't need husbands—"

"Women have no husbands? They have *jobs?* What nonsense is this?" Lydia's shriek shook the window panes. She waved her gloved hands in front of my face. "These fingers are not made for labor! They are for sensuous caresses of my husband's shoulders and slapping the cheeks of impertinent servants!"

"We also don't have servants anymore—"

"No servants? You cook your own meals and turn down your own beds?" Lydia fanned her face, her expression what could only be described as 'aghast'. "I've been in this world but two hours and already I long to return to the mediocrity of Longbourn!"

"That's not possible, so get used to it." Heathcliff's patience had already worn thin.

"You *can* have a husband if you want one," I said, trying not to give her the wrong idea. "It's just that you don't have to think about it now. Most people wait until they're older. You're only sixteen, right? You could go to school and—"

"Who wants to go to school? I've had quite enough of books from my sister Lizzie. I *shall* have a husband. If Wickham is lost forever, then one of you shall have to step up. But which will it be? I shan't like to live in this dingy house, and a shopkeeper's living will not keep me in the manner in which I intend to become accustomed. So Mr. Heathcliff is out of the question." With a wave of her hand, Lydia disregarded literature's greatest romantic hero and turned her gaze to the criminal mastermind. "You, then, Mr. Moriarty. What sort of fortune do you command?"

Morrie laughed. "Darling, I think you're a little young for me."

"I'm not too young, and I am already out."

"Out? Out where?"

"Out in society, you fool. You may be handsome, but you're

terribly simple." Lydia smirked at me. "No wonder Mina here has no clue how to dress like a lady."

I stared down at the Misfits hoodie I'd hastily pulled over my pajama bottoms. "What's wrong with this outfit?"

The shop bell tinkled. "Bloody hell," Heathcliff yelled at Morrie. "I told you to flip the sign while we dealt with this!"

"But where's the fun in that?"

"Don't worry." I held up my hands. "I'll deal with it."

"Please," Morrie clasped his hands to his chest. "Don't leave me alone with her."

"Sorry. She's your future wife and your responsibility. Me and my unladylike attire have to go and do our job." I shut the door to the Classics room in Morrie's face and strolled into the hallway to meet our customer.

"Cynthia, hello." I plastered on the biggest smile as I recognized Cynthia Lachlan, member of the infamous Banned Book Club and wife of big shot developer Grey Lachlan. I hadn't seen Cynthia since the unfortunate day her friend Gladys Scarlett died of arsenic poisoning right here in the shop. "Welcome back to Nevermore Bookshop. What can I do for you today?"

"Mina, you're exactly the woman I wanted to see," Cynthia gushed, grabbing my hands in hers and squeezing my fingers. Her wrists jangled with gold bracelets. "I came by to thank you again for cracking poor Gladys' murder. Grey and I would still be locked up in that rotten police cell if it weren't for you."

Because Cynthia and her husband (who I'd never managed to meet) stood to gain by Gladys' death, and Grey had access to arsenic through his construction contacts, the police had them in custody under suspicion of Mrs. Scarlett's murder until I solved the case for them. "Please, there's no reason to thank me. I wanted to find out the truth and—"

"Nonsense. You've done me a good turn, and I want to make sure you have compensation." Cynthia fished around in her purse and pulled out an envelope. "I know how much you love books and reading. We're hosting the first Argleton Jane Austen Experience at Baddesley Hall. You might've heard about it?"

"A little bit, yes." I choked back a laugh. Mrs. Ellis had been talking about nothing else for the last week. According to her, the Lachlans spared no expense for their extravagant event. The VIP tickets cost thousands of pounds each and included accommodation at the house and cuisine from a Michelin-star chef they flew in from Paris.

"Tickets sold out months ago, of course. But there are certain privileges to running the event." Cynthia pressed the envelope into my hand. "Grey and I would be honored if you and your three lovely friends would attend the Jane Austen Experience as our VIPs. These tickets will get you an all-access pass to all the events, a beautiful suite with two double rooms at Baddesley Hall for the weekend, meals, and a seat at our table for the ball on Saturday night."

"Oh, um..."

"A ball?" A voice called from the end of the hall. Lydia stood in the doorway to the main room, her empire-waist dress sweeping the floor as she jumped up and down with glee. "It's not yet the season of course, but I will acquiesce to attend."

Mrs. Lachlan's eyes widened. "You look as though you're dressed for the ball already, ma'am. Do you not already have a ticket?"

"Who needs a ticket to a private ball? One is either invited or they aren't," Lydia glared at me. "Considering you've cruelly pulled me into your world from one where I would marry the delectable Wickham, this is my best opportunity to secure a husband—"

"This is Lydia, ah... Wilde," I said, thinking fast, as Cynthia peered at Lydia with curiosity. "She's my second cousin. Her parents sent her over for the Christmas holidays to enjoy the festival. She's French, you know, so she's a little..." I made a motion that Cynthia might interpret in a myriad of ways.

"I'm not French." Lydia stamped her foot. "How dare you say such a thing!"

"I told you," I winked. Cynthia nodded and stepped away. She pointed at the envelope in my hand. "I didn't know you had family visiting. I'm afraid I have only four tickets available..."

Lydia scurried forward and grabbed the envelope. She pulled out one of the tickets. "This one's mine. What you do with the rest is your business."

I peered in the envelope at the three remaining tickets. My hand thrust into my pocket, touching the edge of my father's letter. *We just got this big potential clue about the mystery of Nevermore Bookshop, and that something in the future is going to be bloody, and my father is somehow mixed up in it. Is it really the time to spend a weekend away?*

But then I thought about how weird Morrie was being lately, and how maybe it was to do with being shut up in the shop, and how the tension that held Heathcliff together relaxed when he was outside, in the fresh air, and how Quoth hid away in the attic with his paintings and his beautiful sad eyes.

And I couldn't escape the idea of all those rich people with their fancy jewels, all the extra staff, all the people coming and going... the perfect hunting ground for the Argleton Jewel Thief. No way was the burglar going to pass up this opportunity.

As much as I wanted to sit in the bookshop and figure out why my father was sending me notes from the past, and why Victoria had seen me covered in blood, I also wanted to... *not* think about it. Because my head was already a mess. I still hadn't told Heathcliff or Morrie about seeing the neon lights. And when I did... Nevermore would no longer be an escape from my problems. I wasn't sure I was ready to face any of it – my dad, my eyes, my feelings for the guys – yet.

Maybe getting out of Nevermore for a few days would help me prepare, and it might sort out Morrie's bad attitude. That is, if Lydia didn't force him to marry her.

Cynthia glanced from Lydia back to me. "So you'll come?"

Behind her, Heathcliff poked his head through the door and made a throat-slitting motion with his hand. I beamed at him and swiped the three tickets. "Thank you, Cynthia. We wouldn't miss the Jane Austen Experience for the world."

CHAPTER SIX

"*W*hat are we going to do about *her?*" Morrie hissed. The four of us huddled around the flat's blazing fire. Outside the window, light snow fluttered past the window on its way to blanketing Argleton in fluffy holiday ambiance. Empty takeaway containers from the Curry House littered the table, and the air was thick with the scent of rogan josh and Irish coffee.

In case we hadn't figured out to whom he referred, Morrie jabbed his finger at his desk chair, where Lydia slouched, squealing with glee as she punched the keys with a single finger.

"I did it!" she cried. "Lord Moriarty, I have created my first *social media profile.* Look at all the men who've inquired about my friendship already! This is infinitely easier than waiting for Daddy to introduce himself to the eligible men in the neighborhood. I wonder if I can talk to some soldiers..."

The floor at Lydia's feet was littered with empty soft drink cans and chocolate bar wrappers. She'd spent the whole day demanding Morrie (or Lord Moriarty, as she now called him) acquaint her with the pleasures of modern living. After an exhaustive lesson in electricity and microwave popcorn, she dragged Morrie outside and demanded he order her a rideshare 'carriage' so she could experience the wonders of the automobile. They drove off into the countryside and returned with five bags of junk food and a very subdued master criminal. Now Lydia swiveled around in the chair, her eyes sparkling. "Lord Mooooorrrriarty, this man named Ahmed has sent me a letter. Oh, it appears to be some sort of portrait. I wonder if he's handsome..."

"Click the envelope icon and find out," Morrie said with a sigh. "None of our other fictional visitors have been this exhausting."

"Your charge has settled in nicely," Heathcliff said.

"She's not mine," Morrie shot back.

"You might want to tell her that, *Lord Moriarty*," Heathcliff sneered.

"She insisted that if my bank account was as bloated as I claimed, I must have a title!"

Lydia frowned at the screen. "That's not a portrait! It appears to be some kind of wrinkled sausage. But why would this man feel the need to share a likeness of his meat with me?"

I snorted. Lydia had just become the first Bennet sister to receive a dick pic. She had much to learn.

"Apparently, I'm to be *her* escort for this ridiculous weekend," Morrie declared, pinching his temples as if he fought off a headache. "Perhaps I can arrange a convenient suicide."

"Come on, *Lord Moriarty*. it'll be fun," I beamed, even as my own headache flared at the edges of my skull. In the corner of the room, a neon-green light wiggled across the darkened edges of my vision.

"Fun?" Morrie picked up the brochure and read from the list of activities. "What's fun about a costume promenade, or a hat-making workshop, or a lecture on sex and sensuality... no, actually, that one does sound intriguing."

"That's the keynote given by Professor Julius Hathaway." I

pointed to the man's picture over Morrie's shoulder. "He's the historian who first discovered Jane's connection to Argleton. Apparently, he's a bit of a celebrity to the Janeites."

"Janeites?" Morrie's lips curled back in a sneer.

"It's the affectionate term for Jane Austen fans." I directed his attention to a glossary on the back page of the brochure. "Apparently, Janeites walk, talk, dress, and live Austen. The only thing they hate more than movie adaptations with inaccurate costuming are Brontians – those are fans of the Brontë sisters—"

"I deduced that," Morrie said snippily. "I don't need you to explain every little thing. Sex lecture aside, you still haven't convinced me why I should deign to attend."

"Because I want you to. That used to be enough."

"I'm not so blinded to your charms that I follow you like a puppy," Morrie declared. "Or like a raven."

Quoth, who sat cross-legged on the floor beside my chair, his head resting against my leg and a sketchbook open in his lap, stiffened at Morrie's words. I resisted the urge to call him out. Morrie wouldn't give ground and speak of his feelings in front of the other guys, and especially not in front of Lydia. If I wanted the truth from him about his recent rudeness, I'd need to get him alone. And resist his kisses for long enough to draw an answer from him. Neither of those things was going to be easy.

I tossed the newspaper in Morrie's direction. "Fine. How about an appearance by the Argleton Jewel Thief? With all the rich guests, I bet he'll be tempted to show up. If you want something to engage your intellect, we might try to smoke him out, provided your ego hasn't swelled so big you can no longer fit through the doors."

From the desk, Lydia snorted. "That was a truly impressive slander, Mina. I shall have to remember it for future interactions."

Morrie's eyes scanned the article. "Intriguing."

"So not your work, then?" Heathcliff's eyes sparkled. "I was certain these jewels might soon adorn Lydia's thin neck."

"Not me." Morrie tossed the paper on top of the empty cartons. "Okay, I'll go. But I'm not dancing with Lydia."

"Yes, you are!" Lydia shrieked. "I must show you off at the ball, or I won't be able to make any of the other men jealous. You are integral to my plans."

"Let Lydia show you off on the dance floor," I grinned. "I can't very well show up with more than one date, and I'm already taking Heathcliff."

"What?" Heathcliff glowered. "No, you're not."

"I've a fourth ticket in my pocket that says otherwise."

"Not doing it. I'd have to close the shop over the long weekend, and as you've helpfully pointed out, with all these Jane Austen freaks in town, business is booming. All that is beside the fact that there's not a bribe on earth large enough to make me wear a cravat or listen to doddery old professors talk about stockings. Give the ticket to Quoth. He's a bird. They love fanning their plumage and hopping around for ludicrous mating rituals."

I glanced at Quoth, and he nodded. "Quoth and I already discussed it. He doesn't feel comfortable with all the people that are going to be there. He'll stay here and tend the shop, and Jo's promised to come in and help as well. Quoth will visit us in our room at the Hall in the evening and he might join me for some of the lectures if one of you will lend out your lanyard. But I need a date for the ball and you're it."

"Is there any chance of me getting out of this?"

"Not a one."

Heathcliff sighed, folding his arms. "Fine. But I'm not wearing a silly costume."

I crossed my fingers behind my back as I recalled the 'costumes mandatory, and will be supplied to any patron arriving without' written on the back of the ticket. "Oh no, I'm sure that will be fine. Now, if we can move on to something more important—"

My phone beeped with a message. I glanced at the screen. Mum, demanding I come home and help her with her latest get-rich-quick-scheme. She'd had to give up on her pet dictionaries after the dictionary creator discovered he could make more money self-publishing them on The-Store-That-Shall-Not-Be-Named. Now she'd put together create-your-own-soap kits with her friend Sylvia Blume, which meant the kitchen had become a disaster zone and every surface in the house was coated in a layer of glittery soap scum.

But what she was *actually* doing was trying to get me away from the clutches of Heathcliff. Because she couldn't deal with the idea that I might choose the dirty gypsy over the rich and suave Morrie.

Because for some reason, when she looks at Heathcliff, she sees my dad.

The realization hit me like a freight train, slamming out all other thoughts. The words of my father's letter blazed across my mind. If what he said was true, if he really was trying to protect both of us, then did my mother know about it? *Everything in my life is a lie.* I slipped the phone back in my pocket without replying.

"I'm ready for you guys to see this now." I pulled the letter from my pocket and spread it over my knee. Morrie grabbed it, his eyes darting over the words before handing it over to Heathcliff. "What do you make of it?" I asked.

"This paper is unusual," Morrie snatched the letter back, holding it up to the light. "It's rougher than one would expect from Victoria's stationery. The ink has an interesting patina." He licked the tip of his finger and rubbed it against the edge of the letter, then tasted the ink. "As I suspected. This paper and ink predate 1896."

"What else?"

"The drawings in the border support my assertion that the letter is older than when we received it. They look like the kind of drawings one would see on a medieval manuscript."

Hmm... I dug around in the pile of books on the table and pulled out Herman Strepel's volume of Homer's Frog-Mouse War (It had a Greek name, but I still couldn't pronounce it). Flipping through the pages, I stopped at one of the drawings of the mice attacking the frogs. "Like this?"

"Exactly." Morrie picked up a magnifying lens from his desk and held it against the page. "I'd need to study both the paper and the ink under my microscope, but I think this letter might be contemporary with that book. Notice the handwriting?"

My stomach flipped as I compared the writing on both documents. *That's where I've seen it before.* The strange flicks on the letters looked familiar because they exactly matched Herman Strepel's handwriting.

"Does this mean my father is Herman Strepel?" I shook my head. "No, that's impossible."

In my pocket, my phone buzzed again. I ignored it.

"Is it? We know that your father was able to travel both ways through time, since Victoria noted he'd visited her at least once before." Morrie smiled. "And implied they had shared intimacies."

"Yeah, don't say that," I gulped. "You're talking about my father doing things in that bed, and *we* did things in that bed."

"Not nearly enough things," Morrie said with a sigh. "I conclude that Herman popped over to our century-long enough to impregnate your mother and make some kind of powerful enemy before heading back to his own time."

I rubbed my head where the migraine had progressed through my temple and across the left side of my skull. "This sounds like an episode of Doctor Who."

"Doctor who?" Heathcliff grunted.

"Exactly."

Heathcliff glowered at me. "What are you on about?"

"How have you not heard of Doctor Who? It's only the best-loved British science fiction show of all time."

"Heathcliff won't let us have a TV," Morrie said.

"What are you talking about? We have a TV." Heathcliff pointed into a dark corner of the room, where the boys had stacked a mountain of dirty laundry. Morrie dug underneath it and pulled out a tiny box the size of his head. A large, crescent-shaped hole shattered the screen.

"Mr. Simson left that for me. He said I'd enjoy it." Heathcliff stretched out his leg to demonstrate how the hole in the screen exactly corresponded to the toe of his boot. "He was wrong."

My pocket buzzed again. I removed my phone and turned it off. Quoth raised an eyebrow at me.

Morrie held up the letter. "Can I hold on to this? I'll do some investigation and see what we can find out. But it won't be tonight, not if you're staying."

"She's not staying," Quoth said quietly. "I'll walk you home, Mina."

"You don't speak for her, little birdie."

"Neither do you. And Quoth's right. I'm not staying. But I'm not going back to my flat, either. Jo and I are having a sleepover." I lifted my rucksack from behind the chair. "I should get going. She's waiting for me."

"Why go to Jo's when I'm here?" Morrie pouted.

Because you're being a wanker and I need to not be around you right now. Also, because when you're not a wanker, you're a beautiful distraction, but I can't have what happened last night happen again, not with this letter in my hands. "I just need some girl time, is all."

"But I need you..." Morrie's eyes darted to his computer, where Lydia was gyrating against his webcam.

"Have fun with Lydia and Ahmed!" I pecked him on the cheek. Heathcliff wrapped me in a bone-crushing hug, stealing a kiss that left me breathless. Quoth followed me down the stairs.

"Why aren't you going home?" he whispered as he helped me into my coat.

"You know why."

"You're avoiding the guys and ignoring your mother." Fire flickered in Quoth's eyes. "You're going to have to ask her about the letter. And your eyes."

"I know."

"What if the blood Victoria was talking about is hers—"

"I know!" I pulled my wool beanie down over my ears. "Trust me, I know. But not now. Not tonight."

"Why are you avoiding dealing with this? I thought you wanted nothing more than to solve the mystery of Nevermore."

"That was before I knew my father was involved."

"Why does that change things?"

"Because... because *it just does!*"

Quoth winced. Remorse shot through me. "I'm sorry. I didn't mean to yell. This letter has turned my head upside down. And Morrie's being a cock and I just..."

Quoth leaned in and brushed his lips against mine. "I wish I understood. You sure you don't just want to stay here? We could watch the stars through the attic window."

The thought of snuggling up with Quoth made my stomach flip, but I shook my head. "That sounds amazing, but I can't. I need to think, and I can't do that if I'm with any of you. You turn my head all mushy."

"You still want me to come with you in the morning?"

"What's in the morning? Oh."

My heart dropped like a stone.

In the morning.

I'd completely forgotten.

In the chaos of the letter and Lydia and the Jewel Thief and the Jane Austen Experience, it had slipped my mind that I made an appointment with a new ophthalmologist in nearby Barchester General Hospital. She was going to run tests on my eyes and hopefully give me a clue as to how fast I could expect to lose my vision now that I was seeing random neon lights. Only Quoth knew about it because I asked him to come with me. It was the whole reason I was staying at Jo's that night. The appointment was first thing in the morning and I didn't want Mum or the guys to ask questions.

Shit shit shit. On top of everything else, I had to face the news of my impending blindness. Great.

I squeezed Quoth's hand. "Yes, please come with me."

His hands felt warm even through my woolen gloves. He leaned forward, pressing his lips against my forehead. "It's going to be okay, Mina."

I almost believed him.

CHAPTER SEVEN

"*A*re you sure you're going to be okay in the hospital?" I asked Quoth for the fiftieth time as our rideshare joined the dual carriageway heading down to Barchester. "It's a big place, and there'll be lots of people and weird beeping machines."

Quoth leaned across the backseat and squeezed my hand. "You'll be there, and that's all that matters. Stop asking me if I'm okay. That's supposed to be *my* job. Are *you* okay?"

I swallowed hard. Worrying about Quoth accidentally shifting in public was distracting me from the true purpose of our little excursion. I didn't want to think about it.

"I'm fine. Better when I'm not talking about it. How's Morrie coping with his new friend?"

"When I flew down this morning, he was huddled on the chaise lounge under the window. I think he got kicked out of his bed. Lydia bounced down after me. I left as she was measuring him for his wedding top hat."

The driver pulled up in front of a gleaming hospital. I hadn't been inside Barchester General since I was in high school and I broke my arm in the mosh pit at a local punk show. My initial diagnosis of retinitis pigmentosa came from an ophthalmologist in New York City, but since I didn't have two quid to rub together (hilariously, being a bookshop assistant paid even less than my fashion internship), going back to him was out of the question. My new specialist's office informed me that all my records had been successfully moved over.

Now there was nothing to do but face my doom.

My fingers curled around the edge of the seat. Quoth ran around the side of the car and opened the door for me. He took my hand. "You look like you're heading to the gallows."

"Maybe I am."

"You've already had one shock this week," he said. "If you want to go home and leave this for another day, I understand."

My father's letter flashed in front of my eyes. All night I stared at the ceiling in Jo's flat, the words running over and over again, mingling with my fear of losing my sight. Twice last night I'd seen the floating neon lights, in lurid shades of pink and green. I couldn't deal with that right now, but I *had* to deal with this.

I shook my head. "Don't give me the option of turning this car around, because I'll take it. I *have* to do this. Half the fear I have is the not-knowing. When I know, I can face it."

Quoth nodded. He understood that better than anyone. Nothing in Quoth's life had been defined. While Morrie and Heathcliff at least had memories from their book lives to turn to, Quoth had nothing but trochaic octameter, which was the least useful of all the poetic meters.

Quoth's hand gripped mine as we made our way to the ophthalmologist's clinic. A chirpy nurse behind the desk gave me a form to fill out and told me to take a seat. I scribbled some nonsense of the form and flipped through a fashion magazine while we waited for my name to be called. Marcus Ribald's latest collection splashed across the cover. Seeing it felt weird, like another lifetime.

I tugged at the hem of the oversized Misfits shirt I'd made into a bodycon dress. After meeting the guys and learning about the book trade and solving two murders, I hadn't thought about fashion in over a month.

"Mina Wilde, Dr. Clements will see you now."

I stood up, steadying myself against the wall as my legs shook. Quoth rose too, turning toward me. He slipped his hand in mine and flashed me a beautiful, sad smile. I drew strength from his gentle kindness and forced my feet to move forward. We shuffled into a bright corner office overlooking the parking lot and a public garden beyond. The walls were covered with old black-and-white movie posters and vintage LPs. In the corner stood a black birdcage, where a cockatoo hopped along a perch.

Beside me, Quoth stiffened. I glanced at him in concern. Would he be able to remain in human form with another bird so close by? His jaw set hard. He gave a slight nod of his head and shuffled closer to me.

Dr. Clements stood to greet me. She was younger than I expected, with a friendly smile and head of layered red hair shot with bright pink streaks. I liked her immediately.

"Hello, Wilhelmina."

"It's Mina." I pointed to a poster from the 1933 *Dracula* film that hung on the wall behind her. "Like Mina Harker. And this is my friend, Quoth. His parents were goths."

"Mina and Quoth, it's a pleasure to meet both of you." She patted the chair beside her. "Have a seat. I've read your files from your New York specialist. It looks as though you've had all the usual diagnostic tests. I'm assuming you wanted to see me because there's been some change in your vision."

I squeezed Quoth's hand. "I'm seeing these explosions of light," I said. My voice sounded odd, hollow, as though I was listening to it from far away. I detached myself from the words I spoke, my consciousness to hovering above my body, so I looked over my own shoulder while I described my vision. It felt surreal,

as though I spoke about some other person. "They look like fireworks or neon lights. They seem to happen when I'm particularly
emotional or... or..."

*In the middle of sex with one or more of my three fictional
boyfriends*, but I couldn't exactly say that.

"Did Dr. Phillips explain to you about the typical stages of
your type of RP?"

"A little bit." Behind Dr. Clements, the cockatoo pecked at its
feeder, squawking as it drew out a berry. Quoth's fingers tightened against mine, but he remained still and human beside me.

"Your retina is a layer of light-sensitive tissue lining the back
of your eye – they convert light into electrical signals that make
their way to the brain, giving you an image. As the cells in the
retina deteriorate, your brain attempts to create its own image to
explain why it's not getting signals any longer. That's what you're
seeing."

"Dr. Phillips explained that I might see lights or random
shapes in the future, but he said it wouldn't be for years."

"That's correct. I'd like to take a look at your eyes today, and
we might be able to get a better idea of the rate of deterioration."
Dr. Clements wheeled over a diagnostic machine and took me
through a series of tests. I studied graphs and arranged colors
and looked at blinking lights. Quoth held my hand the entire
time.

Back at her desk, Dr. Clements opened a drawer and offered
me a Cadbury chocolate bar. I accepted it, peeling back the
wrapper and shoving half the bar into my mouth. I offered the
rest to Quoth, but he shook his head. While I chewed, Dr.
Clements studied the screen. "I'm just looking at your results,
Mina. What I'm seeing shows that the rate of deterioration on
the retina has increased faster than Dr. Phillips predicted. This
isn't uncommon, as the deterioration can slow down or speed up
during any stage, and we don't know what triggers these
changes."

I nodded, my mouth too full of chocolate to speak. Chew, chew, chew. My stomach churned in knots.

"From this point, it's very hard to give you an exact timeline. Every person is different. But you are progressing more rapidly than we'd usually expect."

I swallowed, the chocolate sinking to my stomach like a stone. "Can you take a stab at a timeline? How long before I go completely blind?"

"With your particular strain of RP, you may never go completely blind," she said. "I've seen many patients who've retained some central vision. You will almost certainly retain light sensitivity. But I think over the next eighteen months you could expect your peripheral vision to recede further and you'll see more of these fireworks."

Eighteen months.

Numbness shot through my body. My temples screamed, as though my head had been dunked in ice water. Quoth's hand squeezed mine, but I barely registered his touch.

Eighteen months.

The only single bright side in this whole mess was that I was *supposed* to have years. 'At least five years', Dr. Philip had said. Five years to deal with the trauma and come to terms with being blind and learn how to read Braille and find a pair of dark sunglasses that suited my face and whatever else I had to do.

Now even that had been taken away from me. *Eighteen months.* Icy panic gripped my chest. What was I going to do? I wasn't ready. I didn't have a plan. I was hanging out in a bookshop and fooling around with three guys and getting mixed up in murders and meeting Lydia Bennet. In eighteen months time, I wouldn't even be able to read *Pride and Prejudice*, let alone sell it to a customer. How will I count money for the till? How will I list books on The-Store-That-Shall-Not-Be-Named?

How will I see the iridescent colors in Quoth's hair as it captures the light, or know when his feelings change because of the orange fire dancing in his eyes? How will I continue to learn chess so I can kick Morrie's smug arse? How will my whole body shudder with ecstasy when Heathcliff locks his gaze on mine?

Quoth winced. I stared down at my lap, noticing with an odd detachment that I'd crushed his fingers so much the tips were turning white.

"I'm sorry." Dr. Clements' leaned across her desk, her eyes wide and open and sad. "It's the worst part of my job, telling people shitty news, especially patients as young and with as good a taste in music and movies as you. I'm glad you have a friend here to support you. I don't want to give you platitudes while you digest this news, but I think it's important you know that all my patients diagnosed around your age go on to live full and happy lives. Every single one. RP does not have to hold you back."

"Okay." I heard her words, but behind the pounding chorus of doom in my head, they meant nothing. *Eighteen months. I've only got eighteen months...*

Dr. Clements leant against her hand. "I don't want to over-whelm you, but have you thought about your adaptive needs?"

"What's that?"

"There are new skills you'll need to learn in order to continue being independent and doing the things you enjoy. You don't need sight to lead a full and happy life. There are tools and support systems designed to help." She slid a stack of pamphlets across the table to me. "This explains some of the adaptations and support you'll need to consider. You're rubbing your temple. Do you get migraines?"

"Sometimes." I dropped my hand from my face.

"That's common as well. Your brain and eyes strain to make use of the available light." She scribbled a prescription on her pad and handed it to me. "These painkillers will help. Be careful not to take more than the recommended dose, as they can become addictive. I can help you with whatever you need." Her pen poised above the pad. "That includes coping with the emotional impact of losing your sight. I'm happy to give you a referral to talk to someone."

Isis' tits, nope. "I'm fine. I don't need a psychologist."

"Are you sure? Many of my patients find it useful to talk to someone."

I nodded, standing up. Quoth's arm jerked as I pulled him up alongside me. "Yes. I... thank you very much, Dr. Clements. I've got to go. I have to get back to my job."

"Of course. Come back to me whenever you want. I'm happy to take another look at your eyes and help you with anything you need." She held out her hand to me. I stared at it, my brain shouting at my body that I was supposed to shake it. My hands remained at my sides, my fingers curled into a fist, crushing Quoth under my grip. I blinked, turned away, dropped Quoth's hand, and fled into the hall.

"Mina, Mina. Slow down." Quoth ran after me as I fled the hospital.

"I'm fine." I jabbed at my phone app to call a driver. "It's all fine."

"That's not what your expression says." Soft fingers touched under my chin, turning my face. Quoth's eyes bore into mine, the irises ringed with fire. "Mina, you're absolutely crushed."

His voice croaked. My shoulders sagged. I sank against his body, resting my head against his chest. His arms went around my shoulders. "I am," I whispered.

Quoth's heart thudded in his chest. I focused on the beat, synching my breathing with his, allowing his realness to bring me back from the brink. Yes, I would be blind in eighteen months, but these arms would still be there when I needed them, this heart would still be beating. And that filled me with the certainty I needed to hold back my pain.

A car pulled up, and the driver honked the horn. Reluctantly, I slid out of Quoth's embrace and got into the backseat. He climbed in beside me, his hand seeking mine again.

"You should consider talking to the psychologist," Quoth said. He didn't look at me.

"Why? It's a shock, but I've accepted it and I'm fine. Besides, if I need to talk to someone, I've got you."

"Are you sure? You've dealt with a lot these past few months, what with seeing Ashley dead, and Mrs. Scarlett and Ginny Button, and finding Mr. Winstone's body, and now your father's letter—"

"I'm *fine.*" I plastered a smile on my face. "Hey, I just realized, you survived that entire hospital visit without changing, even with Dr. Clements' bird in the corner."

"Yeah." Quoth flashed me a brilliant smile. "You're good for me, Mina Wilde."

"And you're good for me, Quoth the Raven."

~

*A*s the car pulled over in front of the village green, my phone beeped. It was a text message from Mum, demanding to know why I hadn't come home for a second night in a row. I tossed it on the seat without replying.

"You should talk to her," Quoth said.

"Of course I should. But I'm in a shite mood and I don't want to."

"She's the only family you've got."

"She's *not* my only family anymore, since apparently my father writes to me now, in addition to being a small-time crook and a time-traveling Lothario."

"Until you speak to your mother, you're not going to get any answers about that letter. She cares about you, and she's worried."

I glared at Quoth. He was right, and I was pissed at him for it. He probably longed to have a meddling mother who constantly tried to ruin his life.

As we walked toward the shop entrance, loud house music blasted my ears. A customer rushed from the store, her hands planted firmly over her ears.

"What's going on?" I yelled at Quoth. He shrugged and followed me inside.

As I made my way down the darkened hallway, Lydia crashed through the room, spinning and jumping like a wild animal. She'd replaced her bonnet and empire line dress with an off-the-shoulder shirt adorned with a sequined penis across her breasts, leopard-print ballet flats, and a pair of the tightest black jeans I'd ever seen.

"Oh, Mina, you have returned." She threw her arms around me. I staggered back under the force of her embrace. "Won't you dance with me? The boys are such spoilsports. All they want to do is rest."

Beside me, Quoth's body shrunk into itself in an explosion of feathers. His bones cracked as they reshaped into wings. A moment later, a large raven took off, seeking the shadows of his lair above the entrance.

I didn't blame him. Lydia *was* a terrifying presence.

"Aren't you freezing?" I asked, disentangling myself and wrapping my scarf tighter around my neck. Even though Heathcliff had the stove in the main room blaring, it wasn't exactly warm in the shop.

"Of course not, silly goose. The dancing keeps me warm!" Lydia laughed and twirled away. "This music is so much more lively than the pianoforte. Why, I should like to dance all day and night."

From the chaise lounge in the corner, Morrie moaned.

I stepped inside, unable to conceal my smile. The criminal

mastermind lay in a messy heap across the couch, a cold compress over his eyes and an expression of existential angst marring his usually-smug features. All around him towered boxes and shopping bags. Makeup and hair straighteners and stacks of clothing and colorful iPhone cases spilled over the tables and cascaded across the floor.

Heathcliff was nowhere to be seen. *I bet he's hiding in the storage room, leaving Morrie to take care of Lydia. Smart man.*

"She made me take her shopping," Morrie whimpered. "She needed things so she could fit into our modern age."

I grinned. *At least he's too exhausted to be a wanker today.*

"Lord Moriarty and I had such good fun." Lydia pulled his credit card from the pocket of her figure-hugging jeans and waved it in his face. "What a wondrous invention this is. I never wish to part with it."

"Give that to me," Morrie held out a limp hand. "It looks tired."

Lydia tossed the card at him, laughing. She grabbed her brand new phone from the table beside the armadillo and changed the song to a death metal track. "This one reminds me of Mary playing the pianoforte at the Netherfield ball!"

I sat down on the end of the couch, my eyes darting over Morrie's features, trying to commit every detail of him to memory. Would I even remember what things looked like when I was blind? Would the full picture of Morrie's high, sharp cheekbones and haughty lips and strong jawline and willowy, muscled frame cease to exist to me, accessible only in fragments through moments of touch and sensation. Would the ice-blue of his eyes no longer pierce my heart?

"Why are you looking so odd?" he asked. "Did Quoth ask you to do something kinky on your date? Did he make you eat a dead mouse?"

"No, I—" I opened my mouth to tell Morrie about the doctor's office, but I bit back the words. As far as Morrie and Heathcliff were aware, Quoth and I had been out on a date. I glanced away, sucking in my breath and blinking away a tear that threatened to spill down my face. If I said something to Morrie now, and he acted the way he'd been acting... I couldn't handle it. So I changed the subject. "Do you have my letter?"

"It's in my pocket." Morrie sighed, flopping back against the pillows. "Can you get it? I can't move right now."

I slid my hand into his pocket and pulled out my father's letter. As soon as my fingers grazed the paper, a cold shiver ran down my spine.

"Did you have time to look over it between trips to the Barchester mall?"

"My investigations have confirmed our suspicions," Morrie said. "The compounds in the ink match those used by Herman Strepel. The person who wrote this note and the person who lettered *Batrachomyomachia* are one and the same."

My father is Herman Strepel.

My chest tightened, and my mouth dried out. For the first time in my life, my father had a name and a profession.

So what? What does it matter that my father is an ancient book-letterer who owned Nevermore over a thousand years ago? He still knocked my mother up and then ran out on us when I was a baby.

And if he is Herman Strepel, then why is he in our time period in the first place? Does he just hop around the different centuries, selling books and breaking hearts? Where is he now? Has he been eaten by dinosaurs?

What does he know about fictional characters coming to life? The two things have to be connected. And who is his enemy?

And what does Mum know about any of this?

Quoth swooped into the room and settled on my shoulder. "Croak?" he asked, nuzzling his head against my cheek.

Your thoughts are all tangled up, he said. *You should speak to your mother.*

"Not going to happen," I said aloud. Quoth shook his head sadly.

"Talking to yourself is the first sign of insanity," Morrie said from the couch.

"I know. Conversing with fictional characters is sign number two, and having a time-traveling dad is number three, so I might as well have myself committed right now."

"The post's arrived." Heathcliff wandered in from the other room and dumped a stack of envelopes on the desk. "There's a letter for Lord Moriarty. Since when do you get mail?"

"Give me that!" Morrie leaped to his feet, knocking over a stack of makeup bags as he grabbed the envelope from Heathcliff's hands.

"Expecting to be drafted?" Heathcliff shot back.

Morrie didn't seem to hear. He tore open the envelope and scanned the letter. "But that's... that's impossible," he muttered.

"What's impossible?" I tried to peer over his shoulder.

Morrie shoved the envelope into his pocket, keeping his hand on top so I couldn't pull it out. "Oh, nothing, nothing. My bank manager messed up one of my Cayman Island transfers, is all. Excuse me."

"Morrie—" But he'd already disappeared upstairs. I glanced at Heathcliff, but he shrugged.

"Don't bother with him. He likes his secrets. You and he are alike in that respect." Heathcliff dropped a book on his desk, picked up the next one from his stack, and left the room again, no doubt to return to whatever foxhole he was hiding in.

What did he mean by that?

"I guess I'm minding the shop, then!" I yelled over Lydia's music. "That's good. It'll give me time to finish this Jane Austen display!"

As I arranged books and festival flyers around the stuffed armadillo, I thought back to the time a week ago, when Morrie had handcuffed me to his ceiling and he and Quoth had done amazing things to my body. It was one of the most intense experiences of my life, and from the way Morrie's voice had wavered,

I'd thought that maybe it meant something to him, too. Afterward, he ran away, leaving me and Quoth snuggling together in his bed. The panicked look in Morrie's eyes before he fled... that was the same look he wore when he'd read that letter.

What's up with Morrie?

CHAPTER EIGHT

"You haven't been home for two nights." Mum pounced as soon as I walked through the door.

"Let me get inside before we have it out. It's freezing." I slammed the door, kicking off my wet boots and peeling off my gloves.

"Don't speak to me like that. I didn't know where you were. You could be lying raped and murdered in the street!"

"You're overreacting. You know I don't walk around here alone. The guys are walking me home, or I take a rideshare, or Jo drops me off. If it's such an issue for you, I could just move into Heathcliff's shop – that way I'd never be out on the mean streets of Argleton."

As soon as I said the words, I regretted them. My mother recoiled as if I'd slapped her.

"If that's how you feel," she said in a chipped tone, backing into the kitchenette.

I sighed, sliding my rucksack off my shoulder and following her into the kitchenette. "It's not. You can always ring the shop if you need me—"

I stopped in my tracks, my jaw dropping as I surveyed the

carnage in our kitchen. Every pot, pan, bowl, and plate we owned was stacked on the counter or scattered across the floor. Pink and purple goop dripped down the cabinets and splattered the walls. It looked like a My Little Pony had exploded in the microwave.

"I did ring the shop!" Mum stood in the middle of the mess with her hands on her hips. A smudge of purple glitter extended across her cheek, like some kind of tribal marking. "I asked for you and that rude gypsy said, 'We don't have any titles with that name', and hung up on me!"

Thank you, Heathcliff. "He probably misunderstood you. Mum, what happened here?"

"I told you I need your help! Sylvia made up these craft kits to make bath bombs and soaps and face creams. She wanted me to test them to make sure the instructions were easy to follow. But everything keeps going wrong and it's all because you weren't here."

"I don't see why my presence would help – I don't know about any of this stuff, either. If you were having trouble, you should have called Sylvia." I picked up a jar of peanut butter on the counter. Glittery pink goo had dried over the lid, forming a seal. I banged it against the counter to loosen the crud. "Aren't some of these chemicals hazardous? Should you really be doing this in our kitchen?"

"These are exactly the questions I needed you to ask!" Mum swept a bunch of dishes into the sink, leaving a rainbow smudge of unicorn poop across the counter. "But you didn't even call—"

"I wrote you a text message." *I didn't send it, but you don't have to know that.* "Morrie and I stayed up late watching a film, so I decided to crash at the shop. And then Jo and I were hanging out last night, and she'd had too much wine to drive me home, so I kipped on the sofa. Here, I'll help."

"I didn't get this text," Mum muttered. I slid in beside her and turned on the hot tap to fill the sink, piling the dishes neatly on the counter to make more room.

Guilt chewed on my gut. I should have texted her. Quoth was right – she worried about me. As I moved, the edge of the letter brushed my leg. All the guilt flew from my mind as my father's words came back to me.

Did you know my father was a time-traveling bookbinder? It was on the tip of my tongue to ask. "I'm sorry, okay? I'll let you know more details next time." It came out more petulant than I'd intended. "Morrie and I are going to the Jane Austen festival this weekend, so I won't be home. There, now you know."

"Are you and Morrie dating?" Mum's eye sparkled. My transgressions were forgotten with the prospect of a son-in-law who was richer than Croesus.

"I've told you a hundred times, no." The lie felt uncomfortable on my lips, but I couldn't very well tell her the truth about the three guys. "We're just friends. I'm capable of being friends with guys without sleeping with them."

"But if you were to date Morrie, I want you to know that I'm okay with it. I think you and he would make a lovely couple."

"What about me and Heathcliff?" I raised an eyebrow. "Or me and Allan?"

"Mina, it's mean to tease your mother like that." She threw a tea towel at me. "You're not serious, are you? Morrie is a much better match. Don't make the same mistakes I did."

The letter dragged against my leg. *What does that mean, Mum?* She didn't elaborate, of course. She never did about my father. She just called him, 'that bastard', then reached for another mug of tea, which was what she did now.

"Speaking of your mistakes," I blurted out. "I received a letter from Dad."

Dad. The word sounded ridiculous. I might as well have said a letter from 'Pope Gregory the Ninth'. I'd never called anyone 'dad' in my life.

SMASH. The mug slipped from Mum's hand and crashed against the countertop. Shards of ceramic flew everywhere. She leaned over the counter, her face white.

"Mum?"

"That's not possible," she whispered, gripping the edge of the counter.

I hadn't meant to tell her about the letter. But now that she knew, I'd see what I could discover. I took her hand and led her over to the table. I pulled out the nearest chair and Mum slumped down into it. "It came to the shop. It's on this weird old-fashioned paper."

"Can I see it? What did it say?"

I paused, my fingers pinching the corner of the envelope in my pocket. I wanted desperately to fling it across the table at her, but her pale face gave me pause.

If what the letter said was true, if my father really was Herman Strepel, then he knew about whatever magic had a hold on Nevermore Bookshop. When I thought about it rationally, I didn't believe my mother knew anything about it; otherwise, she would have tried much harder than she did to keep me away from the place. She was living in Barchester when she was with my father, so she didn't connect him to Argleton or Nevermore.

She doesn't know. The certainty hit me like a punch in the gut. Whatever secrets my father was protecting, he'd kept them from her, too. That made me feel a little better, and I hated myself for that.

I withdrew my hand from my pocket and bent down to clean up the broken mug. "I left it at the shop. I didn't want to look at it, you know? He said that he still loves us, and he left us because he was a danger to us. It kind of sounded as if someone was after him."

"How *dare* he? After all these years." Mum slumped down in her chair. "I suppose it was some elaborate poem surrounded by fiddly drawings. He fancied himself an artistic soul, did your father. Really, he was just a crooked second-rate criminal."

"What kind of crimes? Please, Mum, you've never told me anything about him. Was he a druggie? A thief?"

"Counterfeiting." Mum gritted her teeth, as though she couldn't bear to get the words out. "He sold copies of Banksy paintings and old medieval manuscripts."

I wasn't expecting that. It fit with Herman Strepel's unique skills. "What was he like? What about his family?"

She sniffed. "He didn't have any family, but he got on well with my parents. Dad wanted him to join the family business, but he kept insisting we'd get rich one day off his manuscripts, and he wouldn't need to peddle drugs anymore. Apparently, he was working on a masterpiece. Some never-before-discovered work by Hester or Horatio or something."

"Homer?"

"Maybe. I don't remember. He was always talking nonsense about old writers and artists." I picked up the bigger pieces of broken cup and tossed them into the rubbish bin, my mind whirring. It couldn't be a coincidence that Herman Strepel's copy of The Frog-Mouse War had shown up in the shop when he was counterfeiting Homer in my time. Was it a message from my father somehow?

"That would make sense, then. The letter *was* handwritten, and there were drawings in the border." I hunted out the brush and shovel and swept up the tiny ceramic fragments and as much unicorn poop as I could. My hands shook with excitement. This was more than I'd ever found out about my father. "Do you have any idea what he might be talking about when he says he's in danger?"

Mum shook her head. "He's a criminal, Mina. He's probably pissed off the wrong people. If he writes any more letters to you, he's going to be in danger from *me*."

You never told me before that he was an artist and a writer. That he was a reader.

All my life I'd been the opposite of my mother. She had no imagination. She thought books were stupid and had barely ever set foot in Nevermore Bookshop (except to drag me away as a child or to sell her pet dictionaries), whereas I had practically been raised by those fictional characters. She was the one who talked me out of my English degree at Oxford because she thought I had a better chance of making it as a fashion designer than as a writer. Even when I was being bullied and I hated myself and I felt so completely alone, she never told me that there was someone else out there like me – my father.

Rage boiled up inside me, turning my veins to lava. My hand balled into fists at my sides. I *hated* her. She kept this from me, and I *needed* it. If I'd known I wasn't so completely alone, if I hadn't felt like such a freak, things might've turned out so differently for me...

I slid into the chair across from her. On the stove, the kettle boiled, but both of us ignored it. I studied my mother's face, noting the bags under her eyes, the vein throbbing on her temple – the same one that throbbed when I did something naughty. My fingers itched to slap the expression off her face. *How dare you be angry with me? I have every right to hate you right now.*

"You've never told me this," I whispered, the words hard. "You never told me that I was like my father. All my life you made me think I was a freak because of the things I liked. And it was all because you were angry with him. When you looked at me reading or drawing, you saw him. The only reason you wanted me to pursue fashion was because it was something *you* liked."

"Don't turn this around on me, Mina," she snapped. *"He's* the one who walked out on us and left me to raise you. I did the best I could with what I had. I put you through school and I let you hang out at that musty bookshop you loved more than our home. I did everything I bloody could to give you the life I didn't get to have. And you get one letter from him in twenty-three years and now you hate me."

"Don't you think I might have liked to know I had a father who loved to read? Don't you think I would have wanted some kind of relationship with him? But you made me think he was an evil criminal just so I'd hate him as much as you. Well, congratulations, Mum. I hated him, all right, but not as much as I hated myself!"

"He *was* a criminal!" she screamed. "Just because he did his crime with pretty pictures instead of drugs doesn't mean he was a person you should have in your life."

"I'm twenty-three years old. You don't get to make that decision for me." *And you don't seem to have a problem with Morrie even though he's more than implied he hasn't obtained his fortune legally. A smartly-dressed rich criminal is still a criminal.*

Mum's gripped her head in her hands, her whole body trembling. "This is exactly why I hoped he'd never contact you. Can't you just trust that I know what's best for you? Don't try to see your father. Don't answer his letter. If you think you feel lonely now, wait until you love him and he leaves you. You don't know what lonely is."

I glanced up at the glitter-stained ceiling. It took every ounce of self-control not to roll my eyes. "I'm not you, Mum. I won't fall to pieces just because of some guy. I'm strong enough not to fall into that trap, and you should know that."

"Oh, you are, are you? Then why did you come crawling back from New York City so I could look after you?"

I recoiled, my cheeks stinging, as though she'd slapped me. "I can't believe you said that. I can't believe you just threw the fact *I'm going blind* back in my face."

"Fine," she sniffed. "Do what you want, Mina. You always do. After everything I've sacrificed to give you a good life, go back to the man who abandoned you when you were a baby. But don't come crying to me when he breaks your heart."

69

"Suits me." I stood up. "Don't expect me to come home again."

"Wait, Mina—" Mum grabbed my wrist. I wrenched my hand away, flung myself into the hallway and grabbed my rucksack. It took me all of two minutes to throw in some clean clothes, my current book, my journal, and my tickets for the Jane Austen Extravaganza.

"Come back inside. You don't know who he is, what you could be walking into—"

"Of course I don't, because you won't tell me. You gave me an ultimatum. I've made my choice." I shoved my feet into my Docs and stepped on the front porch.

"You ungrateful bitch!" Mum slammed the door in my face.

Tears streamed down my cheeks. I walked to the corner of the street and called for a rideshare. *Fuck you. If you don't want to tell me about my father, fine. I've solved two murders over the last six weeks. I can solve this, too.*

$\mathcal{I}$ was still fuming about the fight with Mum on Friday as Heathcliff, Morrie, Lydia, and I approached Baddesley Hall along a wide avenue lined with ancient oaks. Another Christmas snow fell during the night, blanketing the vast lawn in a white carpet. I shivered in my red trench coat, thick scarf, two pairs of gloves, red merino sweater, homemade 'Jane Austen is my Homegirl' t shirt, red tartan wool mini skirt, and fleece-lined leggings.

I hope that big old house has modern heating.

"You might have called a carriage," Lydia sniffed at Heathcliff as her silk shoes sank into the snow. Despite how comfortable she'd become in modern clothing, Lydia was back in her empire-line dress and bonnet for the occasion, only with Morrie's leather jacket draped over her shoulders to ward off the chill.

"You might have dressed weather appropriate," he shot back.

"Only another mile to go," I said, my teeth chattering. *Stupid rideshare refusing to go up the driveway because of a tiny amount of snow.* Something heavy fell on my shoulders. Smiling gratefully, I tugged Heathcliff's coat tighter around my body and squeezed his hand. Although his expression remained surly, he pulled me closer, allowing the reassuring warmth of his bulk to heat me through.

Yes, I think this weekend might be good for all of us.

At the end of the avenue, the high and handsome Baddesley Hall awaited us. Backed by a ridge of wooded hills – the trees now bare and glittering with snow – the grand facade stretched out in two high wings, flanked with decorative turrets from which flew flags bearing Jane Austen's likeness. Elegant columns flanked a set of wide marble steps leading up to double-height wooden doors, where a crowd of people in period costume milled about, waving as cars and carriages navigated a tight turning circle around a grand fountain.

Even Lydia was warm in her admiration. "It's as fine a house as I have ever seen. I should think it even finer than that prig Mr. Darcy's Pemberley estate."

"Remember what we told you," Morrie said. "For this weekend, the guests believe this *is* Pemberley, which never actually existed except for in the book. It's very important no one guesses you're a fictional character come to life. If you can make it for the whole weekend without shattering their illusion, I'll let you buy that Prada handbag."

"Yes, yes," Lydia said crossly, leaning into Morrie's arm. "One doesn't like to be constantly reminded of one's impermanence. I have come for the dancing, not to make conversation about books!"

We passed a visitors' parking area off to the left. A stream of people in Regency attire flowed around the fountain, heedless to the traffic as they ambled toward the house. Hired staff from the village in period uniform rushed about, collecting luggage and handing out room keys.

"See?" Lydia pointed to one of the parking attendants, dressed as a footman. "I told you grand families would never give up their servants."

We pushed through the crowd and entered the lobby, which

was even grander than the exterior. Twin staircases swooped down from the upper story, framing a small fountain at the center of the room. My boots *clack-clacked* across the marble as we made our way to the crowded information desk, taking in the decor and soft furnishings that adorned the impressive space.

In the elegant and handsomely-proportioned room, Cynthia Lachlan's "additions" stood out like a nun at a Clash concert. A wingback chair covered in leopard-print fabric sat under one of the windows. Fashion magazines stacked on the reception table. An industrial-looking lamp on the card table beside it. A rug in a garish shade of pink delineated a short hallway. I'd heard from Mrs. Ellis that some people in the village looked down on Cynthia and Grey for being new money pretending to be old money. Looking at this room, I could kind of see what they meant. But at the same time, I liked that Cynthia was having fun with her home. That was what a home should be for.

"Mina, I'm so pleased you could come."

I glanced up. Cynthia descended the stairs, wearing a lilac empire-waist gown and matching bonnet blinged up with sequins. She kissed me on the cheeks and made me re-introduce her to my party. Morrie and Lydia both gave the customary Regency bow and curtsey, but Heathcliff only grunted in acknowledgment. If Cynthia noticed, her meticulous study of Heathcliff's impressive muscles straining against his black dress shirt had convinced her to ignore his rudeness.

"I have your rooms all ready for you," she said, removing a set of keys from the hook on the wall behind the information desk. "You have our finest suite. It won't do for our VIPs to be with the rest of the riff-raff..." her voice trailed off as her eyes swept over my t shirt. "Are your costumes in your bags? You haven't left much time to change before the opening plenary."

"No costumes," Heathcliff barked, moving closer to me as if my body would shield him from rogue cravats.

Cynthia frowned at my tiny backpack covered with band

patches and Morrie's slim-leg trousers. "No, no, those outfits won't do, not for our VIPs. Not to worry, we'll pop along to Adelia Maitland in Netherfield. That's the marketplace room. We've renamed all the rooms after famous places in Jane Austen's books, just for the weekend. Isn't that fabulous?"

"What fun!" Lydia exclaimed.

Cynthia beamed. "Adelia will sort you out with the perfect attire."

"But I don't want to wear—" Heathcliff's protests fell on deaf ears as Cynthia ushered us down a wide hallway and into an enormous receiving room. People bustled back and forth, examining the stalls lining the walls and extending down the center of the cavernous space. Throngs of bonneted women perused the aisle, while yet more costumed ladies stood behind the stalls, selling everything from Austen branded teas, costumes, jewelry, fans, leather notebooks, and even self-published works of Jane Austen erotica. I smirked as my eye caught the title of one woman's book – *Spank Me, Mr. Darcy*. She had a long line of eager customers in front of her stall.

As we went past, Lydia's hand snaked out to grab a copy of the erotica book. Morrie slapped it down.

We stopped at a large stall in the corner. Racks burst with period dresses, cloaks, and breeches. A plump woman with dark cheeks and a yellow bonnet that gave her the appearance of a bloated sunflower bustled over to meet us. "Mrs. Maitland, this party is in need of proper attire. They'll have both outfits for the day and something more dramatic for the ball. Please see to it, and bill me for the rental."

Mrs Maitland gave a short curtsey. "As you wish, M'Lady." She grabbed Heathcliff and thrust a jacket into his arms. "You. Wear this."

"I prefer my own jacket." Heathcliff glowered at her as he whipped his coat off my freezing shoulders and held it in front of his chest like a shield.

Unperturbed, Mrs. Maitland wrestled it from his arms and tossed it into a pile of dirty clothing. "Now you wear this."

"You knew about this?" Heathcliff growled, accepting the stiff blue top-coat with all the terror of a soldier handling a live grenade.

I grinned. "Maybe a little."

"If you're to dance with me, then we shall match." Lydia dragged Morrie over to one of the other racks and flung clothes at him.

Heathcliff tore off his shirt, grumbling under his breath as he fumbled with the collar of the white one Mrs. Maitland handed him. Every female head in the room turned to admire his broad shoulders, toned torso, and the dip of his ab muscles as they descended into the waistband of his jeans. My mouth watered, and a pang of desire shot through my chest. By Astarte, even if I went blind tomorrow I didn't think I'd ever forget that body. Everything about Heathcliff oozed danger, wildness, and unbidden passion.

Mrs Maitland dragged me away from my glorious view to a rack of dresses, pulling out gown after gown and holding them up to my face. "No, not the cream, or the yellow, or the blue. Red, for you, with your hair and complexion," she cooed. "Are you happy with red? In the Regency era, it was a color mainly reserved for older ladies, for white and pastel were all the rage with younger women. This dress would have been seen as quite daring."

"Sounds perfect." I accepted the silk dress with black lace detailing. Mrs. Maitland pulled aside a curtain to reveal a small changing room. I slipped inside, pulled off my t shirt, pullover, and skirt (leaving on my fleece leggings, because it was freezing inside the Hall) and shimmied into the petticoat. My teeth chattered. Women's clothing in the Regency wasn't exactly designed for insulation.

I pulled the red dress over my head. It sat perfectly over the petticoat, nipping in just below my breasts. The scoop neck pushed my tits together so I actually had cleavage. I turned this way and that, admiring the way the skirt swirled around my legs.

Mrs Maitland poked her head inside and handed me a blush-colored gown. "The red is perfect for the ball, and I've set aside matching silk flowers and a string of pearls for your hair. Here are your gloves and a matching fan, but I don't think you'll need the fan in this weather. For daytime wear, you want this simpler dress."

I wasn't a fan of pastel pink, but when I pulled the muslin dress over my head and arranged the puffed sleeves and neckline to best show off what little cleavage I had, I realized how pretty it was. The blush picked up reddish hues in my hair and the color of my cheeks. I tucked my phone and my father's letter into my *decolletage* and smiled at the girl in the mirror. "I feel ready to land a husband of at least five-thousand a year."

"That's the spirit." She threw the curtain open, setting a pair of slippers down on the floor. "Slip your feet into these and you're ready for your Jane Austen Experience."

I winced as I tugged on the silk slippers. They were paper thin and super flimsy. As I stepped out into Mrs. Maitland's stall, every piece of lint and every imperfection in the marble was revealed through the fragile soles.

I miss my Docs already. I am definitely not cut out to be a Regency lady.

I wasn't the only one struggling. While Lydia twirled about in a new cream dress with a neckline so plunging it would be sure to divert attention from my 'racy' color choice, the boys were getting a lesson in pulling on stockings. Morrie had his twisted around his ankle, while Heathcliff had knotted his into a noose and was pretending to hang himself with it. Behind them, a small audience of younger Janeites and an older woman with salt-and-pepper hair that matched her muslin dress stifled laughter. I recognized the woman's face from somewhere, but I couldn't place it.

"You roll them on your fingers, like this..." Mrs. Maitland demonstrated. Heathcliff copied her, and somehow shoved his thumbs through the silk, leaving two gaping holes.

Morrie, at least, got the hang of his, rolling up the stockings and managing to give Mrs. Maitland an eyeful of his crotch, likely on purpose. She didn't even turn away. I guess in her line of work, you saw it all.

"These really do hug everything." Morrie pirouetted, wearing only his stockings and a black flouncy shirt. At the sight of... well... *everything,* several members of our audience tittered and looked bashfully away. "I feel a pleasing sense of support and security."

"Before you prance off, you'll need to be fitted for your breeches." Mrs. Maitland steered him back into the depths of her shop. As one, the audience let out a disappointed sigh.

"Oh dear," the older woman said. "I know whose dance card will be booked solid at the ball."

"I'm sorry for my friends," I said to her. "They don't mean to be so... licentious."

"Nonsense," she smiled back at me. "It's good to see young men enjoying Jane Austen, even if they do need a few lessons in the proper decorum. Honestly, I think mandatory costumes are a little silly myself, but I can't deny the organizers have put on a spectacular event."

"Is this your first Jane Austen event?" I asked.

"Heavens, no. I'm Professor Michaela Carmichael. I'll be giving a lecture on medicine and cosmetics in Jane Austen's fiction this afternoon."

"That's right." I remembered where I'd seen her face before – her picture was in the brochure as one of the invited Austen scholars. "You're a physician turned Janeite. You wrote a famous book on Regency medical practices."

"I'd hardly call it *famous*," she said, with a dismissive flick of her wrist. "My royalties would barely keep one of the Bennet girls in bonnets and bonbons. People would far rather read James Patterson or Jane Austen erotica than any serious academic text."

"I work at a bookshop. I know all about that," I smiled, thinking of the tall stack of James Patterson books we had to send to recycling every month because we got more than we could ever hope to sell. "Still, it must be nice to be surrounded by so many adoring Janeites. I bet everyone in this room is excited about your lecture."

"Oh, I wouldn't say that," her features turned stony. "They're all here to see the *famous and handsome* Professor Julius Hathaway."

"That makes sense. He's the academic who discovered Jane Austen's connection to Baddesley Hall. The local shopkeepers want to hug him for all the extra business he brings to the village with the yearly festival. Plus, I guess you're always guaranteed to pull a crowd with a lecture on sex and sensuality in Regency novels, even if you are an academic and not an erotic novelist." I recalled Professor Hathaway's lecture topic only because it had set Heathcliff off in a tirade about the frivolity of Austen novels that included at least three curse words I'd never heard before.

"I'd hardly refer to Hathaway as an *academic.*" Professor Carmichael visibly stiffened. "His books pander to popular tastes. And between us ladies, that man would be the last person on earth I'd want to listen to on matters of sensuality. But you didn't hear that from me."

"Hear what?" I had no idea academics were so inclined to gossip.

"Far be it for me to speak ill of a colleague." Her eyes lit up, as if that was precisely what she intended to do. "But Professor Hathaway has somewhat of a sordid past. His late wife, may she rest in peace, would turn in her grave to know he had to leave his post at Oxford after sleeping with one of his undergraduate students."

"Heavens!" I gasped, in a perfect mockery of one of Austen's characters reacting to such scandalous news. I remembered I was carrying a fan, and I held it over my face in an expression of surprise.

"Indeed," Professor Carmichael nodded at my fan, acknowledging my joke. "The wife died of an aggressive hereditary bone disease when their daughter was very young, and his bed's never been cold since. I'd watch out if I were you. His taste runs to young, pretty women with Regency manners and little sense, and he's extremely charismatic and manipulative. There's many a whispered story about inappropriate happenings at these Austen events and young women leaving his suite in tears."

"I may not know how to tie a bonnet," I said, resentment creeping into my voice, "but I have enough sense not to be seduced by an aging Lothario."

"Oh, of course. My apologies, but I was referring to your companion." Professor Carmichael pointed to Lydia, who chased Morrie through the crowd, yelling at him to wear his breeches. I nodded.

"Fair point. If Hathaway's as bad as you say... that's an abuse of his power. Why doesn't someone report him?"

"A few brave souls have tried, but he's beloved in the Jane Austen community, and he knows how to spin a story so he ends up as the victim. He fancies himself a handsome Bingley or Darcy, dancing with all the girls and leaving a trail of broken hearts in his wake. In reality, he is worse than Wickham. Hathaway spends more time chasing tail than working on serious scholarship. It might be why his recent book, *Chaste and Carnality*, has been so heavily criticized."

"It has?"

"Oh, yes. Outside of Austen circles, he's something of a laughingstock. His academic work is often juvenile and full of holes, but this recent book is practically nonsensical." Professor Carmichael gestured to the center of the market. "But I have monopolized you too long. It appears at least two of your suitors are now properly attired. It was a pleasure to meet you, Mina Wilde. I hope to see you at my lecture."

I glanced over to where Lydia and Morrie danced in the middle of the aisle, while the string band in the corner played a Regency reel version of Lady Gaga's latest hit. Morrie still wore only his stockings and shirt. Young women in bonnets crowded around, clapping their hands in delight while Lydia tried to pinch his bottom. Behind them, a group of older ladies whispered disapprovingly at the spectacle. *We haven't even got to our rooms yet and we're already more scandalous than the Bennets at the Netherfield ball. This is going to be an interesting weekend.* "I wouldn't miss it."

"I hope you'll bring your delightful friends." Professor Carmichael curtseyed. "At least then I shall have four souls in attendance."

"I'll tell you what, I'll drum up an audience for you if you cut me in on your book royalties."

She laughed. "How about if I buy you a drink at the ball tomorrow night? You're likely to come out better off."

"It's a deal." I curtseyed back, nearly falling over in my ridiculous shoes.

"And stay away from Hathaway!" With a final wave, Professor Carmichael disappeared into the crowd.

CHAPTER TEN

*H*alf an hour and five pairs of stockings later, Heathcliff and Morrie were properly breeched, buckled, and cravated. They looked amazing, even if Heathcliff kept scratching himself and Morrie's voice had risen half an octave from the tight stockings.

Lydia's performance had left her with no shortage of admirers. Young girls fawned about her, excited to make acquaintances with the gregarious socialite who was quickly becoming the talk of the event. But her attentions were diverted by three male graduate students – wearing the red-coated livery of officers – who competed for her attention and made dates for her to sit at their table at breakfast. Lydia Bennet was in her element.

After wrangling Lydia away from her entourage, we presented ourselves to Cynthia, who deemed us properly attired. Finally, she led us up the sweeping staircase and right to the end of a cream-paneled hallway. "Here are your rooms."

I sucked in a breath as I stepped into an extravagant suite. A canopy bed made up with blush-and-gold linens and draped with matching curtains stood on a raised plinth in the center of the room. Delicate vanity screens in the corner surrounded a claw-foot Victorian bath, set beneath a window overlooking the main drive and parterres. An alcove on the right led into a high-ceilinged study and opulent bathroom decorated in gold and white marble.

"Here is the second room." Cynthia pushed open a door behind the bed, revealing a second room with a similar layout, decorated in teal and gold. A lounge suite was arranged around the high window overlooking the grounds. On the table in front of it stood a bottle of Champagne in a silver bucket and a tray of fancy chocolates.

"These are some treats from us. Grey is sorry he couldn't be here to greet you in person. They're pushing ahead with the King's Copse development, and he's on site at all hours trying to get as much done as possible before the weather turns completely dreadful."

"Tell him we'll happily save his bacon anytime." Morrie was already working the cork off the Champagne bottle.

"Let's hope it doesn't come to that." Cynthia held out four lanyards. "These are your passes for the weekend. Wear them at all times to ensure access to the events, except for the ball. You'll find ribbon wristbands inside for that – we can't have these ugly things ruining our outfits! If there's anything you need, speak to one of the staff and they'll accommodate your every whim. Have an Austentacious time!"

Cynthia left in a whirlwind of perfume. As soon as she was out of sight, Heathcliff loosened his cravat. I kicked off the silk slippers and slid on my Docs. *Ah, comfort, how I missed you.*

"The Lachlans certainly are going above and beyond to give us the star treatment," Morrie said, handing me a glass of Champagne. I noticed he wasn't in a hurry to remove his outfit. Heathcliff was already gulping from his hip flask as he stomped on his cravat.

"It's just as well. From your little performance downstairs, I imagine this suite will quickly fill up with Lydia's admirers."

"Perhaps that was my plan all along, to divert her attention away from my own fragile body... speaking of the annoying wench." Morrie held up a third glass. "Lydia, where are you?"

Lydia poked her head around the door. "I have decided Lord Moriarty and I shall take the pink room with the larger bed. It better suits my complexion."

Morrie's hand froze. "We're not sharing a bed."

"There are four of us, and but two beds," Lydia pointed out. "How else do you propose we make our arrangements? Unless, perhaps, you are the kind of man who does not sleep, because he is awake all night taking care of his amorous duties?"

"I don't know what you mean," Morrie said, his words careful.

"Silly goose! I mean that if you're not to share my bed, then where will you sleep?" Lydia's trilling laugh filled the room. "Because you're not going to share with Mina and Heathcliff. Whatever would people say?"

"People wouldn't say anything, because you wouldn't tell them," Heathcliff growled. "Our sleeping arrangements are none of their business."

"And is your true origin none of their business, too?" Lydia asked sweetly, her eyes sparkling with malice.

I glanced at Morrie and Heathcliff, and read everything I needed to know on their careful expressions. Lydia's presence had highlighted a key flaw in their operation – their honesty in the hands of the wrong book character might lead to their downfall.

I had assumed we three would share and leave Lydia on her own, but it occurred to me that even as flirtatious as Lydia was, she would not react well to the idea of a woman with multiple partners. And if Lydia chose to make her opinions public or make too much of a spectacle, as she seemed inclined to do, she could cause big trouble for all of us.

I sighed. *Perhaps there's a way we can solve this on Lydia's terms?*

"None of us are married, Lydia. It wouldn't be proper. Think what your poor father would say!"

She stamped her foot. "Damn their pomp and propriety. You have feminism now, you told me. And they're not here! I shall never see them again."

"Be that as it may, if you share with Morrie, word will get around that you're committed to him, and your three suitors will quickly lose interest. The key is to incite jealousy, but not to deter them completely."

"Yes, I suppose that makes sense."

Ah, now I've got her. "You and I will share the pink room, and the boys will have this room."

Lydia gasped.

"What?" I demanded. "What's wrong with that idea?"

"Two women, sharing a chamber? Won't people gossip?"

"Exactly," I grinned. A slow smile passed over Lydia's face as she contemplated my words.

"Oh, I do adore your century." She downed her champagne in a single gulp and held out her glass for more.

CHAPTER ELEVEN

*B*etween them, Morrie and Lydia polished off the rest of the Champagne, and we adjourned to our separate rooms to put our things away and prepare for the day's schedule of activities. I took a moment to text Quoth and ask him how his day was going. A moment later, my phone beeped.

"The first customer today asked for a book called Far from the Maddening Crowd. He grew irate when I tried to tell him the title is actually Far from the Madding Crowd, and insisted on speaking it incorrectly even when I presented him with the book cover as evidence. It's not even eleven am yet and already I long to defecate on people. I fear I've turned into Heathcliff.

Stifling a giggle, I sent back a text telling him how much I missed him already.

Once Lydia had fixed my bonnet and demonstrated the proper way to wear a muff, we met Heathcliff and Morrie in the hallway. The pair of them couldn't have been more different. With his stiff collar and black shirt, Morrie had an air of the clergy about him, which was hilarious given his personality. His ice eyes surveyed my outfit with a piercing attention that – were he a real Regency priest – would've seen him excommunicated on the spot. I couldn't help but think all that black would look particularly striking on Quoth, as well.

The military tailoring on Heathcliff's topcoat perfectly flattered his physique, drawing attention to his broad shoulders and narrow waist. His wild hair hung free about his face, and the line of stubble along his chin that he refused to shave and the gleam in his dark eyes gave him an air of danger. His bronze buttons glittered, and at his side hung a thin sword.

"I thought Victoria had your blade?" I asked, touching the elaborate basket hilt.

"This is a spare."

"A spare sword? In case you have more people to stab than weapons available for the task?"

Heathcliff was about to respond, but Lydia twirled around Morrie, dragging him toward the staircase. "Quickly! My new friend David is saving a seat for me."

I linked arms with Heathcliff. "To Pemberley!"

In keeping with her word to name the event's rooms after famous locations from the books, Cynthia had named the grand ballroom Pemberley. It was located off the rear of the entrance hall, accessed through a wide hallway between the staircases that led into a marble anteroom (Uppercross) where the refreshments and goody bags were stationed. Off either side of the entrance hall were two drawing rooms to be used for the smaller workshops – Northanger Abbey and Mansfield Park, and just along from Mansfield Park was Netherfield, which we'd already had cause to visit.

We followed the train of costumed people into Uppercross, where we waited for the doors to the grand ballroom to be opened. While Lydia stole Morrie away for photographs, Heathcliff and I took a turn around the room (mostly for the benefit of scoping out the food being offered). A row of tall, narrow windows along one side let in bright light from the snow-covered lawns outside.

Although stately in proportions and decoration – the high ceiling boasted a mural of songbirds sitting amongst gilded vines – Uppercross bore more touches of Cynthia's eclectic interior design, with some odd choices of furniture. Gilded portraits hung from the walls, and plaques beside each one described the exploits of its subject. That was where the English Heritage ended and the bling began. One wall was dominated by an enormous stone fireplace that had been gilded in gold. It reflected light from the enormous crystal chandeliers. In front of the fire, on a shaggy cream rug, stood a wingback chair in bright cherry red, the wings oversized, pointing up to the ceiling as if the chair hoped to fly away and join the birds.

"Do you think everyone in this room has their breeches up their arse?" Heathcliff muttered under his breath. "Or just me?"

"At least seven people have given me dirty looks for wearing my Docs under my dress," I added. "We make quite the pair."

"As long as you're as miserable as I am," he whispered back, "this weekend won't be a complete turd."

"Want to stuff our pockets full of tiny sandwiches?" I asked.

"Bloody hell, yes."

Heathcliff and I made our way to the buffet. I lined the front pocket of my purse with tissue and dropped several sandwiches and four slices of brownie inside. Meanwhile, Heathcliff shoved macarons up his sleeves. All around me, conversation flowed, discussing everything from historical accuracy in the film adaptations to 'fuck, marry, kill' their favorite male characters. Gold necklaces glittered from bare throats and pearl earrings dangled from every lobe.

The Argleton Jewel Thief could be in this room right now, sizing up his or her next victim.

"... the old Don Juan is at it again. He makes me sick."

My ears pricked at Professor Carmichael's voice. She was on

the opposite side of the food table, her head bent low as she spoke to a young Asian woman wearing a bright blue muslin dress and a string of colorful beads around her neck. They both frowned at a blonde man at the end of the table. He had his back to us, but from the way he kept bending down to touch a young Janeite on her arm and swipe a rogue curl off her face, I knew I was looking at the infamous Professor Hathaway.

Curious now, I moved closer to Professor Carmichael and the other woman. I hovered my hand over a tray of sweets and slices, pretending to be utterly preoccupied with the choice of red velvet cupcake vs miniature lemon curd tart (in reality, I had four of each wrapped up in my purse).

"...it's the absolute last straw," Professor Carmichael hissed to her friend. From this angle, I could see she was a slight woman with high cheekbones and strong chin of Korean features wearing a simple dress that perfectly showed off her creamy skin. "He will pay for what he's done. I won't sit back any longer. I don't know if I can even wait until your article comes out."

"Are you sure?" the Korean woman leaned toward the professor. "If you go to press with this, your own reputation will be on the line. You know how these things usually go. They will say you are jealous of his success, that you are trying to besmirch his name. If you could get a victim to speak, it would be better, but even then it is a big risk."

"I've reached out to everyone I can, but they won't speak against him, for all the reasons you've stated. If I must be the voice, then so be it. The evidence I have to show is scientifically undeniable—"

Before I had a chance to wonder what their conversation was about, the doors opened and the crowd surged into the ballroom. Heathcliff and I were swept along with the tide. No less than three women shot me filthy looks when my Docs crushed their dainty slippers.

Heathcliff choose seats at the back of the room. I squinted at the stage, unable to read the words on the projector from this distance. I rose to move forward, but Lydia dragged a defeated-looking Morrie into our row and plonked him down beside me. One of her new admirers trailed after her and took the seat on the end of our group. Now we were trapped. I sat back down.

"May I introduce my new friend, David Winter," Lydia said, arching her back so her cleavage jutted out into David's field of vision. "David is a graduate student and personal assistant to the fine Professor Hathaway. He is also, I've been told, somewhat of a demon on the dance floor."

"Pleasure to meet you, David." I reached out my hand to shake with him. My cheeks flushed as he turned my hand over, raised it to his lips, and offered a light kiss on top of my knuckles. He really was taking this Regency manners thing quite seriously. "What are you studying?"

"History. My thesis is on currency and measurement in Regency England." His face lit up, like the idea of looking at old coins was exciting or something. "I'm actually giving a lecture on the subject this afternoon, in Mansfield Park, if you're interested in learning about the fascinating world of numismatics. That's what we call the study of currency—"

"Yes, yes." Lydia waved her hand in front of his face. "While I'm sure that's *terribly* fascinating, what Mina and I are really interested in is finding partners for the ball. I am a very accomplished dancer and need someone who can keep up, whereas Mina's utter lack of grace and refinement will need to be tempered with an experienced partner, and her Heathcliff is not up to the task."

"That's not true at all—" I started, but then my elbow knocked my purse off the end of my chair, and Lydia grinned at me in triumph.

"You must reserve a set for me, Lydia." David's eyes wandered to the front of the room, where they rested on a slim, blonde figure chatting with some of the older academics off to the side of the stage. "However, I am sorry to tell Mina that I'm engaged for the rest of the ball. I'll be dancing most dances with Christina—"

"But of course you are. Mina doesn't care, do you, Mina? She doesn't even know how to dance. Whereas I have been dancing practically since I could walk..." David nodded as Lydia prattled on, his eyes glued to the blonde's head. *He's besotted. Whoever the blonde is, I hope for her sake she has a passing interest in currency.*

Beside me, Heathcliff leaned over. "Too bad you didn't pack any chocolate-covered coins into your purse," he whispered. "You'd be beating him off with a stick." I broke down into giggles.

Lydia frowned at Heathcliff's sleeve. "What's that on your cuff?"

"Macaron crumbs?" Heathcliff dumped four slightly-smushed biscuits onto his lap. "Do you want one?"

"I'd rather have my head gruesomely bashed in than eat something from your sleeve."

"That can be arranged."

I waved to Professor Carmichael as she strode past to sit down at the front of the room. The Korean woman she'd been speaking to settled into a seat directly in front of me. Her bold blue dress stood out amongst the pastel colors. She pulled out a rainbow-colored notepad and set up a dictaphone app on her phone. From the conversation I'd overheard earlier, I gathered she was no Hathaway superfan, so that left two possible options – academic or journalist.

After a few moments, Cynthia stepped onto the stage and tapped the microphone to get everyone's attention. "Welcome scholars and makers, ladies and gentlemen, Janeites and long-suffering partners, to the first annual Jane Austen Experience here at Baddesley Hall. I know you're all excited to experience a fine home where Jane herself spent a magical Christmas with her friends. Here, she danced, and dined, and played the pianoforte after breakfast, although never in company—"

A smattering of titters echoed through the hall. "That's a reference to her niece Caroline Austen's biography," I overheard Mrs. Maitland two rows in front of us explain to her bonneted friend. "Jane was introduced to the piano at the Abbey school, aged nine. Caroline said, 'Aunt Jane began her day with music, 'tho she had no one to teach; was never induced to play in company; and none of her family cared much for it'."

Beside me, Heathcliff groaned. I elbowed him. "Let's do a shot every time someone makes an obscure reference," I whispered.

"What, and keel over before lunchtime?" he snorted. "At least let me survive until I can pick these stockings out from my arse—"

"Shhhh!" Lydia hissed.

Cynthia continued. "... perhaps she even penned a few pages under this very roof. My staff and I have done everything we can to recreate a magical Regency event, complete with lectures on every aspect of Jane Austen's world, craft workshops, a costume promenade, and of course, tomorrow night's ball."

At the mention of the ball, the audience clapped. Heathcliff whispered in my ear. "We could drink every time people clap for things that aren't worth clapping over."

"At this rate, we'll be sloshed before the end of the lecture."

The clapping died away, and Cynthia swept her arms in a dramatic arc toward the side of the stage. "It is my pleasure to open our proceedings by inviting our honored guest to present his award-winning lecture on sex and sensuality in Austen. Please welcome to the stage Professor Julius Hathaway."

Lively piano music played from a band in the corner as the man I'd noticed earlier strode his way confidently on stage, escorted on one arm by David's blonde love interest. And no wonder he could not be swayed by Lydia's ample breasts. From the front, I could see how pretty the woman was. She had a figure made for empire-waist dresses. Her blonde hair was piled on top of her head in an arrangement of becoming curls, and a hint of blush lipstick colored her bow-shaped lips.

She shared the same facial structure and hair color as Professor Hathaway, who had a full head of straw-blond hair and sparkling, intelligent eye. Daughter? Niece? Weird coincidence?

Professor Carmichael's words ran through my head as I watched the famous historian take the stage. The professor seemed to grow in height as the applause rolled over him. By the time he reached the podium, he wore a smile so smug he could have given Morrie a run for his money.

"Thank you," he beamed out at the crowd. He had one of those posh Oxbridge voices, because of course he did. He ran a hand through his blond hair and shuffled his notes, and for a moment I saw why he had the power to seduce young women. Intelligence combined with haughty arrogance and a gravelly voice turned a certain kind of woman (i.e., me) to mush. It was why I kept finding myself in Morrie's bed, even though all evidence suggested he was a bit of an emotionally-unavailable wanker. "I'd say it's a pleasure to be here, but really the pleasure is all yours."

Women in the crowd tittered. Because of course they did. Heathcliff pretended to hang himself, and I stifled a laugh as a woman two rows over shot us a filthy look.

Professor Hathaway launched into a lewd and hilarious lecture, which mostly consisted of taking dialogue from the books out of context and making suggestive remarks about the size of Jane Austen's breasts. His delivery was such a triumph of wit and charisma that I doubted anyone in the room noticed just how little actual scholarship he expounded.

All except one. After Professor Hathaway mentioned her name for the umpteenth time, Lydia leaned toward me. "Who does this gentleman think he is?" she whispered. "Why does he keep talking about me as though I'm some kind of rabid dog?"

"He's a renowned historian and Austen scholar. He believes he knows more about your habits than you do. He even wrote a book about you."

"But that's preposterous, otherwise he wouldn't have called me 'a caterwauling strumpet.'" Lydia shrieked. "I resent it. I have a mild and agreeable voice! I have a mind to stand up right now and give him a piece of my mind."

Now more heads were turning to frown at us.

Morrie threw out his hand. "You do that, and you risk exposing us all. Remember, no one can know you're the real Lydia Bennet. Now sit back, and stay *silent*. Or we'll sick Professor Hathaway on you. I heard he has quite the reputation as a lover of young women."

"Really?" Lydia eyed the professor with interest, her previous outrage forgotten. "He is awfully rich."

"Morrie, don't even kid about that," I snapped. "If what's been said about that man is true, he's abusing his power and may be sexually harassing young women. That's not funny."

"What is funny is how a man that old even gets stiff enough to do everything he's accused of," Morrie mused, his voice a little louder than I thought wise.

"He's not that old. Only in his fifties—"

"Yes he is," Morrie huffed. "He looks like he'd be just the right age for Jane Austen herself, and she's *dead*."

"I've heard it on good authority he's a fan of little blue pills," an unfamiliar voice cut in.

I turned to meet the piercing eyes of the Korean woman. Up close, I could see she had one of those faces with the startling symmetry and intense cheekbones that made men stop in their tracks. She clutched her phone in her hand, and the dictaphone continued to record. The pages of her open notebook were already filled with scribbles. Around her neck was her lanyard and a camera I recognized as the same model my friend Ashley used to shoot her social media selfies.

I snorted. "That doesn't surprise me."

"I can't believe I have to sit here and listen to this waste of oxygen speak." She flipped her lanyard around to show me her press credentials. Alice Yo – she was with the *Custodian*, an online news site famous for award-winning journalism. They'd once done an exposé into transgender models that had nearly derailed Paris Fashion Week.

I stretched out my leg and lifted the hem of my skirt to show her my boots. "It's not exactly my usual scene, either." I grinned. "I'm far more comfortable in boots than bonnets. Want a sandwich?"

I held out my purse. Alice shook her head, smiling as she showed me the pocket of her jacket, also lined with napkins and filled with a variety of food items.

"At least the food is decent." Alice rolled her eyes. "A good thing too, because my flat fridge is completely empty. Maybe that could be my headline – LET JANEITES EAT CAKE. My boss didn't even have an angle for this story. He basically wants me to write a piece about these sad spinsters and virgin LARPers. I've been in war zones and covered international politics, but I had to take it because I need the work. That's what happens when you're a woman in my business. You get given the fluff stories."

"Are you sure it's just because none of the male journalists know how to tie a cravat?"

We both giggled. I liked this reporter already. From the stage, the professor shot us a filthy look, but continued to drone on.

"My name's Mina Wilde. I work at Nevermore Bookshop, in the village. Although I used to work in fashion, so I know a little about industry-sanctioned misogyny."

"I recognize your name. You're on my table for the ball. My editor got me these expensive VIP tickets. An all-access pass, he told me. 'It's going to be like Woodstock, except with bonnets. You'll love it, Alice'." She mimicked his voice. Then she leaned forward, her eyes sparkling. "He's expecting a fluffy story about

94

how endearingly colonial this weekend is, but I've got a *real* story for him instead."

"Oh, intrigue."

"I can't say anything now, but there's a scandal brewing among the Janeites, and I intend to bring it to light."

A woman in the row in front of Alice, sporting a rather magnificent bonnet resplendent with fabric flowers turned in her seat to shush us. Alice turned back to the front. I straightened my back and tried to pay attention to Professor Hathaway.

"... and when Captain Wentworth lays hands on Anne Elliot for the first time following their estrangement, it's with an act of authority that leaves her perfectly speechless and of the most disordered feelings. The man in charge left any Regency woman hot under the bodice—"

CRASH.

The ballroom door burst open. I jumped in my seat as a rotund man sporting an impressive goatee and a floor-length black leather trench coat thundered up the aisle, followed by three women in gothic-style black dresses and corsets.

"In the words of one of the greatest writers in the English language, Jane Austen was nothing but an accurate daguerreo-typed portrait of a commonplace face," he sneered.

Professor Hathaway's expression remained even, but anger flashed in his eyes. "What are you doing here, Gerald? This event is for Janeites only."

"Not so. This event is for anyone who has a ticket." Gerald held up his lanyard with glee. "And since I am in possession of such a ticket, the Argleton branch of the Brontë Society will enjoy the weekend as we wish."

The man on stage bristled. "Very well. Take a seat, for I wish to continue my lecture."

Gerald held up a finger. "Not so fast. We should like to correct you on one or two salient points. Namely, that your Mr. Darcy is in any way a romantic hero and a sexual being."

"Lord Fitzwilliam Darcy was the greatest romantic hero of all time." Mrs. Maitland stood up, her face red with anger.

"Darcy was a shit!" yelled a girl wearing black fishnet top over a PVC bra. "He's an uptight, bullish snob who gets off on manipulating people, and he needs to check his privilege!"

"He was also a monumental bore at parties," added another girl in a black-and-white striped Beetlejuice dress of which I was deeply envious. "At least you know Heathcliff would be spiking the punch and participating in reckless skullduggery."

Heathcliff leaned forward. "Now I'm interested," he whispered.

"Just so you know, I'd choose you over Darcy any day," I whispered back. "And not just because this dress is ridiculously impractical for running about the moors."

"As much as I admire your enthusiasm, Gerald, and as much as there are those among us who may secretly feel Emily Brontë to be the superior writer, Heathcliff was never meant to be held up as an example of a romantic hero," Professor Carmichael said from the front of the room. "*Wuthering Heights* is a story of toxic obsession and bitter revenge, and of the next generation washing away the sins of the past—"

"All Heathcliff was good for was headbutting trees and snogging skeletons," Professor Hathaway sneered, rudely cutting off his colleague. "If you like your sexual partners twisted by jealousy and made ugly by their desire for revenge, Hannah, well, then, I can see why you chose Gerald."

Gerald's face blazed. He wrenched himself from Hannah's grip and stormed toward the stage, his hands balled into fists at his sides. The crowd surged as it became apparent a fight was about to break out. David leaped to his feet and rushed toward the stage. Two of Lydia's graduate student admirers moved in front of the steps that accessed the stage. Gerald whirled on his heels.

"Come down here and say that to my face, old man." Gerald's words dripped with menace.

"Go home, Gerald," Hathaway said. "I can smell the alcohol on your breath. This is not the forum to stir up dissent about our beloved Mr. Darcy."

"Yeah!" A Janeite in the middle of the room stood up. "Darcy is a thoroughly decent man underneath his pompous exterior, far more worthy of admiration than that vicious, dog-murdering sociopath—"

"Ouch," Heathcliff muttered.

"*Decent?*" Hannah scoffed. "If decent gets you off, lady, then why are you all here fawning over *that* man?" She jabbed an accusatory finger at Professor Hathaway. "Nothing he does with graduate students could be described as decent—"

"Careful," warned Hathaway. "That's an accusation against my good character that could ruin my career. If I were a less congenial man, I might consider legal repercussions for this baseless accusation—"

"It's hardly baseless!" Carmichael yelled. "You'll soon find out just how little tolerance the world has for your behavior."

"Are you threatening me, Professor?" Hathaway's voice sounded amused. "If this is revenge because I rejected your sexual advances, then it's very petty, rather like Gerald's hero Heathcliff."

"I resent that," Heathcliff muttered.

"That never happened!" Carmichael roared. "You're lying, just like you've been lying to your daughter! But we'll get you."

In front of me, Alice stiffened. I wondered if Carmichael's comment had something to do with what they'd been discussing earlier. *Hathaway must be the subject of Alice's article.*

"Bring on your legal repercussions, old man!" Gerald yelled back. "I'm not afraid of you and your horde of Austen sycophants!"

"That's enough!" Cynthia yelled. "Gentleman, ladies, please be civilized. Unfortunately, I cannot allow you to block the aisle in this fashion, as it's a fire hazard. I see some empty seats near the back. If you and your entourage would but take a seat and be silent, we can continue with the proceedings. You'll have plenty of time to debate the questionable merits of Heathcliff outside of the plenary sessions."

Gerald cast his gaze between Hathaway and Cynthia, and to the blonde girl – Hathaway's aforementioned daughter, I guessed – cowering in David's arms. His shoulders sagged. "Very well. But I'm watching you and your wandering hands, old man."

As the group slid into the seats opposite us, I noticed Alice frantically scribbling. I leaned over her chair and tapped her on the shoulder. "Do you know what just happened?" I asked Alice.

"I should think you'd recognize Gerald Bromley," she replied. "He's a bit of a local character. He's president of the local Brontë Society. Those gothic beauties are his executive committee and they hang off every word he says. Apparently, he used to be one of Hathaway's graduate students, before they had a falling out and Gerald was dismissed from his graduate program. He works locally as a consultant for English Heritage properties and grand estates, helping them run events and tours with historical accuracy. Cynthia offered him a handsome sum to be on the committee for this event, but when he heard Hathaway was the guest of honor, he threw a big stink and quit."

"Then why is he here?"

She shrugged. "Janeites and Brontians have a famous rivalry, but I suspect it's personal. Gerald's probably here just to rattle Professor Hathaway."

If that was Gerald's intention, he succeeded. Hathaway stumbled through the rest of his speech without his previous *joy de vivre*. On two occasions, David even had to point to his place in his notes.

The audience remained subdued after Gerald's outburst, no longer clapping and laughing at every Austen reference. Gerald and his three gothic maidens whispered amongst themselves throughout the lecture, passing around a hip flask between them. I didn't speak to Alice for the rest of the lecture and lost her in the crowd when it was over. I hoped we'd see her again – she seemed like my kind of person.

After the plenary, we had a choice of lectures on various aspects of Austen's world or a fencing demonstration on the back lawn. I had no intention of going outside in the freezing weather, but Cynthia swept past us on the stairs and informed me that as VIPs we were welcome to watch from the covered balcony in her first-floor office. Eager to explore more of the house and watch men swing swords around, I dragged Heathcliff after her. Morrie and Lydia followed us, leading a trail of Lydia's admirers.

A roof over the balcony kept out the worst of the snow. I gravitated toward the large brazier at one end, where a man in period costume handed out small cups of hot chocolate. I collected two for myself and leaned over the side to view the fencers below while listening to the commentary on Regency fencing techniques. In the open courtyard below us, Lydia's friend David parried with another gent in period attire. He deflected a thrust and lunged at his opponent, touching the point of his sword to the man's heart. They bowed to each other and resumed another match.

After several more rounds, it was clear the mousy graduate student was no amateur with a blade. Again and again he deprived his opponent of his weapon, and twice knocked him on his arse. He didn't utter a word of mockery, and even apologized and disqualified himself from a win for an imagined infraction. *What a gentleman. He'd be swoon-worthy if he didn't study coins for a living.*

After twenty minutes of fighting, David removed his fencing mask to take a drink of water. Hathaway's blonde daughter rushed over to him, offering him an embroidered handkerchief to wipe the sweat from his face.

"What do you think of the fighting?" Heathcliff asked.

"It's exciting, but rather vicious," I remarked.

"Please," Morrie quipped. "I could take them all down with my middle finger."

"You fence, do you?" I lifted an eyebrow.

"Please. I was champion of my college at Oxford. Although, I did always prefer dueling with a cane. It makes a satisfying sound when it splits a man's skull."

Beside him, Lydia shivered with delight. "Lord Moriarty, you say such wicked things!"

"What about you?" I asked Heathcliff. "You've got a sword hanging off your belt. Do you know how to use it?"

"I'm not schooled in that fancy sort of fencing with flimsy foils," he muttered. "But I've slit a man open with a blade, if that's what you're asking."

I shivered. Unlike Lydia, it wasn't from delight. "When did you do that?"

"There were blades enough lying around in the North, and I'm an angry man who picked a lot of fights," he replied. "I'm not proud of it, but you must never forget that I am Heathcliff. What did that woman call me just before – a vicious, dog-murdering sociopath."

"I know that's not who you are."

Heathcliff turned his head away. I placed my hand on his, and he shrugged it off. I hadn't realized that this weekend might be difficult for him in this way – being confronted with the legacy of the actions he took inside the pages of a book.

I wanted so badly for Heathcliff to see that man I saw in him – the one who took a stray cat in and cared for her, who locked his heart inside an iron chest and threw away the key because he'd been driven low and made into a beast by a brother who should have loved him, who may be a bit of a grump (okay, a lot of a grump) but would go to the ends of the earth to protect the people he cared about. Sometimes I caught a glimmer of hope in

Heathcliff's eyes, and the wild passion with which he kissed told me that maybe his edges were crumbling. But then...

But then he looked dark and dangerous – like he did now – and I wasn't sure what to believe.

I needed to talk to him, but I couldn't with Morrie and Lydia and all the Janeites around. So I changed the subject. "I wonder who that blonde woman is. I see a family resemblance, but Professor Carmichael did say he liked to date graduate students."

"While he would be exactly her type, it's highly unlikely that they are dating." A soft American accent broke in behind me. "That's Christina Hathaway."

I glanced around to see Professor Carmichael clutching a hot chocolate in her hand. A fur-lined bonnet was tied around her salt-and-pepper hair.

"Let me guess, relation to the eminent professor?" Morrie inquired.

"His daughter." Professor Carmichael sniffed. "He's raised her to be his perfect Regency girl, based on his own studies of parenting and fatherhood in Jane Austen's books. The poor girl probably believes she needs his permission in order to even have coffee alone with young David."

"You're serious?"

"Oh yes. Christina's been utterly indoctrinated. She's by Julius' side at every event and book signing. She seems to have no life outside of him and his interests, and she defers to him always. In many ways, she's more his wife than his daughter. Of course, he has seen to it that she has a thorough education in all pursuits deemed appropriate for young ladies, and is quite accomplished at the pianoforte, needlework, sewing, that sort of thing. She has that certain something in her air and manner of walking, in her address and expressions, that would have even Mr. Darcy award her with the title of 'accomplished'. But I do not believe she's ever once binge-watched *Gilmore Girls* or snogged someone entirely inappropriate after too much wine."

I laughed at her description. "That sounds like a lonely life."

"Indeed. Although to many here this weekend, it is the life to aspire to."

"But not you?"

She waved a hand. "Oh, don't get me wrong. I am a Janeite through and through. For all my academic posturing about Austen's popularity being a kind of moral nostalgia, I fell in love with her heroes as a little girl. If Mr. Darcy were to ask for my hand, I would accept without hesitation. I just don't go in for all this silly *pageantry*." She pointed at the toe of my boot sticking out from the hem of my dress. "I see you and I share a similar disposition."

I laughed again, loving how all the rebellious Janeites seemed to be finding me.

The bell sounded from within the house, alerting us that the hour had come to move to our next activity of choice. Lydia insisted on Regency dance lessons. "I shall show you all how we danced at Netherfield," she declared. "But first, we should pay a quick visit to David's lecture. I should wish to offer him my ribbon for winning all of his duels."

When we entered Mansfield Park, David's eyes lit up. He stood at the front of the room, laying out trays of old coins nestled in velvet pouches. Even though he'd been soaked in sweat only minutes ago, he appeared fresh-faced, his hair perfectly tamed and his clothing immaculate, right down to his ruffled cravat. Apart from an old man peering at the coins with mild interest while his wife tugged on his arm, we were the only other people.

"Lydia, I'm so pleased you came." David gave a deep bow. "I was beginning to think they'd placed my lecture alongside the dancing as they were certain no one was interested enough to show up, but I knew the world of numismatics was too exciting to keep you away—"

"We're not staying," Lydia said. "My friends are in desperate need of dancing instruction, and I wish to be there to laugh at their foils. But we did want to visit with you beforehand and congratulate you on your fencing prowess."

"Yes, that was an impressive performance," Morrie put in. "Tell me, how do you fare with a gentleman's cane? Or the bare knuckles?"

"Bare-knuckle boxing is illegal in this country," David said. He offered his arm to Lydia, who took it with a smile and a tilt of her head. "Come, Lydia. Let me quickly show you this fascinating world of numismatics. Coins really do bring the Regency era to life…"

We crowded around and tried to look interested as David held up different coins and explained their denomination and mineral composition, and the significance of their designs. Heathcliff pretended to hang himself behind David's back. Ignoring him, I bent down to examine the tiny coins.

"Um, Mina? You shouldn't get so close," David said. "Your breath contains droplets of water, which can damage the delicate metal."

"Oh." I stood up so fast I crashed into the old man, who stumbled into his wife. They both glared at me and hurried off.

"Now you've scared away my only other attendees," David said sadly. "That man was going to buy a copy of my book."

I noticed a table in the corner with a massive stack of books on it. My cheeks blazed with heat. I hadn't realized I'd been looking so closely. Instinctively, my hand flew to my chest, where my father's letter still rested between my breasts, reminding me that this was *his* fault.

"While it's very fascinating watching Mina sniff the coins," Lydia said. "I use these coins every day and I don't need them explained to me when I could be dancing. I expect to see you this evening, David. I look forward to dancing the quadrille with you."

The four of us raced out of the drawing room. As I turned I

caught a glimpse of David, staring after us with wide, sad eyes. But after he'd drawn attention to my eyesight, I didn't feel any sympathy for him.

"Oh, what a dreadful bore." Lydia laughed. "If she were here, I think I might offer him my sister Mary. She seems quite his type. Why, he keeps his money in little pouches and doesn't even spend it. What a fool."

"Why do modern people find coins so fascinating?" Morrie mused. "The only time currency interests me is when I'm attempting to launder it."

"You wash your money?" Lydia gasped. "But why?"

I rolled my eyes. "Not that kind of laundering, Lydia."

"Well, what kind of laundering?"

Isis save us.

"Oh look, we've reached the ballroom." Morrie offered Lydia an elbow, and she immediately shut up. "Shall we?"

"Are you sure you want to go in there?" The pensive look on Heathcliff's face during the fencing, and the way he slunk away from me, played on my mind. "We could go somewhere quiet and talk—"

Heathcliff sighed. "If you're insisting on attending this godawful ball, I guess we'd best not make fools of ourselves."

Given the ball was tomorrow evening, and the only dancing I knew how to do involved throwing myself around a circle pit at a punk show, I agreed it was a good idea. As we passed through the entrance hall, I noticed Christina Hathaway standing with her father while he signed autographs for a gaggle of giggling Janeites. "Wait here," I told Heathcliff, curious about the professor.

I pushed myself through the crowd and extended a hand. "It's a pleasure to meet you, Professor Hathaway," I said. "I enjoyed your lecture. The first part, at least."

He held my hand several moments longer than was polite, his finger sliding over my knuckles in a way that made my skin crawl. "Thank you, my dear. Tell me, do you consider yourself a scholar of Regency society, or are you here for the fun and frivolity?"

"Oh, no. I just came because I like books. 'I declare after all that there is no enjoyment like reading.'" Proud of slipping in an Austen quote, I patted Heathcliff's shoulder. "We're from Nevermore Bookshop in the village."

"Really?" His eyes lit up in a predatory way. "Mr. Simson's old establishment? I swear that place is so ancient it was probably around when dear Jane visited the village. It's nice to see it in such *delightful* young hands. You should speak to David about having me do a signing. I'd be pleased to support the local arts in *any way* I can." His words were accompanied by a super unsubtle wink.

Gross. I deflected the professor's attention by curtseying to Christina. "Pardon me, I don't believe I've had the pleasure."

"Christina Hathaway." She curtseyed back. I caught a peek at her dainty feet inside a pair of pristine silk slippers. No Docs for Christina Hathaway.

I scrambled for something to say to her, so I wouldn't have to speak to Hathaway again. "I've heard you're a talented musician. Will you be gracing us with a song over the weekend?"

"Oh, I couldn't possibly." Christina looked to her father.

"Nonsense. You must give us a song or two. Christina is accomplished in all that she does," the professor beamed. "She has a thorough knowledge of music, singing, drawing, dancing, and several languages. Her embroidery wins national awards, her performance on the pianoforte is exquisite, and she makes all her own clothes, as well as my own humble wardrobe."

It was on the tip of my tongue to quote Mr. Darcy that the word accomplished 'is applied to many a woman who deserves it no otherwise than by netting a purse or covering a screen', but then I took in the professor's elaborate embroidered waistcoat and lace cravat. The work that must've gone into that outfit was astounding. Christina must indeed be very accomplished.

"Mina, there you are." Cynthia grabbed my shoulder and spun me around. "I was just telling Michaela here all about your skill at solving murders."

Professor Carmichael's harangued expression changed to sympathy as she recognized me.

"I just got lucky," I said, searching the room for Heathcliff or Morrie, someone who might be able to save me. Gerald stood in the corner, a glass of wine paused at his lips. When he noticed our merry group, he slid closer.

What's his game? Why would anyone pay hundreds of pounds for tickets to an event they didn't even want to attend just to psych out their old professor? Does Gerald have something else planned?

I was drawn back to the present by Cynthia's gushing about me. "...no, no, Mina's being modest. Those incompetent detectives were going to have Grey and I charged with the murder of my dear friend, Gladys Scarlett. Can you imagine such a thing! While we were at the station, fighting for justice to be done, Mina single-handedly chased down not one, but *two* murderers. And just five weeks ago she figured out that the local market bagboy killed a girl in the bookshop. Why, I say that Argleton Jewel Thief better watch out if Mina ever decides to get on his case. Wouldn't you say so, Michaela?"

Cynthia stopped talking long enough to suck in a breath. Professor Carmichael seemed unaware that she had been left to pick up the conversation. Her body stood rigid with anger as she stared at Professor Hathaway.

"Michaela," he nodded in a businesslike way, smiling that creepy smile of his.

"Julius," she shot back, her voice frosty.

The conversation stalled with the two academics staring daggers at each other. Cynthia opened her mouth, likely to continue her gushing praise for my mystery-solving prowess. To cut her off, I turned to Christina. "You're very talented. I know a little about fashion. I studied at New York Fashion School, and worked with the designer Marcus Ribald for a year. I know how much skill must've gone into these outfits."

"Thank you," she beamed. "Did you live in New York City all by yourself?"

"Of course! Well, I lived with my friend Ashley. We had this tiny place off Greenwich Avenue, so we were close to the West Village and all the great shopping and bars. I got to work Fashion Week, and it was amazing."

"But weren't you afraid? I've read that New York City is dangerous for a young woman on her own. Did you not have an escort?"

"It can be dangerous. You've just got to be sensible and prepared. Ashley and I took a self-defense class. I learned how to kick a man in the balls. I'm a little bit disappointed I never got to use it."

"I took fencing classes!" Christina blurted out. She seemed shocked. Beside her, Hathaway stiffened. "But Father prefers I stick to ladylike pursuits."

Um, okay.

"Well, if you want to sit down over lunch or dinner, I could tell you all about fashion school. I could even give you some application tips if you wanted to get in." I turned to Cynthia. "Are Christina and her father seated near us at the ball tomorrow?"

"Of course. You are both at the VIP table for our most honored guests," Cynthia beamed.

"Perfect. We can talk more at the ball."

Christina beamed. "I'd like that very—"

"Thank you, but Christine has a full weekend already," Professor Hathaway touched his daughter's hand. "Please escort me back to my room, dear. I don't wish to derail the dance practice with my presence. When the ladies see me on the dance floor, they tend to go a bit silly."

Christina rearranged her face into a placid expression. "Of course, Father. Please, excuse us." He took her arm, leaning into her to whisper something in her ear, and they ascended the staircase.

Heathcliff stared after them. "That scoundrel."

"Who?"

"Hindley," he whispered. His body shuddered with rage.

"What do you mean?" Hindley was the brother of Catherine Earnshaw and Heathcliff's sworn enemy in his book, but I didn't know why his name came up now.

"Watch her walk away," Heathcliff said through gritted teeth. "See how her body stiffens at his touch? See how she shrinks away as he leans close?"

I followed his gaze to Christina and Professor Hathaway as they ascended the staircase, squinting as I tried to follow her movements. My shrinking peripheral vision limited what I could see, but I thought I saw her step outward in order to place another inch of space between her arm and his.

"I think I see what you mean," I whispered. "But I don't understand what it has to do with Hindley."

"He does not see her," Heathcliff whispered, his voice tight. "He only sees what he wants to see. The pain he causes because of his own misery will break her, too."

I cast my mind back to *Wuthering Heights*, to Heathcliff's hatred for the man who terrorized him, how it was that hatred, combined with the pain of Cathy's death, that trapped Heathcliff in his destructive pattern. He was saying that Christina was trapped by her father's Regency ideals, and I had to agree.

A shudder rocked through Heathcliff's body. A line of sweat streaked across his brow. A thunderstorm raged inside his eyes as he stared ahead at the spot where Hathaway and Christina had been.

I snapped my fingers in front of his face. "Oi, come back to me. That wasn't Hindley."

Heathcliff blinked. "What?"

"You went somewhere else for a moment. I think you believed Christina's father *was* Hindley."

Heathcliff ran a hand through his tousled hair. "Yes. I did. His manner to his daughter... the way he sought to control her... I'm back now. I think it's all these costumes, all this grandeur. It's doing my head in."

"Come on," I grabbed Heathcliff by the hand. "No more thinking of Hindley. We've not at Wuthering Heights now. This is Jane Austen, where all can be forgiven with a ball and a marriage proposal. If we're to attend the dance tomorrow, you're going to need to know all the moves."

CHAPTER TWELVE

"Ow," Heathcliff muttered as I trod on his foot again.

"You don't have to say that every time I stand on you," I muttered as Heathcliff and I crossed places. "It doesn't hurt *that* much."

"You're not the one whose shins are being battered around by steel-capped toes," Heathcliff growled as he turned around the man behind him. I turned too, only I got the direction wrong, and ended up spinning right into a woman's shoulder. "At least now we know why women wore those dainty slippers. It's so they didn't hobble the men in the room."

"You're such a twat." I stretched out my hand to meet him again in the middle. "Shut up and spin me."

As I ducked under Heathcliff's arm in an awkward circle, Morrie and Lydia glided past us, lifting their arms as they crossed over to swap partners. *At least someone's having no trouble at all learning the moves.* I glowered at them both as I swung around Heathcliff and stood on his foot again. It didn't surprise me – Morrie had to control every aspect of his life, so of course he'd have a perfect sense of rhythm and grace.

As he turned back to the set, Morrie's eyes met mine. What I saw there startled me. He looked *frightened*.

Weird. Fear was not an emotion on Morrie's radar. Even when he'd leaped out at Darren as he tried to stab me, his eyes blazed with a kind of brutal intensity. Morrie knew exactly what he was doing at every moment. He had a solution for everything. He never had a reason to feel fear.

What about this dance has him so on-edge? My mind flashed back to the letter Morrie received earlier this week, the letter that he refused to explain to anyone. *It can't have anything to do with this ball, can it?*

Still thinking about Morrie, I lost my step and crashed into David.

"Yeooow!" David winced, breaking his Regency cool to grab his injured foot, which was encased only in a buckled fabric shoe. He'd finally given up hope of anyone attending his numismatics lecture and joined the dancing fifteen minutes ago, a decision he was probably right this moment regretting as he hobbled across the dance floor. He knocked into Cynthia, sending her sprawling into a waiter, who knocked a tray of glasses.

"I'm sorry!" I bent down to help Cynthia to her feet.

"Thank you, Mina." Cynthia dusted off her muslin gown. "My, this dancing is harder than I imagined."

"You were supposed to go *under*," Heathcliff smirked at me. "Not go down and take everyone in the room with you."

"I'll do it better next time," I grumbled, watching Morrie and Lydia spinning away. I couldn't see his face.

"No, you won't. We're getting off this dance floor before you put someone's eye out." Heathcliff took me under the arm and dragged me off. Behind me, the dancers applauded.

Ingrates.

I dragged Heathcliff toward the front of the room, where Morrie and Lydia were still dancing the set. "It turns out that

Regency dancing is much more complicated than moshing to punk music." I glowered at Morrie as he spun Lydia around in perfect time. Morrie glanced up at me. His body stiffened. Although he didn't step out of time, his focus wavered for a moment, and his perfect features crumpled back into a look of such despair that sent a chill down my spine.

Why is he looking at me like that, as though I've just stomped on his pet puppy? It can't be that he's finally realized his behavior has been upsetting me – this is Morrie we're talking about. He wouldn't care. So what's wrong?

Heathcliff's foot came down on my boot. "What are you staring at?"

"Morrie. Something's up with him."

Heathcliff peered at our friend as he and Lydia switched places. As he skipped past her, he pinched her bum. She squealed in delight and chased after Morrie to get him back, causing two dancers to lose their time and crash into each other. "True. He's a bigger wanker than usual."

"That's not it." I squinted at Morrie as he came around to do the twirl and swap again. His eyes fell on mine. He plastered his usual sublime grin on his face, but too late – I'd seen the darkness lurking there. "I mean, you're right. He's been a massive wanker lately, but I think something else is going on. There was that weird letter he got the other day, and some things he's said and done."

Like the way he ran away from me after that threesome—

At the thought of that night – of being sandwiched between Morrie and Quoth while they did delicious things to my body, of surrendering my senses to dwell in the dark places beneath their hands and lips – a delicious shiver ran through my body. *By Aphrodite, not now. I'm trying to figure out Morrie, not relive one of the hottest moments of my entire life so that I become a puddle of mush on the ballroom floor—*

"From MENSA," Heathcliff cut into my memories.

"What?"

"I saw the envelope in the rubbish bin," Heathcliff shrugged. "It was from some organization called MENSA. I assumed Morrie was blackmailing them."

MENSA? I wasn't surprised that Morrie was a member. He liked people to know exactly how clever he was. But I *was* surprised that he kept the letter secret. Morrie wouldn't waste a moment telling everyone in Argleton that he'd been accepted into MENSA. *So then why did he hide the letter? And what does it have to do with the weird way he'd been acting?*

"What if he took an IQ test, and he *failed*." My mind whirred. Yes, it could explain why Morrie was so snappy, especially when one of us implied he didn't have the answer to something. "Maybe he's worried he's not as clever as he thinks he is, and he's taking it out on us?"

"But this weirdness started well before that letter arrived," Heathcliff pointed out.

"True. Do you think he—"

"Do you want a drink?" Heathcliff growled in my ear.

"Hell yes."

He gripped my hand and dragged me off the dance floor. Cynthia yelled after us to come back and dance in the next set, but my shins hurt so much I no longer cared. Heathcliff tugged me into the Uppercross antechamber, now empty of people, unless you counted the two staff members clearing away the discarded napkins and cocktail sticks. Heathcliff steadied himself against the gilded fireplace and jammed his hands down the front of his breeches. A moment later, he produced a silver flask, popped the cork, and offered it to me.

"I'm not drinking that. It's been against your testicles."

"Suit yourself." Heathcliff knocked back a shot. "There's barely any room to hide booze in these ridiculous clothes. Give me a greatcoat and some proper trousers and I could mix you a right posh cocktail."

"By the end of *Wuthering Heights* you were quite the gentleman," I teased him. "You'd have worn clothes like this all the time."

"Luckily I got out before my life became so dire." Heathcliff took another sip. I paused, wondering if I should ask him about his odd moment earlier, but then he said, "I've been thinking about your letter."

"You have?" Instinctively, my hand flew to my chest, where my father's letter pinched between my breasts. Between all the costumes and warring academics and running around after Lydia, I'd barely thought about it or the fight with my mother all day. At that moment, it all came rushing back to me – that I was at Baddesley Hall dressed in this ridiculous outfit and forcing Heathcliff through the ordeal of a Regency ball because I was desperate to avoid the subject.

I still hadn't told Heathcliff, Morrie, or my mother about the fireworks and what Dr. Clements had said. I hadn't even tried to research the letter beyond Morrie's examination of the paper. I'd been so distracted by balls and bonnets that I hadn't given any more thought to my father and the time-travelling room and Victoria's comment about me being covered in blood. For someone who'd faced down three murderers, I sure was running away from a hell of a lot.

Examining my behavior from the outside, I made about as much sense to myself as Morrie did right now. All my life I'd wanted to know who my father was. The only thing holding me back from hunting him down in earnest was knowing how much it would hurt my mother and how disappointed I'd be that I'd find a criminal.

But if my father *was* Herman Strepel, the time-traveling bookseller, and whatever disguise he'd presented for my mother had been designed to help hide him from the nameless enemy, then the next move was obvious to me – I *had* to find him.

Heathcliff snapped his fingers in front of my face. "Now it was you who went off somewhere."

"Yes, sorry. You were saying?"

"Your father and Mr. Simson both spoke about you being in danger. Victoria also said your father purchased occult volumes from her. Mr. Simson acquired a large occult book collection in the shop. It stands to reason that they knew each other."

"You're right." I hadn't made that connection. Another coincidence that couldn't possibly be a coincidence at all. I patted Heathcliff's arm. "That's very wise. *Too* wise for someone as ungentlemanly as you. Did you and Morrie somehow swap bodies in the time-travel bedroom? It would explain why you're being all clever and he's being a mega grump."

"I *am* clever," Heathcliff growled.

"Yes, but your cleverness is hidden behind your surly and arseholeish exterior."

"Fine. I concede your point. But grumpy or not, I'm on to something here. If your father is intent on staying away from you, perhaps we should attempt to track down the old man? You said he treated you as a special helper in the shop when you were a kid. Perhaps it was his way of trying to protect you. At the very least, Morrie can look into his life, see which retirement home he's holed up in." Heathcliff shrugged. "If we can find him, Mr. Simson might tell us more about this supposed danger."

"You're right. We will do that as soon as we get back. Maybe sooner, if I get sick of wearing these clothes and decide to bail early."

"Please do. Mina?" Heathcliff leaned closer. His deep voice rumbled in my chest. I loved when he said my name.

"Yeah?" An electric charge leaped from my body to his.

"I've been thinking about the other night, in the time-travel bedroom."

My heart thudded. I'd been thinking about it too, non-stop, all the time. How if Victoria Bainbridge hadn't interrupted us, and Morrie hadn't been such a wanker, we might've... things could have...

I might have slept with all three of them.

At once.

I gulped. Why did the idea of it make my body flush with desire and quiver with fear at the same time?

I'd already been with Morrie and Quoth together, and with Heathcliff on the same night. But that was a one-off threesome while I was tied up and then this was... another thing entirely.

There was the way Heathcliff unleashed himself when we were together, as though being with me kept him teetered on the edge of insanity. There was Quoth's impossible kindness and his desperate, silent plea to be loved, and Morrie's battle to control his emotions and conceal his dual nature. There was the way the three of them made me feel like I was invincible, like I could do anything. When I was with them, I wasn't poor friendless Mina, the sad girl who was going blind. I was a goddess. And by Astarte that felt good.

I could never choose one of them. I needed them all, as I'd come to suspect they needed me. But did that mean all four of us, in bed, together? Would that even work?

"What were you thinking?" I managed to choke out.

Another guy might've turned away from such a proposal, but this was *Heathcliff.* His eyes blazed, boring into mine like they intended to flush out a bit of my soul. "I've already texted Quoth to tell him to head straight to Baddesley Hall after he closes the shop. If you want to finish what we started, you should wait until Lydia is asleep and sneak into our room tonight."

"Okay," I whispered, my heart in my throat.

Behind Heathcliff, the ballroom doors burst open. Attendees spilled out, chatting and laughing, demonstrating their dance moves to each other. Waiters swept in to offer refreshments, and maids ducked into the ballroom to clean up after the session. The noise swirled around us, bouncing off the high roof. All I saw was Heathcliff's dark eyes boring into mine, devouring me. Heat pooled between my legs as I accepted the promise of what I would receive tonight from my three fictional men.

CHAPTER THIRTEEN

"A couple just left the shop. The wife wore her Regency finery and informed me they were in the village for the festival. She trotted around the shop, exclaiming over every little thing, and ended up buying that complete set of Folio Society Austen from your display for £150. The husband dragged his feet after her, weighed down by shopping bags. He leaned over the counter with a look of utter despair and asked if we any books in the craft section about how to build a gun, as he wished to shoot himself in the head. On a positive note, absolutely no one has quoted 'The Raven' today, and I look forward with rare and radiant anticipation to seeing you later this evening."

*A*fter speaking with Heathcliff, I found Quoth's text on my phone. It only increased the maelstrom of excitement and nerves swirling around inside my stomach.

I barely heard a word the rest of the day. I sat through two more lectures with Heathcliff's invitation blaring inside my skull. Every time Morrie brushed past me in the hall, his hand grazed the small of my back.

Our VIP tickets included dinner. I was tempted to skip it, but Heathcliff pointed out that if we skipped out on Lydia, she'd likely drag us back by our ears or worse, sit by herself and blab all our secrets.

As we took our seats, Heathcliff's hand brushed my thigh under the table, and my breath hitched.

Morrie, not to be outdone, dropped his fork on the floor. "Whoops, I'm such a butterfingers." His eyes sparkled as he slid under the table, his body hidden from the others by the floor-length tablecloth. As I reached for the bread basket, hands frantically flung up my skirt and shoved aside my underwear. I yelped as Morrie buried his face between my legs.

"Something wrong?" Cynthia looked at me in concern.

"Nothing, nothing." I held up my wine glass. "The wine was just er... warmer than I expected."

I can't believe this is happening. I can't...

Morrie's tongue twirled over my clit, like a ballerina taking the stage for a breathtaking *fouetté*. The sheer audacity of what he was doing combined with that relentless rhythm sent my head spinning and my body pulsing with an ache that needed to be sated. I tried to pick up my knife to butter my bread, but Morrie pounded the flat of his tongue against me and ended up swiping the butter across the front of Heathcliff's jacket.

Oh Isis oh Isis his tongue...

"...Grey likes to joke that I'm his Lady Catherine de Bourgh, but I really do think my personality is more in tune with the kind-hearted and quiet nature of Anne Elliot, do you agree, Mina?"

"Um..." I gasped, gripping the edge of the table as heat pooled in my stomach. Morrie fed the growing ache inside me, driving me closer... closer...

"That friend of yours has been hunting for his fork for an awful long time." Cynthia bent down. "I hope he hasn't passed out down there."

"I'm sure... he's fine..." I gasped.

Right there... please... keep going...

Cynthia lifted the edge of the tablecloth. Morrie pulled away, scrambling out from under the table with his fork in his hand. My whole body shuddered with need. *Damn you, I was right there...* My fingers itched to slide between my legs and finish the job. All it would take was a single touch and I'd be over the edge. I squeezed my legs together, but that only made me more desperate.

"Your hair is all rumpled," Lydia scolded Morrie. "Really now, you should let the servants run after stray forks."

I wanted to correct her on the use of servants, but my body buzzed too much. I knew if I opened my mouth, I might scream with frustration. Across the table, Morrie grinned at me and raised his glass.

You wanker. You did this on purpose.

I scoffed my dinner as fast as I could, drowned three glasses of wine in quick succession, and waited with my nails digging into my palms for an appropriate time to leave the table. On either side of me, neither Heathcliff nor Morrie seemed fazed by the fact dinner was dragging on for seven centuries. By the time Cynthia stood up to give a rundown of the events for the following day. I was close to swooning.

"I'm feeling a little faint," I managed to choke out, as the wait staff emerged with platters of cakes and slowly moved around the room. "I think it was all that vigorous dancing today. Thank you for your company tonight, everyone, but I think I'll go up to my room and lie down."

"Please, Mina, you should stay," Cynthia cooed. "After dessert, some of the graduate students will be giving an amateur production of a story from the *Juvenilia*."

Lydia frowned. "What's the *Juvenilia*?"

"It's a collection of stories, scenes, and novel fragments Jane Austen wrote between the ages of eleven and seventeen," explained David. "They're a unique glimpse into Jane's literary origins and her unpredictable, snarky humor. When they lived at the Rectory, Jane and her family loved to perform plays and poems for the delight of their neighbors. Our resident expert, Professor Hathaway, is certain that similar dramatics would have been performed by the family and guests while Jane stayed at Baddesley Hall—"

"There's no record of that," Professor Carmichael cut in from the table behind us.

David continued as if she hadn't spoken. "—therefore, it's only fitting that we Janeites continue the tradition."

"Sounds delightful." Lydia accepted a second plate of dessert. "I shall most definitely attend. Goodnight, Mina. I hope you a feeling more up to dancing tomorrow, for you have a lot of practice to attend to."

"Thanks, Lydia." I waved goodbye to everyone at the table, and practically sprinted across the room.

As I climbed the staircase, Heathcliff and Morrie appeared at my sides. "Are you certain you don't want to watch the amateur dramatics, gorgeous?"

"Not even remotely," I replied, linking my arms in theirs. "How have you disentangled yourself from Lydia?"

"David is escorting her. I figure she can't say anything too outrageous to that drip, although I heard a rumor that one of her other suitors intends to steal her away."

We passed Gerald coming down the stairs, deep in discussion with Fishnet Girl. She glanced up as we went past, her eyes trailing after Heathcliff. Her tongue reached out to lick her scarlet lips. I almost expected it to be forked.

We ascended the grand staircase as quickly as was possible in my dress. Morrie flung open the door to their room and shoved me inside. Quoth already lounged on the bed, flipping through the TV channels, a bowl of blueberries beside him.

"Don't you have an amateur dramatic performance to attend?" Quoth arched a perfect eyebrow.

I threw myself down on the bed, turned Quoth's face toward mine, and devoured his lips. His tongue tasted tart, like the berries. My body ached with the need to be touched by him. The bed creaked as the other two guys climbed on. Heathcliff's strong arms stole around my middle, unlacing the delicate gown with deft strokes. Morrie pressed his chest to my back, his hands falling over my shoulders and under the neckline to cup my bare breasts.

"When you didn't speak of this again, I thought..." Quoth's words died away under my kisses.

"Don't think," I whispered back, kicking off my Docs and allowing Heathcliff to tug off my skeleton socks. "I'm not."

I closed my eyes, surrendering myself to Quoth's lips and to the urgent kisses and caresses of Heathcliff and Morrie. My mind whirred with questions. Should we do this? Was this what I really wanted? Would this bring us closer together? Would it break down Morrie's walls and burst Heathcliff wide open and make Quoth see how beautiful he really was? Or would it be the end of the special thing we have?

Would it give me the strength to face all the things I was running from? Or was losing myself in them just another way of running?

No. Don't think. I focused on my breath heaving in my chest, on Morrie's teeth scraping against my collarbone, on Heathcliff sliding the dress over my head, his lips closing around a nipple, rolling it and sucking it until I moaned and all thoughts and doubts fled my mind.

"How do you feel, gorgeous?" Morrie's breath caressed my earlobe.

"I feel fucking amazing now that I'm out of the dress," I whispered back, my words fading into a moan as Quoth's lips took my other nipple.

"You're not the only one desperate to get out of these ridiculous clothes," Heathcliff muttered. After some considerable fumbling and cursing, both Heathcliff and Morrie tossed their topcoats and breeches on the floor, and Quoth rid himself of his silk boxers. I lay back on the pillow. Heathcliff leaned over me, his mouth claiming mine in one of his breathless, passionate kisses. Morrie's hands snaked up my bare legs, kissing a trail of fire along the inside of my thighs.

"Let's give those Jane Austen erotica writers downstairs some inspiration," he murmured as he plunged his face between my legs.

Stoked by what he had done to me at the dinner table, my clit hummed and throbbed beneath Morrie's lips. Each slight touch from him sent a new shudder of delight through me. I moaned against Heathcliff's relentless lips as Morrie drove me close to the edge.

Quoth sat back, his legs crossed, his eyes locked with mine. "You're so beautiful," he whispered, the words catching in his throat.

I reached out to Quoth and took his hand in mine, placing it on my breast, above my heart. Morrie plunged his tongue inside me, teasing the ache that begged for more, before he battered against my desperate, throbbing clit. I squeezed Quoth's fingers as an orgasm shuddered through me.

My back arched. My core exploded with warm shivers that spread down my limbs to touch my fingers and toes. The world blurred and blackened, and a streak of bright blue neon color arced across my vision. My own personal fireworks display, courtesy of my men.

As quickly as the blue light appeared, it flicked off, and I could see again. Morrie sat back, flashing me with his wicked grin. Heathcliff continued to kiss me, as though no one else was in the room. Quoth just watched, his eyes ablaze with things he desperately wanted to say and do.

I wish... I wish he could feel as free around Morrie and Heathcliff as he does when it's just the two of us... maybe there's some way I can draw the real Quoth to the surface...

When I'd recovered enough to move again, I flopped forward and wrapped my arms around Quoth's shoulders, pulling him down with me. I leaned him against the pillows, meeting his lips with mine, tangling my hands in his luxurious hair as we fed on each other.

When Quoth kissed me, a well of emotion bubbled up in my stomach, rising through my chest to flow through my mouth, along my tongue. I fed him all the dark thoughts that hid inside me, and he gave me his. I tasted him – not his physical self but his soul. All the emotion he usually poured into his artwork flowed into me – dark and broken and terrifying. But I wasn't afraid of him. How could I be, when he cared so much and so deeply?

This was Quoth, my caged bird, slowly, slowly learning to be free.

I knelt back on my knees and wrapped my hands around his shaft. Quoth's lips parted. His black lashes tangled together as he watched me through heavy-lidded eyes. I leaned forward and took Quoth into my mouth, tasting the sweetness of him, running my tongue around the tip of his cock. He sighed, the sound so full of bliss it cracked my heart.

I kept my eyes locked on his, demanding he watch me, knowing that he knew I watched him take his pleasure in me. I wanted Quoth to know that I would find a way to make him as happy as he made me. That he was worth caring about.

Rocking back and forth on my feet, I took more of Quoth inside me, relishing the stretch of my lips around him, the way his cock strained and jerked against my tongue. He tasted amazing, like wind and butter, like the softness of falling into a pile of autumn leaves.

"Mina," Quoth's voice shuddered. His hands clawed at the sheets. I moved with the same sedate pace Morrie adopted, drawing Quoth deep into my throat before releasing him in a long, slow stroke. Each time his cock slid inside my mouth, I imagined myself drawing all his darkness inside me, leaving him only with the bright, shining light of his heart.

Warm hands stroked my bare legs. *Heathcliff.* I recognized his unrestrained touch, the way he clung to me as though I was the only thing holding him upright. A condom wrapper tore, and then Heathcliff wrapped an arm around my chest, and his cock rubbed between my legs, seeking the entrance.

"Yes," Morrie said, from somewhere to the right. "This is hot."

"Wait your turn," Heathcliff growled, his deep voice reverberating through my whole body. As I took Quoth in, I shifted my legs further apart to give Heathcliff better access. My whole body ached with need of him, of them.

Heathcliff held my torso rigid and entered me in a single deep stroke. I gasped against Quoth's cock as my body accepted him.

I had two of them inside me.

Wow.

This is glorious.

With an animalistic growl, Heathcliff moved, drawing himself out and plunging deep again, tearing my body and heart open in all the best ways. His darkness twisted through mine, finding a melancholy partner in Quoth and in me. I was cracking them open, exposing the hidden things they didn't want anyone else to see. But I saw them, because they reflected my own fears and my own strength back on me.

Quoth's hand on my shoulder steadied me, and the orange fire in his eyes burned through every regret I'd ever had, turning them all to ashes. Heathcliff's body on mine was hot, slick, drenched with sweat and pain and instinct. Unlike Morrie, he relished his lack of control, giving himself over completely to the animal side of him, to the dark aspects that made some call him a brute, a cruel and twisted thing.

But not me. I called him only Heathcliff.

I called him myself.

"I don't mean to break up the party," Morrie pouted. "But I'd like to point out that one of us is feeling a little left out."

"She's got one mouth and one cunt, and we're currently occupying both of them," Heathcliff growled. "Unless you have another suggestion, wait your turn."

"Oh Heathcliff, Heathcliff. How sheltered you are." Morrie held up a tube of lube. It took me a moment to realize what he wanted to use it for.

My lips slid off Quoth's cock as a ripple of unease slid through me. "Do you carry that around everywhere with you, just in case an opportunity presents itself?" I asked.

"Of course." Morrie twirled the bottle around, his eyes dancing. "What do you say, gorgeous?"

You're not getting anywhere near my arse, James Moriarty, until you give me the piece of yourself that you've been holding back.

But I wasn't going to give him that answer now. Morrie deserved to sweat a little longer. I bent my head back to Quoth, taking him in deep and slow. Quoth's eyes widened, and his fingers clamped on my shoulder. "Mina, I think..."

I gripped him tighter, pumping with my hand while I swirled my tongue around the tip of his cock. His body stiffened, muscles clenching as he came, hard, in my mouth. I swallowed down the taste of him, taking everything he would give me as if it were a gift I'd been hoping and praying for. In many ways, it was. Quoth *was* a gift, one I hoped to unwrap every single day.

"Now that you're done with the bird, focus on me." Morrie shoved a slumped Quoth aside and waved the bottle in my face. His easy smile tightened with desire. "What do you say? Yes?"

I shook my head. "Not this time."

Morrie lifted an eyebrow. "But perhaps next time?"

I laughed as I kissed him. *Your cock isn't the only thing I want. I demand nothing less than your whole heart, James Moriarty. And I'll get it, one day.*

Morrie wrapped his arms around me. He sighed. "Fine. But if

I'm not inside you by the end of the night, I'm going to be very upset."

In response, I rocked my hips against Heathcliff. "We can't have that."

"So... what are we going to do about it?"

"Do you ever shut up?" I rose up on my knees and grabbed his shoulder, yanking him against me and stoppering his protests between my lips. Morrie clung to me, his body pressed against mine even as Heathcliff drove deeper.

Pressed between their bodies, their hands and flesh all over me, a fire blazed inside me. Stoked by their raw, primal need, I became Sekhmet, protector of the sun, warrior goddess of fire, healer of wounds, because this fire... it was healing fire. Over my shoulder, Heathcliff and Morrie locked eyes, and the look that passed between them was something otherworldly. It seemed that the fire touched them, too.

Heathcliff's nails dug into me as his body tensed. He buried his face in my shoulder, teeth dragging against my skin. A shudder rolled through his body. Inside me, his cock quivered, driving deep as he released, the power of his final thrusts jerking me against Morrie, as though he drove his cock through both of us.

Heathcliff held me for a moment, leaning down to claim me with another breathtaking kiss. That moment and that kiss tell me everything I ever needed to know about him. He slid off me and flopped against the bed.

"My turn." Morrie grabbed my hip and spun me around so that he too came at me from behind. I yelped as he plunged inside me with a deep thrust. Gone was his control, his casual indifference. Morrie unleashed the chaos inside him that he'd held back for so long. Nails dragged down my back. Teeth snagged my neck. He bucked against me like a man possessed, like he was fucking a demon from his own body.

I arched my back and rocked against every thrust, relinquishing myself to his abandon. If this was Morrie's chaos, if this was what he was trying to protect me from, then he could forget it. I wanted this. I needed it, needed him. Whatever was going on in Morrie's head right now, something had broken him. The floodgates had opened. About bloody time.

A hand snaked around my neck, the finger pressing against my lips. "Bite me, gorgeous," Morrie murmured, quiet and far away, lost in his own inner turmoil. I sank my teeth into his skin as he plunged his hand between my legs, flicking my clit with the end of his finger. As he drove me to the edge with finger and cock and the orgasm swept over me, I bit down hard on his finger, tasting the tang of his blood on my tongue. Morrie's body stiffened, and he finally released.

Does he need the pain that much?

As he slumped against the bed, I turned my face toward Morrie, meeting his eyes. "Mina," he whispered. His face glazed over with a strange, faraway look, tinged with the kind of sadness Quoth usually carried with him.

I kissed him, long and slow, trying to draw out an answer. Something in Morrie felt different. Quieter, more vulnerable.

Wow.

Morrie drew away, his eyes widening.

"Morrie, what—"

He yanked his head back, turning away from me and sliding off the bed. I reached for him, but he jerked his arm away.

No, Morrie, don't do this. Don't pull back when you were so close.

"Where's the fire?" Heathcliff grunted. Morrie didn't reply. He thrust his long legs into his breeches and hobbled toward the door.

I sat up, concern bubbling in my chest. "What's wrong?"

"I just… I have to go." Morrie threw a shirt over his shoulders and stumbled into the hall. The door slammed behind him.

CHAPTER FOURTEEN

"*M*orrie, wait!" I threw myself off the bed, scrambling around on the floor for my clothes. I grabbed my dress, then realized it would take far too long to fasten with any degree of propriety. My rucksack was in the other room, and we'd locked the door between the two in case Lydia decided she had to join us. I couldn't risk opening it if she was on the other side, having her discover what was going on.

I swiped Heathcliff's flouncy shirt off the floor and flung it over my head. He was so broad and tall that it came down nearly to my knees. It wasn't exactly Regency appropriate, but it was at least somewhat decent.

"Mina, what are you doing?"

"I'm going after him." I pulled on Heathcliff's enormous topcoat and shoved my feet into my Docs.

"Why?" Heathcliff demanded. "He's just being Morrie. He can't handle it if he doesn't get to be in charge."

"I don't think that's it this time." I yanked the door open and jogged into the hall. It was empty. At the top of the staircase, I paused, looking down over the edge. Couples milled around in the entranceway below, holding wine glasses and making chit chat. Piano music floated in from Uppercross. If Morrie was upset, he wouldn't have gone downstairs. *Where, then?*

I remembered the covered balcony where we'd watched the fencing. At this time of night, it would be completely deserted. I raced across the upper landing, ducking down one hallway and then another until I found my way back to the small study that led to the balcony.

I didn't want to turn any lights on and risk scaring Morrie off. I shuffled my way through the dark study, wincing as I smashed my hip against a large oak desk. Moonlight shone in from the windows outside, and a headache bloomed in my temples as my eyes focused on the squares of pale light, obliterating everything else within my narrowed field of vision.

"Ow!" My knee slammed into a stone plinth. I thrust out my hands and managed to catch a terracotta vase before it toppled onto the floor. As I righted the plinth and set the vase back onto its stand, a shadow passed through the moonlight.

"Mina?"

I glanced up. A tall figure stood in the doorway leading out onto the balcony. In the dark, I couldn't make out any features beyond a vague shadow, but I knew that voice anywhere.

"I came to find you." I straightened up. "I thought we could talk."

"Go back to the room. I'll be along in a minute." The figure disappeared.

Oh no, you don't. I made my way to the doorway, leaning against the frame and watching Morrie. He leaned against the railing, staring out into the snow-cloaked night. In the gloom, I couldn't discern his features, but the shape of him was unmistakable.

"Morrie?" I stepped up beside him.

"I'd prefer to be alone," he said, without turning.

"Is that true, though?" I took another step closer. "You're always alone, even when you're with me. You hold something back and you fight against yourself. I think maybe you don't know any better, but whatever the reason, you've built this space between us. I hate it. Tonight, you closed that space and let me see you, *really* see you. And I think you're scared of that."

Morrie didn't speak for a long time. I took my chances and shuffled across the balcony to stand beside him. He wouldn't look at me, so I leaned over the railing, trying to glimpse his face. His mouth set in a firm line and his eyes formed ice-crystals – cold and hard, but fragile. Morrie bit his lower lip, and I dared to hope that something I said got through to him.

"What's going on with you? Why've you been acting so strange these past few weeks? Ever since we solved Mrs. Scarlett's murder you've been surly and mean."

Morrie drew a paper from his pocket, folding it and unfolding it in his hands. He sighed.

"I put you in danger." He didn't whisper or choke. His words came out clear, confident. Whatever he was about to tell me, he had a fundamental conviction that it was true.

"What do you mean?"

"When you went to Mrs. Winstone's house and found her husband's body. It took me too long to figure out there were two different killers, and I should have seen her as the killer immediately. All the clues were there – the missing husband, the conflict with Ginny Button, the walking stick attack that didn't fit with the killer's pattern. But I missed it." He shook his head in disbelief.

"It doesn't matter. We figured it out together and caught Mrs. Winstone *and* Greta. We solved the case thanks to your cleverness, and no one else got murdered."

"Don't you see? It matters very much. I should have figured it out, but I didn't, and I've been racking my considerable intellect trying to figure out why. The terrifying thought occurred to me – that perhaps I was losing my mind. For the last couple of months, I've been addled, mixed up, stupefied. Perhaps it was an undiagnosed medical condition. I needed to find out, and the first part of the equation was to understand just how badly my brain was depleting." Morrie handed the letter to me. "So I re-took the MENSA IQ test. I sat this test a year ago, for the sole purpose of winning a bet with Heathcliff, which I did in fact win. I tested with an IQ of 172."

The envelope from MENSA. It was his test results. But he wouldn't be this upset unless...

Yikes. I knew Morrie was clever, but an IQ of 172 was off-the-charts. Morrie's lip quivered, and my heart ached from him as all his erratic behavior and snide comments came into sharp focus.

Morrie prized his intelligence above everything else, and if for some reason he was losing it, that would feel like losing a core part of who he was. I knew enough of what that felt like to know that it felt like utter shite.

"Morrie," I touched his shoulder. "I'm so sorry. I wish you'd said something. You don't have to deal with this alone. I can help. I—"

He laughed, but the sound had no mirth in it. He held out the letter. "Read it."

I took the paper, flipped it open, and scanned the results. The number leaped out at me.

Standardized IQ score: 173

Huh?

"Morrie, did you even read this? It's one point *higher* than your last exam. You have nothing to worry about."

"Of course I'm worrying. That paper proves that my brain is in perfect working order. The problem is that my heart is getting in the way."

My own heart hammered against my chest. I had so many questions, but I kept silent. If I spooked Morrie now, he'd never open up again.

"I care about you." Morrie rested his cheek on his hand, shaking his head as though he couldn't believe any of it. "I promised myself I'd never make that mistake again. I only cared about one other person my entire life, and, according to the record, he pushed me over a waterfall."

By Isis, he's talking about the Reichenbach Falls.

"Morrie..." I didn't want to press him and spook him off, but I had to know. "Are you saying that you were in love with Sherlock Holmes?"

"How could I not be? He was the only one who ever vexed me, whoever made my life interesting." Morrie looked up then. "Until you."

My heart thundered in my ears. Morrie's eyes locked with mine. The icicles inside them shattered to pieces. Here he was, my amoral criminal, stripped bare of all his bravado, and I understood his pain. Morrie's emotions were a tidal wave, pulling him under. He needed to hold on to that tiny shred of control he had left, or he was going to drown. Admitting he cared meant admitting that he'd been wrong before, that he'd loved someone who he knew from a book committed the ultimate betrayal.

Arthur Conan Doyle only relayed what happened on the Reichenbach Falls through Sherlock's short account to Watson. We never knew what had really been said or done on that ledge. Morrie didn't know, either, because he'd been pulled from his story into our world before it happened. All he knew was that the man he loved pushed him over a cliff.

I wanted to tell him that I'd never do that, but I knew, and he knew, that reassuring someone you weren't going to hurt them wasn't the answer.

"Caring about someone doesn't make you weak," I whispered. "It makes you human."

"Humans are weak," Morrie said, in that cold voice. "I cared once before, and it cost me my life. This time my caring nearly cost you yours, Mina. When I look at you, all I see is my weakness. I'll be driven mad by it if I don't—"

His gaze slid to the side, following something across the courtyard below.

"What?" I turned my head too, but I couldn't make out anything in the dark. Frustration welled up inside me that I couldn't share in the interesting thing he'd seen.

"It's Christina Hathaway." Morrie lowered his voice and narrowed his eyes. He dropped low behind the balcony so only the top of his head was visible over the railing. I dropped down beside him, caught up in the excitement of the moment. *Give Morrie a puzzle to solve, and he's happy.*

I crouched down beside him, my heart hammering. "What's she doing?"

"She's with that journalist. They're walking under the trees at the far end of the courtyard, talking in low voices."

That's not exactly exciting. "Don't change the subject. They probably just went outside for some air. Or a cigarette. Wouldn't it be hilarious if Miss Perfect Regency lady was a secret chain smoker?"

"She has a secret all right, but it's not a nicotine addiction." Morrie grinned. "They're kissing."

CHAPTER FIFTEEN

"*W*hat?"

"Yeah." Morrie leaned over the balcony and peered out to the end of the courtyard, where I could just make out two shapes huddled under one of the trees. "It's a pity you can't see. There's some serious snogging going on. We could get tips."

"Morrie!" I grabbed his hand and dragged him back into the house. "We shouldn't be spying on them. They deserve a bit of privacy."

"Relax, gorgeous. They have no idea we're up here, otherwise they wouldn't have been so desperate to eat each other's faces."

"Do you think Christina's father knows?" I found it hard to believe a man like Hathaway with his adherence to Regency values would approve of his daughter's apparent sexuality.

"I doubt it, otherwise they wouldn't feel the need to venture out into minus four-degree weather in order to lock lips."

"Interesting. I wonder if it's got anything to do with the story Alice is working on. She's definitely trying to bring down Hathaway—" I shook my head. "No, I'm not doing this. It's none of our business what people get up to behind closed doors."

"Or under trees."

"Yes. Or under trees. Speaking of which," I punched him in the arm. "You can't keep running away every time you get emotional. I can't deal with this on top of everything else – you're either in this, or you're out."

"What does that mean?"

"It means…" I closed my eyes. Was this really what I wanted? If I pushed Morrie too much, I might end up pushing him away. But on the other hand, Morrie wasn't the only one who was getting emotionally entangled against his better judgment. A certain master criminal had already got under *my* skin, and the more time I spent with him, the harder I fell – not for the cocky guy on the surface, but the broken man underneath. I needed Morrie to trust me enough to show me more of that guy. "It means that I want all of you or none of you. You have to give in to what you're feeling for me, or you're out. No more sex. No more… what happened tonight—"

"It's called an orgy," Morrie said. "Or a foursome. A harem in reverse. Some people prefer gangb—"

"Don't be crass." My face flushed. "You were the one who started this, Morrie. And you're right. I *don't* want to choose. I want you, and Heathcliff, and Quoth. I want you not just because you're clever, but because I care deeply about you. I maybe even possibly love you." My tongue slipped on the word, a word I'd been dancing around, not yet ready to say to any of them, even though it was probably true. I'd loved very few people in my life, and apart from my mum, they either abandoned me or stabbed me in the back. "And you're not the only one throwing your heart on the line here, or the one with a monopoly on pain. I get your heart, or you walk away. That's my final offer."

I spun around and stalked from the room, leaving a stunned and silent James Moriarty on the balcony, his icicle eyes boring into my back.

CHAPTER SIXTEEN

"Get up, get up!" A pillow hit me across the face.

"Croak, croak, croak!" A raven hopped across the bed, flapping its wings frantically.

"Er, um, what?" I reached up to rub my eye. Black and white feathers sailed through the air around me.

"How dare you sleep in here with *my* escort, and on the day of the ball, too!" Lydia smashed me in the head with the pillow again.

"What's going on?" Morrie muttered, opening his eyes. "How did she get in here? We locked the door."

"Morrie taught me how to pick a lock!" Lydia screeched, hitting Morrie over the head for good measure.

"Ow! That was because you were annoying and I wanted you to shut up for twenty minutes," Morrie cowered under the blankets. "You weren't supposed to use it against me."

"Well, she did, and now she's trying to murder us with goose down." I pulled a feather from between my lips. "Lydia, hold on for a sec. Lydia!"

She whomped me over the head again, muffling my words with 400-count Egyptian linen. I tore the pillow from her grasp and hugged it to my naked chest. Lydia glared at me from the end of the bed.

"Sit down." I jabbed my finger at the lounge suite arranged under the window. Lydia flopped onto the sofa and glared at me defiantly. "Let me find some jeans, then I can explain."

"You are not even wearing bloomers?" Lydia screeched.

"Turn down the volume," Heathcliff muttered. "Some of us are trying to get our beauty sleep."

"I'd give up now, because not even a decade of sleep is going to help you any," Morrie said.

"Croak!" Quoth hopped in circles around the bedsheets.

"Right. I'm sorting it." I grabbed Lydia by the hair and dragged her into the other bedroom, slamming the door behind me.

"Ow. Unhand me, you harlot!" Lydia raked at my face with her hands. I slapped them away. "I'm going to tell everyone about your scandalous behavior—"

"No," I said, dropping her on the bed. I went over to the mini-bar under the desk and pulled out a small bottle of whisky. I tossed one to her, and broke the cap on the other. "You're not. Drink that."

Lydia stared at the bottle in her hand, and then at the fridge. "Is that some kind of… futuristic icebox?"

"That's exactly what it is." I held up my bottle. "And it is one of the many joys of the modern world. Bottoms up."

"Why are we drinking? You're supposed to be explaining why I found you in a compromising state with my escort. You have your own escort – the grumpy one. Why did you have to take mine, too?"

"I'm getting to that. I just need a little liquid courage first. And you might want a little too, for what I'm about to tell you."

"Very well." Lydia held up her bottle to me, and knocked the whole thing back, slamming the glass down on the table. I tossed mine back too, the cheap whisky burning all the way down. I tossed the bottle on the desk and leaned forward.

"Here's the thing, Lydia. A lot of stuff has changed since Jane Austen wrote your story. For one thing, we have refrigerators now, and we can keep our shitty whisky cold for occasions like this." I coughed as the alcohol burned through my chest. "We also have feminism, which means you don't have to find a husband in order to lead a rich and secure life."

"Not this feminism lark *again*." Lydia's lip curled back. "It sounds horrible."

"I can assure you it's actually quite fun. Feminism means that you don't have to make decisions based on how amicable and eligible you will be to men. For example, you don't know this yet, but when you ran away with Wickham, your family had to tear up and down the countryside to find you because they were worried about your reputation. Now, you can do whatever you want, and your reputation is fine. You could go to bed with Wickham and talk about it with your girlfriends the next day, and it would make you no less desirable as a wife. You can go to bed with anyone you choose and you don't have to marry them."

Lydia's lip curled back. "Is this true?"

"Yes. Well, sort of. People love to gossip. They might say mean things about you behind your back, and call you a slut, because we haven't quite smashed the patriarchy yet. That's a whole other conversation." Sensing Lydia glazing over, I gestured to the door that separated our rooms. ""The *point* is, Morrie may be your escort, but he's already taken. By me." *At least, I hope he is.* I thought of the ultimatum I'd given him last night. "And so is Heathcliff. And Quoth. I'm not married to any of them, but that doesn't mean we can't date and sleep together. We could even live together if we wanted."

Lydia's eyes were so large and round she should have had orbiting moons. "I never believed such a thing would be possible."

"Why not? Lots of old stories have men with harems of women. Why shouldn't it be the other way around? That's feminism – equal rights for all. Now, the thing is, this having multiple partners thing is still not entirely socially acceptable. It's the kind of thing we all know happens but we don't talk about it."

Lydia's face perked up. "Oh, yes. Like how Father caught my sister Mary kissing Maria Lucas behind the stables."

Okay, wow. I stifled a laugh. "Yes, exactly like that. It's very important that you don't tell anyone about me and the guys. This town is small, like Meryton, and some people won't approve. Their disapproval could hurt all of us, including you."

"But you just said—"

"I know what I just said." I rubbed my temple, where a headache had started to blossom. "By Isis, it's too early in the morning for this. It's that patriarchy thing I told you about. I'll give you a book to read when we get back to the shop. For now, let's just say you can do whatever you want, as long as you aren't flaunting it. Think of it this way – knowing Morrie is off the table only frees you up to enjoy any other man you might desire. Or a woman," I added, thinking of what Morrie and I had unwittingly witnessed last night, and of what Lydia had just told me about her sister. "You could even have a woman, if you so chose."

"Women freely cavort with other women?" Lydia gasped. "My mother is at this moment rolling in her grave, and I *love* it."

I grinned. "Lydia, I think you're going to really enjoy being a teenager in these times. There's a reason 'It's complicated' is the most popular relationship status on Facebook. Now, will you stop holding on so tight to Morrie – there's a ball tonight, and a whole house filled with weird costumed freaks who would love to bed an actual Regency lady."

"Then what are we waiting for?" Lydia threw open her suitcase and started throwing dresses over her head. "Help me into this outfit. I need to look *sensational* today if I'm to fill up the rest of my dance card for tonight. And we must hurry, for I don't want to miss an opportunity to speak with David over breakfast."

~

*L*ydia dressed in the muslin gown she'd arrived in, pinned her hair and adorned it with silk flowers she'd purchased from the market in Netherfield. As soon as she was satisfied that she was ready to receive an onslaught of gushing admirers, the three of us rose to make our way to the day's activities. I kissed Quoth goodbye, running my hands through his black hair.

"I'll think of you all day long," he said between kisses.

"You do that," I kissed him. "We have the ball tonight, so—"

Quoth pointed to the bedroom window behind his head. "I've left that open wide enough so I can come in. But I think I'll probably sit outside the ballroom and watch the ball. It'll be fun to see the costumes and hear the band and watch you batter Heathcliff's shins."

I placed my hands on my hips and glared at him. "I'll have you know I'm a fantastic dancer, thank you."

"That's a lie," Heathcliff called from the hallway.

"Mina, let's go!" Lydia dragged a distraught Moriarty toward the stairs.

I clung to Quoth, not wanting a whole day to go by where I didn't see him. He laughed, pressing his lips to my forehead. "Just know that when you clomp around that dance floor tonight, I'll be watching you."

A delicious shiver ran down my spine at the thought. "I like that."

Lydia barged through the door and grabbed my arm, dragging me away. "Christ, you're more of a dawdler than my sister Jane, always with her head in the clouds."

I waved goodbye as Lydia dragged me from the room and slammed the door behind me. Heathcliff wrenched me from her grasp and settled my hand on his arm. "Her method leaves much to be desired," he murmured. "But I can't argue with her logic. I heard the breakfast is quite something to behold, and my grumbling stomach has a mind to behold it."

Breakfast was served in two large rooms off the main house kitchen. The walls had been whitewashed, and the normal furnishings removed and replaced with long banquet tables. My mouth watered when we approached the buffet. I hadn't realized how hungry I was. Having a foursome must've worked off a hell of a lot of calories.

The food was arrayed in silver chafing dishes, with labels written in tiny print attached to the tops. I leaned over to read my choices. *Scrambled egg? Yes, please.* I dumped a spoonful on my plate. *Pork and fennel breakfast sausages? Don't mind if I do. Croissants with ham and cheese? I'll take three—*

"Excuse me, dear, but you shouldn't breathe all over the food like that."

I jumped in surprise, tipping my plate forward and spilling eggs and sausage down the front of my dress. Color flared in my cheeks as I turned to meet a group of older ladies in their Regency finery. I hadn't realized how close I'd been leaning over the food in my attempt to read the labels. "Oh, right, sorry."

"Leave her alone," Heathcliff glowered at the dowagers. "She's blind."

I bristled at Heathcliff's words. "I'm not blind. I'm only partially—"

"I don't care if she's blind, deaf, and dumb, it's unhygienic."

"Don't you dare speak to Mina like that." Storms brewed in Heathcliff's eyes.

"It's fine." I shoved my plate into Heathcliff's hands. "I have to go clean up, anyway."

"Mina—"

I raced from the room, keeping my eyes glued on the floor, not wanting to see if anyone followed me. In the bathroom, I dabbed at the front of my dress with a wad of toilet paper, but that only spread the stains across my chest. As I glared at my reflection in the mirror, a flash of green neon light flashed across my vision.

"Aaaaarrrrh!" I gripped the edge of the sink and stared at myself in the mirror. I couldn't see the labels on the chafing dishes.

I remembered Lydia's weird look when I was looking at David's coins the other day. I hadn't even noticed how close I was leaning in to look at things. My cheeks burned with embarrassment. *I've been making a fool of myself in front of everyone, sniffing the coins, breathing on the food...*

This is my father's legacy.

A corner of his note stuck out of the top of my bra. I pulled it out and smoothed it on the edge of the sink. A tear rolled down the side of my face as I read over the words. It dropped onto the border of leaping animals, smudging the ink.

Who are you, Father? Why couldn't you have been there from the beginning? Maybe if you had been, I wouldn't have to go through this alone.

The bathroom door banged behind me. I jumped, my heart pounding. "I'm fine," I dabbed at my face with the wet tissue. "Just trying to get this bloody eyelash out of my eye."

"Mina."

At the sound of Heathcliff's dark, gravelly voice, I dropped the tissue into the sink. My hands trembled harder. *Get a hold of yourself, Mina.*

"You're not supposed to be in here." I didn't turn around. I couldn't move. But in the mirror, I could just make out the edges of his silhouette, his black clothes and dark features camouflaged in the shadow of the door. "This is the ladies bathroom."

"I don't care," Heathcliff growled. "I had to see you."

"I'm fine. I just can't get this blasted stain out of my dress."

Heathcliff stepped forward, standing under the downlight, throwing his body into full view. The shadows on his face etched a story of pain.

"Don't do this," he growled. "If you choose this path, you'll live to regret it."

"What?"

"Don't be driven low by petty people and their prejudice and hatred." Heathcliff's hands balled into fists. "Don't take all that rage and turn it inward, until you hate yourself so much you become incapable of feeling anything else. You're no monster, Mina. This path is not for you. I'd leave you before I drag you down into the darkness with me."

My chest tightened. I spun around to face him, to stare down this wonderful man who believed he was a monster. Heathcliff's eyes bore into me, full of storms and ghosts.

"You were always more than the darkness," I whispered. "Before I even met you, you, Heathcliff, were the first true hero I had. On my bleakest days, I looked to your love for Cathy and believed that one day someone could love me like that."

"You call that *love?*" he spat. "It is nothing but a wild, maddening, dangerous passion."

"If you don't think that's love, then what is?" I faced him. "Love isn't this high, noble act reserved for sedate dances and quiet moments. Real love is primal, and savage, and human."

"What are you saying?" Heathcliff demanded, sweeping across the room to press his body against mine. His heart thudded against my chest, perfectly in time with mine.

"I'm saying that if it's monstrous to love you, then I will happily become that monster," I shot back, my arms trembling. "Because I love you."

I barely got the words out when Heathcliff mashed his mouth against mine, sweeping me into his arms. We slammed against the wall. My elbow hit the hand dryer, but I barely felt it, so enraptured was I with Heathcliff's fire and with the surge of emotion welling inside me.

I love him. I hadn't said the words to shut him up or make him forget about Hindley and the evil things he'd done in his book. I said them because every syllable rang true inside me, and every fiber of my body begged for the fire of his passion to engulf me.

The words unleashed something in Heathcliff – if this was what his monster was capable of when stoked with love and kindness instead of cruelty, then how different might his story have ended if he hadn't been denied so much. He ravaged my mouth with his, rendering me completely senseless, lost to his violent devotion.

His hand pawed at my dress, dragging it up my hips. Someone could walk in at any moment. But I didn't care. I had Heathcliff. We belonged to each other and it felt like my entire life had been waiting for this moment. I needed Heathcliff inside me, right now.

Clearly, Heathcliff had the same idea. In seconds he had my skirts up around my torso, tearing my panties away. He clawed at his breeches, popping off a button in his haste. It ricocheted off the toilet stall and skidded out of sight. Heathcliff yanked down his breeches, pressing his hardness against my hip. "Bloody stockings," he muttered, fighting to roll them down over his rigid cock.

I slashed the thin silk with the edge of my nail, tearing a hole wide enough for the head of his cock to poke through. Heathcliff's dark eyes crinkled as he laughed. "Now who is the feral one?"

"They don't call me Mina Wilde for nothing." I wrapped my arms around his neck, pulling him close, pressing together our beating hearts.

After rolling on a condom, Heathcliff leaned his weight against me and lifted my arse in his hands. I wrapped my legs around him and clamped my thighs tight. The hilt of his sword jabbed against the back of my thigh. He found my opening, sliding inside me. I gasped as he claimed me, body and soul.

We found each other in the storm of our love, driving rain and hard hail and winds that tore at our skin. Heathcliff said with his kisses what he could never utter. His monster rushed boldly to the surface, pushing out through his skin, and Heathcliff and the monster became one, and they were fierce, and storm-tossed, and utterly beautiful.

My Heathcliff.

Heathcliff reached up with dark fingers to cup my face, dragging my lips to his. "Mina, I love you," he cried out, slamming his cock inside me.

Somewhere in the recesses of my mind, I remembered Ashley telling me to never believe a bloke who uttered those words during sex. The haze of endorphins was bound to make people go a bit loopy.

But when that bloke was Heathcliff, and his dark eyes were filled with storms that matched the tempest inside me, and a corner of my father's letter jabbed into my chest, I knew Ashley was wrong.

"I love you," I whispered back.

Heathcliff's body shuddered. He held me close as his orgasm claimed him. We came together in a shower of sparks and rage and fireworks.

Even when he'd pumped himself dry, he remained inside me, holding me against that wall as if it were the only thing tethering us to earth. An electric charge buzzed through my body – the aftermath of an incredible orgasm, but something more, something deeper. From the way Heathcliff's eyes bore into mine, he felt it, too.

"Whatever souls are made of," he whispered, "yours and mine are the same."

CHAPTER SEVENTEEN

*H*eathcliff and I cleaned up and straightened our clothes as best we could in the bathroom. I peered out the door, looking in both directions. People wandered past the end of the hall toward the breakfast buffet, but no one headed toward us.

"It's safe." I slipped out and held open the door. "Come on."

Heathcliff walked out, using his handkerchief to hide where the button had popped off his breeches. "These bloody clothes don't leave anything to the imagination."

"Nope, and I'm glad of it," I smiled, pinching his bum. "Let's go."

"There's my Mina." Heathcliff offered his arm, and I took it. My thighs made a pleasing tingling sensation as they rubbed together, reminding me of what we'd just done. I'd had to throw my ruined underwear away. *Going commando in a Regency dress – this might be the most punk rock thing I've ever done.*

Raised voices echoed down the corridor. A crowd milled at the entrance to the breakfast room. I stood on tiptoes, trying to see over them. Professor Carmichael stood with Alice near the back of the crowd, and I dragged Heathcliff over to them.

"What's going on?" I whispered.

"It's fantastic. That Gerald character walked right up to Professor Hathaway and accused him of plagiarizing his work."

"Possibly you shouldn't look quite so gleeful," Heathcliff murmured. Professor Carmichael rearranged her face into a concerned expression.

"Of course you're right. I'd hate for this to come to blows, especially with ladies present. But it couldn't happen to a nicer person."

Heathcliff sighed. He dropped my arm and shoved his way through the crowd, ignoring the yelps of protest from ladies as he tossed them aside. I followed him, grateful I'd chosen to wear my Docs again this morning.

We reached the front of the crowd and for the first time could see the scene unfolding. Gerald and Hathaway glared at each other from opposite sides of the buffet. Christina stood behind her father, tugging on his sleeve in a pitiful attempt to calm him down. Hannah and the two other goth girls stood behind Gerald with their arms folded and fierce expressions on their pale faces. Hathaway smirked at Gerald, whose skin burned as dark as the tomato sauce swirls decorating his plate.

"Why don't you tell them all, Hathaway?" Gerald was saying. "Tell all these people who worship you that your entire life is a lie. I don't know who you've got writing your books and speeches now, but you should probably fire them because your last book had more holes in it than Hannah's fishnet tights. All I know for a fact is that it cannot possibly be your own words."

"Really, now, Gerald. Must we dig up this ancient history again? The university investigated and found me innocent of plagiarism."

"That's because you were sleeping with the head of the committee!" Gerald yelled. Behind him, Christina gasped and hid her face behind her fan.

David shoved his way in front of Hathaway and glared at Gerard. "Don't do this. You're upsetting Christina."

"She's a big girl, David. She can look after herself." Gerard shoved him aside. "She needs to know what kind of man her beloved father really is."

"And what kind of a man is that, Gerald?" Professor Hathaway said. Unlike Gerald, his tone was reasonable, sensible, carrying an air of authority. Even if what Gerald said was true, Hathaway was going to come away looking like the winner. "The kind of man who takes pity on a failing graduate student, offers him a place even though his grades weren't high enough to qualify, tutors him extensively and creates every opportunity for him to shine, only to have that attention thrown back in my face when I'm falsely accused?"

"You only did that because you wanted to get in good with my girlfriend. You knew she wouldn't continue graduate study unless I did, and then you wouldn't be able to have your chance at her." Gerald grabbed the goth girl by the hand and shoved her forward. "Tell them, Hannah. Tell them how that bastard touched you."

A collective gasp traveled through the crowd. Hathaway's confident expression faltered for a moment. Beside me, Heathcliff tensed, ready to pounce on Hathaway if necessary. All eyes fell on the girl as Gerald dragged her beside him.

"Gerald, stop it!" Hannah wrenched her hand away. "It's bad enough you made us come along this weekend, but now you're saying that in front of everyone. He just touched my breast in the elevator. He said it was an accident, and I believe him. Don't bring it up again!"

"Listen to her, Gerald," Professor Hathaway cooed. "You wouldn't want a slander suit brought against you for things you cannot understand."

"I understand perfectly! I understand what you've done to

your own daughter, making her into this Regency doormat just so she would remind you of your wife."

Christine's face paled. "Please, gentlemen. Let's not make a scene."

"Yes, Gerald." Hathaway nodded. "Let's step back and collect ourselves. Anger is an ugly emotion to air in public. Accusations of plagiarism are best left for a university ethics committee to deal with, and not solved by a duel over breakfast. Come along, Christina." He placed a hand on the small of her back and led her away. Guests stepped aside to let them pass, and I heard a ripple of whispers in the crowd of how Hathaway had dealt with the situation like a gentleman.

I'm not so sure. Hannah's face as she watched them walk away was etched with pain. The story she told and what really happened weren't the same.

The silent room stared daggers at Gerald. He growled, swiping his hand over the breakfast buffet, scattering platters and chafing dishes, and sending a waterfall of sausages and eggs cascading across the carpet.

"Enjoy your breakfast," Gerald snarled at the crowd, stomping away, his leather trench coat flapping behind him.

Staff rushed in to clean up the buffet. The crowd milled around, drifting back to the tables and gossiping about what had just transpired. I turned to Heathcliff. "What you do suppose that was about?"

"Looks like the Brontë Society is here for personal reasons after all," Heathcliff said.

I noticed Morrie and Lydia sitting at a table by the window, enjoying plates piled high with food. My stomach rumbled. I hadn't had a chance to eat because of what that old lady said, and what happened in the bathroom afterward, and now the food was all over the floor. I slid into a chair next to Morrie and plucked a rasher of bacon from his plate.

"Heathcliff, Mina, I'm so pleased you found us." Lydia beamed up from their breakfast "What frightful good fun! I thought there would be a duel for sure—"

"Your name is *Heathcliff*?"

Hannah wrapped her red-tipped claws around Heathcliff's arm, her eyes locked on his like she was seeing him from the first time. From the way her body arched toward him and her tongue ran along her lips, I knew she liked what she saw.

Heathcliff grunted in reply.

She tugged on his arm. "You should consider joining the Brontë society. We're a lot more fun than this crowd."

"I'm not sure I like your costumes any better," Heathcliff growled.

"This isn't a costume." She gestured to the black-and-red damask corset and black tulle skirt she wore over fishnet stockings and New Rock boots. "I dress to express the darkness and existential angst within me."

"Good luck with that." Heathcliff tried to free his arm, but she sank her nails deeper.

"It's my destiny to one day marry a Heathcliff," she whispered. "I want my future children to be sons and daughters of Heathcliff. Every day I pull tarot cards and look at my horoscope to find out when he will arrive. I thought Gerald might be a good contender if he would just agree to change his name, but that was before I knew an *actual* Heathcliff existed. And my horoscope did say I would meet a dark stranger who wasn't a stranger at all! Tell me, Mr. Heathcliff, were you an orphan? Do you love the wild moors? Would I need to change my name to Cathy? Because I would do it. I would!"

"This Heathcliff is all those things, *and* he owns a bookshop in the village," I said, taking perverse delight in watching Heathcliff squirm.

"You're supposed to be helping me," he growled. In response, I nicked a sausage off Morrie's plate and chomped down on it.

"A bookshop?" Hannah's eyes sparkled. I felt a kinship with

her – another outcast book nerd who dreamed of a passionate, grumpy man. "You must tell me all about it. Do you mind?" Hannah asked me, indicating the empty chair at the end of our table.

"Not at all." I grinned, shoving back my own chair. "In fact, I think I'll go to the kitchens and see if I can get some more food, if you'd both like to sit together. Perhaps you could take Heathcliff for a walk around the courtyard after breakfast?"

Heathcliff glared at me. "Why are you making things worse?"

"Have fun!" I waved as I stood up. I grabbed an empty plate off the end of the buffet, maneuvered my way around the staff cleaning the carpets, and entered the short hallway leading toward the kitchens.

Gerald stood in the middle of the hall, his bulk blocking my way. He had his head bent low, whispering with Alice Yo and Professor Carmichael. As I cleared my throat to indicate they might shuffle over and let me pass, all three snapped their heads up, eyes wide. They scattered in three directions, leaving the hall deserted.

What are they up to?

CHAPTER EIGHTEEN

I barely saw Heathcliff for the rest of the day. The one time I glanced at him across the room during a lecture on spinster tropes, Hannah was practically sitting in his lap and he'd acquired two more black-clad admirers. It looked as though the Argleton Brontë society had found their new leader. I wondered what Gerald thought of it all, but I hadn't seen him in any lectures, either. Maybe Cynthia had asked him to leave.

While I waited for Professor Carmichael's lecture – the final lecture of the day – to begin, I scanned the tiny room for Morrie. He'd been absent all day as well. Lydia led him from activity to activity, showing him off and breaking into impromptu dances in the halls. He seemed perfectly content to bask in her growing popularity and cater to her whims. I tried not to feel jealous. *It's probably for the best.* Although Morrie had come back to the room last night and fallen asleep in bed with us, he hadn't said a word to me all day. He had to be thinking about what I told him last night.

Maybe I read him all wrong. Maybe he really doesn't care about me. I've made a big mistake—

Morrie dropped down into the chair beside me. "Good afternoon, gorgeous."

My stomach did a little dance. "You've sprung yourself free." A horrible thought occurred to me. "Wait a second, you haven't stuffed Lydia in a closet, have you?"

Morrie winked at me. "Would I do that?"

"In a heartbeat."

"*Touché.*" Morrie pointed across the room. "However, in this instance, I am innocent. Our little miscreant has acquired more admirers. She didn't even notice when I slipped away. I've officially been demoted."

I followed his gaze to a throng of people across the aisle, the only other people in the room. They were too far away for me to recognize, but Lydia's high-pitched laugh echoed across the room. "Do you need to cry into my shoulder?"

"Yes, please." Morrie dropped his head onto my shoulder and pretended to be wracked with sobs. As his lips grazed my neck, a shiver ran through my body. I reached up a hand to push him away, to remind him that I hadn't been kidding about what I'd asked, when he spoke first.

"I thought about what you told me last night," he whispered against my hair, his lips brushing the lobe.

"And?" My body went rigid. An ache danced between my legs.

"And I think you're playing a dangerous game."

His breath tickled along my neck, sending another delicious shiver through my body. "Oh yes?"

"People don't usually issue ultimatums to James Moriarty and live to speak of it."

"Be that as it may." My body ached for him to keep going. I pressed my hand against Morrie's chest. It took all my self-control, but I pushed him away. "You're not touching me until you give me an answer. What's it to be, Moriarty – spill your feelings, or suffer the blue balls?"

Morrie drew back and puffed out his lower lip. "You're mean."

"You love it. And as soon as you tell me you love me," I patted my arse, "you can have a piece of this."

"Bloody hell, gorgeous." Morrie stood up.

"Where are you going?"

"Cold shower," he muttered as he ducked out of the room. "See you at the ball."

Cynthia, acting as MC, called for silence. Professor Carmichael took the stage. "Thank you very much for coming. I wasn't expecting to see so many of you here for the last lecture of the day, instead of taking an extra hour for ball preparation—"

"Oh, no, I didn't see the time. I have to get ready for the ball!" Lydia leaped up, pushing her way through her gaggle of admirers and fleeing the room. A few other women followed her, muttering about curling irons and petticoat lengths.

Professor Carmichael's shoulders sagged, but she straightened her back, pushed her glasses up her nose, and began her lecture on medicine in Jane Austen's life. She spoke with passion and authority, and her joy for the subject made her whole face light up, becoming more animated and youthful as she dug deeper, telling us how vinegar was distilled and used on a range of ailments, from reviving a fainted person, to croup, dropsy, and stomach aches. She had lots of charts and medical facts to back up her conclusions, no doubt gleaned from her previous occupation as a doctor.

As she talked, more and more people left the room, heading toward their suites to prepare for the ball. My heart went out to Professor Carmichael. As the end of the hour neared, all who was left was me, Alice Yo, Gerald, and Professor Hathaway and Christina right in the front row.

When she presented her conclusion and clicked off her slide, Professor Hathaway stood, clapping over his head as if she was a rock star finishing her encore at Earl's Court.

"Go to hell," she glared at him.

By Isis, there's no love lost there. Alice gave me a pained look. I wanted to stick around and ask her more about her article and if it had anything to do with Gerald and Professor Hathaway's argument and the subsequent clandestine meeting, but a glance at my phone screen revealed I only had an hour left to get ready for the ball. I packed up my things in a hurry and raced off to my room to change, frantically trying to remember all the steps to the dances I'd learned yesterday.

~

"*H*ave either of you seen Lydia?" I asked as we milled around in the antechamber. By the time I'd returned to our room after Professor Carmichael's lecture, Lydia was already gone. She'd left every towel sopping wet and had somehow looped my favorite bra over the ceiling fan. I had to call a staff member to help me get it down. Without Lydia's help, I'd barely managed to pull on the beautiful red dress and get my hair up in time.

"Maybe she's on the roof, polishing her broom," Morrie said.

I punched him in the arm. "Don't say that."

"She'll be here somewhere," Heathcliff said, indicating the crowd of people who packed every corner of Undercross. "I wish they'd open the windows. All the hairspray fumes are doing my head in."

I peered at the series of high windows along the wall, remembering that Quoth had promised he'd be here. "I want to look for Lydia and see if Quoth's here yet. Let's take a turn about the room." I looped my arms in Heathcliff and Morrie and dragged them toward the windows. I peered outside, but the windows revealed only a dark void. If Quoth was looking in at me, I'd be none the wiser, thanks to my stupid eyes. Inside, at least, the chandelier was bright enough that I could make out most faces. *There's Gerald and the rest of the Brontë society. There's Professor*

Carmichael in a beautiful blue dress, and Cynthia looking stunning in blue.

"I see Lydia." Morrie pulled me in the direction of the fireplace.

"Oh no," I breathed. Professor Hathaway sat in the crimson chair in front of the fire, wearing a fine topcoat with gold details and an elaborate sword on his belt. In his lap, Lydia bounced on his knee, whispering something in his ear. "When she said she'd acquired new suitors, it never occurred to me that she'd be after *him*."

Behind me, I heard a disgusted sigh. I turned around in time to see Professor Carmichael make a disgusted face and push her way through the crowd to get away from Hathaway and his sycophants.

"Well, he is a bachelor, and definitely eligible." Morrie grinned. "I bet he has a fortune of ten thousand a year."

"He's also old – even under that dyed hair – and *gross*. I told you what Professor Carmichael said about him, and there was Gerald's outburst this morning."

"Indeed, although I'd be careful to believe the words of rival academics. I've read at a top university, and I can tell you that the dons bicker incessantly and constantly try to throw each other under the bus in order to score a book deal, speaking slot, or professional accolade for themselves. It's a lot like Hollywood, except that the fashion leans more toward, 'tweed and tipsy'."

I watched Lydia toss her head back and laugh at something Professor Hathaway said. Beside her, David leaned down and handed her a drink. "I can't stop thinking about Hannah's face when she was confronting Hathaway. She looked scared. That makes me worry about Lydia. She's only *sixteen*. Should we rescue her?"

"No," said Heathcliff and Morrie in unison.

It appeared we didn't need to. As well as David, three other men hovered around her, offering food and wine and to fill up her dance card. It appeared Lydia had wasted no time in taking my advice. I made a note to speak to her about the dangers of men like Hathaway as soon as I got the chance.

"It's a terrible tragedy," a woman behind me gushed. I turned around, wondering if she was talking about Hathaway. But no, for she held on to Christina Hathaway's hand. "For you to be without your jewels for the ball. Are you certain you're not a victim of the Argleton Jewel Thief?"

"No, no. Father keeps them on his person at all times. I just don't want to disturb his conversation," Christina replied in her high, breathless voice. She looked absolutely radiant in a cream dress covered in fine lace. Rows of pearl beads dotted her demure neckline and edged her gloves, but I noticed she wore no earrings or necklace, as the other woman did. Behind her, Gerald moved closer, with Hannah on his arm. "Those jewels belonged to my mother. He would be terribly upset if something were to happen to them."

Perhaps if your father wasn't so busy trying to seduce sixteen-year-old girls, he might be able to find your jewels.

I didn't get to eavesdrop any longer. Excitement rippled through the crowd as the doors swung open. Janeites surged toward the entrance, sweeping us along with the crowd. I held tight to Heathcliff and Morrie and gazed around the room in wonder.

The ballroom had been transformed. Gone were the folding chairs arranged in neat rows. Instead, the grand marble floor shone from a fresh polish, ready for dancing feet. Floral arrangements wound around the columns, drawing the eye upward to the ornate paintings of nymphs and satyrs that adorned the ceiling. A band set up in one corner, playing a jaunty reel to welcome us. In front of them, a microphone had been set up for Cynthia to call the dances. Round tables down one end waited for the guests, adorned with towering flower arrangements and glittering with crystal and silver dinnerware.

"Mina, there you are!" Lydia grinned at me. Beside her, David held her hand. "Isn't this great fun?"

"What happened to Professor Hathaway? I saw you two getting friendly together." At the mention of his boss' name, David frowned. Christina rushed over and took David's other arm. "I heard you say that you saw my father. He keeps Mummy's jewels on his person, and I wish to wear her pearl earrings tonight."

"I think he's had too much alcohol! He was nodding off by the fire, so I left him. David is a much better dancer, anyway, isn't that right, David? What are those lights?" Lydia stared at the ceiling.

"They're called fairy lights."

"How delightful! Like fireflies except more... glamorous. I look forward to dancing beneath them. They will make my dress look most fetching."

"Should I worry about Father?" Christina asked David. "I don't want him to miss the ball."

"He's probably still surrounded by his fans," David said. "We'll take our seats and I'm sure he'll be along presently. Shall I get you a drink from the bar?"

"Thank you. I'd appreciate that." They disappeared into the crowd. I couldn't help but think they'd be perfect for each other with their lovely Regency manners, but then I remembered Morrie had seen Christina and Alice snogging in the courtyard. I wondered again what her father would think if he knew.

My phone – which still sat in my bra, along with my father's letter – buzzed. I ignored it. I'd already received fifty-one texts from my mother this weekend, all of them ignored.

"Here's our table. After you, ladies." Morrie held out two chairs. Lydia slid into one and put her purse on the other. Morrie went to move her purse, and she glared at him.

"David will be sitting there. Now, go away," she waved her

hands at us. "I'm saving this table for my other suitors. You'll find plenty of other seats around the room."

"Lydia, you can't just sit wherever you want. You have to find your name on your place setting—"

Lydia's cheeks reddened. "I said, move! Don't force me to say something I'll regret."

Before I could give Lydia a piece of my mind, Morrie looped an arm in mine and led me away. "Why, I'm almost offended. I thought I was supposed to be her escort."

"I think we're supposed to sit at Cynthia's table, anyway," I said.

Heathcliff smirked as he took my other hand. "If your ego can't take the bruising, you could go back and insist upon dueling David for her affections."

"Not on your life. That guy is brutal with a foil. If our charge doesn't wish to sit with me, who am I to deny her?" Morrie steered us to a table near the front of the room, where we found our names on the list. Alice sat on one side of the circle, staring down at her phone. On the other side, two women and a man I didn't recognize hooted with laughter while Christina and David talked with their heads bent close together. *I guess he won't be joining Lydia after all.* "Shall we join the other VIPs?"

I nodded. Morrie pulled out the chair next to Alice, and I sank down into it. She looked up from her phone and smiled. "I was hoping you'd sit with me. I don't know how much talk of bonnets and calligraphy I can stand."

"You've already exhausted conversation with our table-mates?"

"Let's see. Christina and David won't speak to me, because they don't like the questions I've been asking about Professor Hathaway." It was on the tip of my tongue to ask her if that was true after their make-out session last night. But I didn't want to make either of them into a spectacle if they'd chosen to keep it private. "We've also got Barbara, the tarot reader. Gina over there writes Jane Austen erotica. Quentin is a scholar of political science and a Marxist and has just spent the last fifteen minutes explaining to me in the most passionate terms the political history of the top hat."

"At least you can't say this is a gathering 'too numerous for intimacy, too few for variety'," I joked, quoting from *Persuasion*.

Alice rolled her eyes. "Not you, too."

"Do you have an angle for your fluffy article yet?"

She jerked her head toward a couple of women at a nearby table who waited for their male escort to pull out their chairs and pour their drinks. "I'm thinking, 'sexism still alive and well in Argleton'."

I smiled, topping up her wine glass after filling my own. *Solidarity, sister.* "I'm guessing your other piece has something to do with Hathaway? I saw you speaking to Professor Carmichael yesterday, and after Gerald's performance this morning—"

"Good guess." Alice set down her phone on the table, turning the screen down so I couldn't see what was on it. "Hathaway has had several inappropriate relationships with female students, and that's only scratching the surface of that man's depravity. Professor Carmichael was the one who came to me with information in the first place, and it was even more damning than she'd initially suggested. Gerald's story could only add fuel to the fire. Hathaway's been allowed to get away with too much for too long. This is going to be the #metoo story of the year. I want—"

Something dived under the table. Alice reached out to save our wine before it splashed on the pristine tablecloth.

I peered under the table. "Heathcliff, what are you doing?"

"Put the cloth down!" He wrenched it from my fingers and yanked it to the floor. The flower arrangement teetered dangerously. Hannah and her goth friends appeared at my side.

"Do you have any idea where Heathcliff got to?" Hannah asked. She flaunted the Regency theme of the ball and wore a fishtail-style black gown with a plunging neckline that would earn the Morticia Addams seal of approval. Her hair was teased out in a wild 80s style, her fake lashes so long they touched her cheeks when she widened her eyes to search the room. "He promised me the first dance."

"Sure. He's under the table," I said. From beneath my feet, something bellowed.

Heathcliff yanked the tablecloth up on the other side of the table. Christina yelped in surprise as he barreled out and dashed off. A moment later, three black-clad goth girls raced after him. Morrie, Alice and I burst out laughing.

"David," Christina folded her napkin on the table. "I need to go to the bathroom. Will you accompany me?"

"It would be my pleasure." David rose and offered his arm. "Perhaps we will find your father on the way." Just as they disappeared, Cynthia stopped by our table and wished us a fun night. I couldn't help but feel a little flutter of excitement as the band struck up a jaunty tune. This really was quite fun.

When everyone in the room had taken their seats and the waiters came around with appetizers – smoked quail breast with Asian pear gel, cauliflower puree, and spelt grains – Cynthia took to the stage to welcome us and explain how the evening would work. There would be a round of dancing between appetizers and the main course, and then the music would continue through dessert and long into the evening. The band struck up one of the popular tunes, the 'Duke of Kent's Waltz', and two lines of dancers took to the floor.

Heathcliff hadn't returned by the time I finished my quail. Morrie swiped Heathcliff's plate and refilled mine and Alice's glasses. "We must take the opportunity to have the next dance together," Morrie's eyes sparkled at me.

"Standing close, staring adoringly into each other's eyes while we remember a complex pattern of steps?" I raised a suggestive eyebrow. "Are you sure the world's foremost criminal mind is up to the challenge?"

The band finished their song, and Morrie held out his hand. "Let us find out."

Morrie led me onto the dance floor and we lined up alongside the other couples. Luckily, the next dance was 'A Fig for Bonaparte', which was one of the easier country dances we learned the previous day. Even so, I managed to begin by stepping the wrong way.

"Ooops, sorry, sorry," I apologized as I bumped my way through the frowning dancers and found my way back to Morrie.

"At least when you go blind, you'll have an excuse for your appalling sense of direction," he grinned.

Weirdly, that comment that might've upset me on any other day just made me poke my tongue out at him. I stuck my foot out as Morrie swept past. He tripped and skidded into Lydia, who shoved him away with a grimace.

We wound our way down the line without any other disasters. The next dance was more complex, and I hadn't been able to see the instructor very well. I shuffled us to the back of the line so I could watch the other couples first. When it came to our turn, I managed to spin the right way. As I twirled around the couple behind me, my gaze flicked to the bar. Gerald slumped over the hardwood surface, a piña colada in his hand. When I spun around again, he was still there, this time with a pink drink. On the next spin, he had a glass of clear liquid that I guessed wasn't water.

"Morrie? Do you see Gerald?" I pointed toward the bar.

"He's wearing an awfully cheap cotton shirt for the ball. And it hasn't escaped my attention he's trying to drink his way through the Baddesley cellars," Morrie observed as he lifted his arm so I could pass under. "Heathcliff will not be amused if there's nothing left for tomorrow's whisky tasting."

"Do you think he's upset about that incident with Professor Hathaway this morning?" I turned back and noticed Gerald accepting an Old-Fashioned.

"He certainly appears agitated—ow." Morrie winced as my boot landed on his foot. "Focus on the dance, gorgeous. My shins are not as robust as Heathcliff's."

I was puffing by the time we finished the set. Cynthia bade us return to our seats amidst raucous applause. I beamed from my place on Morrie's arm. That was actually heaps of fun.

My breasts vibrated. Another text message from Mum. I resisted the temptation to toss my phone into the nearest punch bowl.

Our main course was served – wild duck confit, quince poached in mulled wine, white bean puree – and I dug in, ravenous from all the dancing. Cynthia took the stage again. "We have a very special treat tonight. It is my pleasure as the President of the Jane Austen Appreciation Society Argleton chapter to present our Lifetime Achievement Award for the pursuit of Austen scholarship and the furtherance of the society's aims to promote her work to a new generation. I think it's no surprise that I stand here tonight to present this honor to Professor Julius Hathaway."

The room erupted into applause – all except Professor Carmichael and Alice, who glared at the stage. I turned around to see what Gerald thought of this announcement. He scowled at the bartender and swiped another cocktail.

Cynthia beamed, scanning the crowd as the applause died down. "If Professor Hathaway could come to the stage and accept his award. Where is he?"

"I don't think he's arrived yet," David called out. "Christina and I haven't seen him at our table, although his dinner's gone, so maybe he came by while we were taking a turn of the room—"

"Nope. That was me," Morrie said, rubbing his stomach. "I couldn't very well let a perfectly decent duck confit go to waste."

"So no one's seen the good professor all evening?" Cynthia looked confused. Murmurs stole through the crowd.

"He attended the final lecture of the day," said Christina. "I left to prepare for the ball, and he stayed behind to correct Professor Carmichael on one or two points of scholarship. I went to his room immediately before the ball to collect my mother's jewels, but he wasn't there. Professor Carmichael must've been the last to see him."

"That's hardly what happened," Professor Carmichael stood up, her face flushed with anger. "He expounded on some problematic theories and I corrected him on *facts*. I left him to continue with his favorite activity – blowing hot air out of his arse to a circle of adoring young women."

Nervous whispers circled the room.

"He attended me in Uppercross," Lydia stood up, her face aglow as she realized all eyes in the room were on her. "He was sitting by the fire and seemed in good spirits, although exceptionally tired. Perhaps he retired early?"

"Perhaps he retired with some new young conquest?" Alice muttered into her phone without looking up. The woman at the table behind her heard the comment and leaned forward to whisper it to her friends. On the other side of our table, David bristled. Christina's face reddened. Gerald slammed his drink down on the counter and strode toward the stage.

"I'll accept the award on his behalf," he bellowed. "Seeing as it's really *my* work that you're awarding."

"Oh, this is going to get ugly," Morrie leaned forward, steepling his hands together in gleeful anticipation.

Christina's face fell, her whole body crumpling as her father's reputation become the talk of the room. And even though I thought the guy was a creep, I didn't want to see her hurt, especially among her peers. "I saw him nodding off in his chair just before the ball," I called out. "Perhaps he's fallen asleep after the excitement of the day. I'll go fetch him."

Thinking it best to get the professor onto the stage before the room erupted into chaos, I raced into the antechamber where Professor Hathaway had been sitting with Lydia draped across his lap. The chair still sat beside the roaring fireplace. Tufts of his blonde hair poked over the top.

I knew it. I knew he must have fallen asleep. That fire looks so warm and cozy.

"Professor Hathaway?" I approached the chair, hoping I wouldn't startle him.

Something dark spread around his feet. Was the rug dark crimson, too? *I could have sworn it was white.* I smiled to myself. That would be just Cynthia's taste to add red everywhere. I rested my hand on the back of the chair and leaned down to gently wake the professor.

"Professor Hathaway, everyone's waiting for you in the ball-room. You've won a prize—"

No. Oh, no.

It's not a red rug.

I staggered back, bile rising in my throat. I opened my mouth, and screamed and screamed.

Professor Hathaway's eyes bugged out of his head, his mouth frozen open in a grisly and silent shriek. The hilt of his sword stuck out of his chest, and blood dribbled between his legs to stain the rug at his feet.

CHAPTER NINETEEN

$\mathcal{I}$ sank to my knees, my legs no longer able to support my weight. Footsteps thundered on the marble behind me. "Mina, did you find him—Oh, *shite.*"

Morrie's arms went around me, pulling me into him, swallowing me in the warmth and safety of his body. He swore again as he too noticed the sword quivering in the professor's chest.

He's dead. He's dead.

Those wide, terrified eyes, that jaw frozen in his death cry. He must have yelled out, but no one heard him over the frivolities in the ballroom.

The room spun. I buried my face in Morrie's chest, wishing I could step back in time so someone, *anyone* else could have come out here instead of me. The professor's expression would haunt my dreams. Even when I went blind I'd still see that horror behind my eyes.

"Well, this weekend finally got interesting," Morrie murmured into my hair. "We were hoping for a jewel thief, but this is infinitely more intoxicating."

Don't say that. I never wished for this. I never—

More footsteps clattered behind us. "Whatever is the matter

—" Cynthia's words cut off in a piercing shriek as she too saw the professor's body. More people crowded around, shrieking and exclaiming as they saw what had transpired.

"It's Professor Hathaway!"

"He's been stabbed!"

"Stabbed through with his own sword."

"Everybody, stay back," Morrie cried. "Heathcliff, call Inspector Hayes. Tell him there's been a murder."

"And a theft!" Christina yelled. "My jewels have been stolen."

I opened my eyes. Christina stood, picking up a velvet pouch from the floor directly behind the chair. Her whole body trembled as she held it up so we could see. "We kept my mother's jewels in this pouch," she sobbed. "Daddy was going to give them to me at the ball. But it's empty. This rotten person has come in here and killed my only daddy because of a few baubles."

"Look behind you," Morrie said. "That window is open. It looks as though the murderer might have escaped through it with the jewels."

Heathcliff went to the window and pushed open the frame. "There's a torn piece of fabric snagged on the latch, and a couple of beads on the ledge."

Christina howled. "How could someone do this? How could they kill my daddy over a bunch of jewels? I just saw him this afternoon and he was so beautiful and full-of-life."

David rushed over, wrapping her arms around her. "There, there. The police are on their way and they will catch the villain who did this."

Cynthia wrung her hands. "I can't believe it. The Argleton Jewel Thief has hit our house, and murdered the good Professor Hathaway!"

As Cynthia fretted and Christina wailed, I cast my eyes around the room, and couldn't help but notice both Professor Carmichael's calm expression and Alice frantically scribbling on her pad. A sinister thought leaped into my head, but I stuffed it down. This was clearly the work of an opportunist – someone rambling around the grounds took a peek in the window, saw the professor lying asleep by the fire and the jewels beside him, and took a chance. Perhaps the professor awoke and this assailant stood over him, so he lashed out with his sword, but the killer got it out of his hands and plunged it into his chest.

So if that was true, then why did I have such an awful feeling in my gut?

~

*I*nspector Hayes and DS Wilson showed up soon afterward and ushered everyone back into the ballroom so they could take our statements. I waved to Jo – the pathologist and my friend – from across the room. She lifted an eyebrow as if to say, "not another one?"

I poked my tongue out at her. I did seem to collect murder victims the way other people collected shoes.

"Mina Wilde, stop making faces at my pathologist, or I'll haul you off to a cell again," Hayes growled, only half-joking. I'd been close to too many murders in Argleton in recent months. I nodded in obedience and allowed Morrie to usher me to my seat. Beside me, Alice's face was as white as a sheet. She tapped notes on her phone with lightning speed.

"Can you talk to me about what you saw?" she asked. "At last, this story got actually interesting."

"Maybe... I don't know." I rubbed my head.

"Let us get through the questioning first," Morrie told her. "We don't want to accidentally say something the police don't want revealed."

Alice nodded, but she looked disappointed. I knew that as the person who found the body, I'd make a compelling source for her article, but her mercenary attitude was a little shocking. A man had just been murdered in the very same house as us, and all she was thinking about was her byline?

In an attempt to keep our spirits up, Cynthia had the band continue the music and the desserts brought out, but the party atmosphere had been shattered. Everyone huddled together in small groups, whispering in hushed voices and weeping into their handkerchiefs.

All except the Brontë society. The three goth girls stood beside the dance floor, peering over their black veils at Heathcliff and giggling to each other. Gerald scanned the length of the bar, pouring cocktails down his throat at the rate of one a minute. I noticed a smudge of red on the hem of his leather jacket. Blood?

I nudged Morrie. "Gerald's still drinking."

"That he is. And there's a smudge of something dark on his coat," Morrie squinted. "And I detect a few hairs on his cuff that appear to match the shaggy rug under the good professor's chair."

I reached across the table to Heathcliff. "Get over there and talk to your girlfriends. We need to know Gerald's movements over the evening."

"No way." Heathcliff glowered. "Thanks to the two of you abandoning me, I've already suffered through two marriage proposals and a catfight over which one of them has a right to use the 'I am Heathcliff' line as their social media status. I'm not spending another moment of my time with the ghoul girls. Besides, this case isn't any of our concern. If the professor has been murdered, it's up to the police to solve it, not us."

Morrie nudged him in the direction of the bar. "Aw, go on. You know Mina was only keen on this weekend because she needed a distraction from her father's letter. Well, solving the professor's murder is the perfect kind of distraction, much better than shagging you in a bathroom."

"Hey, how did you know about that?"

"The scent of hyacinth soap when Heathcliff returned to the breakfast table – the flavour of which is not present in the male bathrooms – and an indent of the hand dryer on the back of your shoulder. It was a simple deduction." Morrie waved a hand. "Go on, Sir Snarkypuss, work your charms on the young Miss Hannah. If you don't get over there soon, Gerald will have drank the place dry."

Heathcliff folded his arms. "If I go over there now, I'm going to be cravat-deep in marriage proposals. I even heard Hannah talking to Cynthia about the possibility of holding a wedding at Baddesley Hall. If you're so desperate, *you* talk to them."

"Fine." I shoved my chair back and stood up.

"No, Mina." Heathcliff reached for my hand, but I jerked it away. *If I sit here and do nothing, Professor Hathaway's face is going to haunt me all night, mixed with all my ugly thoughts about my father and his letter, and I'll feel even worse tomorrow.*

While Hayes and Wilson were otherwise occupied, I could help by getting a little information out of Gerald.

My legs still trembled as I made my way across the room, but I managed to hold my poise as I swept up to the bar, nonchalantly picking up a piña colada from the dwindling supply.

"Can you believe this?" I said to Gerald, sipping my drink as I leaned in close to him. "A real murder right here in Baddesley Hall. This never happened in Jane Austen."

"True enough, but in Austen novels, the rakes and scoundrels always end up tamed in the end." Gerald knocked back another cocktail. "The only way to tame a first-class git like Hathaway was to drive a sword through his gut."

Wow, that's harsh. "You can't mean that. I know you had your academic differences, but that's no reason to wish someone dead."

"Academic differences?" Gerald scoffed. "I admired the man once. He was my advisor for my Masters' degree. But that was before he tried to steal my girlfriend and plagiarized my work."

"His speech over breakfast this morning indicated he'd been acquitted of that crime."

But Gerald wasn't listening to me. "...can you just imagine? I open the Jane Austen periodical, and what do I find but excerpts of my Masters' thesis – rough drafts that I'd sent him for his feedback – polished and published as if he himself had written them. I complained to the university. They set up a farce of an academic trial, with a jury of his sycophants who lapped up his explanation that, in fact, it was *I* who'd copied *him*. They kicked me out of the graduate program and refused to grant me credit for the papers I'd already written." Gerald shook his head. "Luckily, Hannah has more sense, and she's not interested in Hathaway unless he'll read lines from *Wuthering Heights* to her while they shag. And since he probably only wanks to his own books, that was never going to happen. Unfortunately, her rejection came too late to save my career. Thanks to Hathaway, my name is mud in academia. I can't get another university to accept me for graduate studies. But I'll not go quietly into the dark night. I'll get my revenge."

Maybe you already did, I thought but didn't say. Instead, I pointed to the stain on the hem of his jacket. "You've got something there."

Gerald picked up the corner and rubbed the stain, so it disappeared. As he did, I noticed the cuff of his shirt was torn, with a triangle of fabric missing. "Oh, yes, mulled wine reduction. The food here's a bit ostentatious." He eyed my drink. "You going to finish that?"

I handed it to Gerald, and he knocked it back, gripping the edge of the bar to remain upright. "It's just so distressing," he said, his speech slurred. "Hathaway is murdered, and it looks as though this jewel thief has made off with another fine haul. That's why I'm drinking so much. I need it to nerve my calms. I mean... calm my nerves."

"Of course. We've all had a nasty shock."

"I work in historic houses, you know... and if I get in his way I could be... could be next..." Gerald slurred. "Oh, I appear to be a little tipsy. I think I'll go... down lie. Lie down, I mean. Of course, that's it."

Gerald stumbled off. I watched him make his way over to Hannah and the other Brontë Society members. *It's interesting that he's been drinking heavily all night, and looking nervous and upset, too, even though I didn't find Hathaway's body until a few minutes ago.*

Something tapped at the window above my head. A dark shape silhouetted against the moonlight. "Quoth!" I cried. I lifted the latch and swung the window outward to admit him. Quoth hopped on my shoulder, croaking in concern.

I heard screaming and commotion, he said inside my head. *And the police are here. Is something wrong?*

"That scream you heard was mine," I whispered to him. "Professor Hathaway was murdered. I found him in the antechamber. Someone stabbed him with his own sword."

As discreetly as I could, I moved to a table in the corner of the room and set Quoth down on the back of a chair. Morrie and Heathcliff made their way over to me, and together we filled Quoth in on what happened.

I'll fly around the grounds, see if I can spot where the murderer got away. He unfurled a midnight wing.

"Don't bother," Heathcliff growled. "All the alcohol and quail breast has gone to Mina's head. She's forgotten that we're not actually detectives and we're not getting mixed up in this."

I sighed. He was right. Just because there was a murder at the Jane Austen Experience didn't mean I had to jump in and try to solve it. In the last two murders, I'd had a personal reason for getting involved – the police blamed me for Ashley's murder, and my friend Mrs. Ellis was in danger. But this time, I didn't have any skin in the game. Judging from the horror I'd just seen, this murderer was one of the most dangerous I'd known. I didn't want to come face-to-face with him or her any time soon.

"Please, everyone, if I may have your attention!" Cynthia stood behind the microphone, waving her arms about. "We've had quite a nasty surprise tonight, I'm afraid. We need you all the cooperate with the police detectives and answer their questions. They're going to keep us in here while they secure the scene and conduct their interviews, and then we'll all be allowed to go to our rooms."

"I'm not staying in this house another moment!" cried one lady. "Not with a murderer on the loose!" A chorus of agreement cascaded through the ballroom.

"Unfortunately, it's not possible for anyone to leave just yet, but the police will do their best to finish the interviews quickly. Of course, Grey and I understand that this is not how anyone expected the first annual Jane Austen Experience to go! If anyone wishes to leave tonight, my staff will be on hand to help with your bags and to arrange transportation and alternative accommodations. However, we do hope you will stay. Tonight's incident looks to be a crime of opportunity undertaken by the Argleton Jewel Thief – a known criminal who the police assure me they are close to apprehending. We'll be putting on extra security – there's nothing we care about more than the safety of our guests. I know our dear Professor Hathaway would want the Jane Austen Experience to continue. With that in mind, we shall forgo the morning's lecture program and instead host a memorial garden party tomorrow in the orangery in his honor!"

"This is ridiculous," Alice said. "A man was just run through with a sword. The murderer is probably someone in this room, and all they can think about is tea parties and country dances."

"What makes you think the murderer is in this room?" I asked.

"Professor Hathaway had a lot of enemies," she whispered. "More than anyone here realizes."

"Do you think this has to do with your story?" I asked. "You're going to tell the police, right?"

"I'm not sure. But I can't tell them what I know," her eyes flashed at me, and she gripped my hands in hers. "Please, Mina, don't mention the fact that I was talking to Professor Carmichael or planning a story about Hathaway. Someone else's life is at stake if the information I have gets out."

"Um..." *That's a weird thing to ask someone who's just seen a dead body.*

I was saved from answering by Hannah, who bustled past me and fell into Heathcliff's lap. "Oh, it's a tragedy! Heathcliff, please hold me. Hey, why is there a raven in here?" She reached out a hand to stroke Quoth's back. He stiffened as she pawed at his feathers. A prickle of rage traveled up my spine. I knew Quoth wouldn't like her touching him.

"Go on," Morrie urged. "He particularly loves it when you quote Poe's famous poem."

"Croak!" The raven warned, darting from Hannah's grip and settling on the chandelier above our table.

"Do you mean, 'The Raven'? I know all the words, of course." Hannah straightened her back. "Listen, Heathcliff. 'Once upon a midnight dreary, while I pondered, weak and weary, over many a quaint and curious volume of forgotten lore—'"

SPLAT.

"Argh!" Hannah leaped up and clawed at her head. "He shat in my hair. That filthy bird defecated in my *hair.*"

"In that case, you should thank it," Lydia called out. "It has improved your hairstyle."

"Aeeeeeeeee!" Hannah screamed, clutching her head and fleeing the table.

"Croak!"

CHAPTER TWENTY

*S*ince I was the one who found the body, Hayes and Wilson interviewed me first. I gave them as true an account as I could remember, shuddering as I had to recall the details of the blade stuck deep in Hathaway's chest, the hilt quivering in the brisk breeze blowing in from the window. I also told them about Gerald and the stain on his jacket and the tear in his cuff. Beside me, Morrie's hand never left mine.

After they dismissed me, and Morrie and Heathcliff had given their statements, we had to walk back through the antechamber to get to our rooms. They'd roped off three-quarters of the room with crime scene tape, leaving the guests a narrow strip to walk. Morrie and Heathcliff flanked me, Quoth on Heathcliff's shoulder, keeping up a steady barrage of insults to each other as a way of distracting me as we walked past the fireplace. It didn't work, but I appreciated the effort.

"Should we wait for Lydia?" I asked weakly. "I'm worried about what she'll say—"

"No," both boys said in unison. Heathcliff picked up his pace, as though anxious to place even more distance between us and Lydia Bennet.

"Mina!"

I turned my head. Jo stood up from behind the red chair and ran over to the edge of the tape.

"Hey." She wiped a strand of blonde hair behind her ear. Her PPE crinkled as she leaned in to pat my shoulder. "I heard you found him. At the rate you trip over corpses, your friendship alone is going to keep me in work for the rest of my life. I'd give you a hug, but I don't want to get crime scene goo on your pretty dress."

I backed away, holding up my hands. "Please no."

"You look smokin', by the way." Jo winked at Morrie, who gave her a thumbs up and a wicked grin. "I'm sorry your ball was ruined. Are you doing okay?"

"It was *horrible*. There was so much blood – I thought the white rug had been replaced with a red one." I gave a strangled laugh. "I guess I don't need to tell you that."

"Not really. But I do appreciate a civilian's perspective of the crime scene. Anything else you noticed?"

"Yeah. He had this awful expression on his face, frozen mid-scream like some hideous Edvard Munch painting come to life."

Jo nodded. "The dead do that, especially if they expire in a sitting position. Immediately after death, the muscles in the body relax, and the mouth falls open. If the body remains in the same position when rigor mortis kicks in, the open-mouthed expression is frozen in place. In funeral homes, they have to wire their mouths shut for viewings."

I shuddered. "I did *not* need to know that."

"Sorry," she grinned. "I forget you don't find this stuff quite as fascinating as I do. In this victim's case, his open mouth was the expression on his face when he died. Apparently, whoever killed him took him completely by surprise. As for the blood, the sword severed one of his main arteries. I'll know more after the autopsy, but it looks as though he died from blood loss—" Jo waved over my shoulder. I turned and squinted at a throng of people walking toward us from the ballroom. The police must've released them after giving their statements. Alice Yo waved back before returning her gaze to her phone screen.

"You know her?" I asked Jo.

"Sort of. She's Alice somebody-or-other. We go to the lesbian film club over in Barchester," Jo replied. "In small communities like this, us queer folk stick together."

"Alice has been assigned to do a story on the Jane Austen fan community, but apparently she's really snooping after another story, something to do with Professor Hathaway."

"Interesting. I'm surprised to see her here. She was saying last month that she was thinking of leaving journalism for corporate copywriting. Her boss is a complete homophobic creep who keeps giving her the worst assignments and cutting her hours. She's been trying to find another job, but journalism is a hard sell these days. If she can't break a big story or find something new by the end of the month, she's going to lose her flat."

"That sucks."

"Yeah. She was asking around the movie night last month if anyone had any ideas for a worthwhile story, especially one on a trending topic like #metoo. We kept telling her to do an expose on sexism and homophobia in journalism, but she said that if she exposed her boss she'd never work in the industry again." Jo picked up her crime scene bag. "I've got to head back to the lab. I'll text you with what I can reveal when I know more. If you need someone to talk to, you know where to find me. But I know you've got those boys to take your mind off things."

"I do. Thanks, Jo."

She waved goodbye and followed the rest of the SOCO team outside. Morrie and Heathcliff dragged me toward the hall. Quoth hopped from Heathcliff's shoulder onto mine, croaking softly as he nuzzled my neck.

"Do you want to go home, gorgeous?" Morrie asked.

Home. Odd that as soon as he said that, I thought of Nevermore Bookshop instead of my dingy conservatory room back at Mum's flat.

My bones ached with weariness and shock. I pulled my phone out of my cleavage and noted the time (and the string of unanswered texts from Mum). "It's already late, and who knows what time it will be when the police finally let us leave the building. Let's just stay the night here and we'll go home in the morning."

CHAPTER TWENTY-ONE

*H*eathcliff swept me into his arms, grunting as he carried me up the sprawling staircase. Along the way, we passed Mrs. Maitland hauling a large pink suitcase down the stairs and one of the erotica writers struggling with a large box of books. Apart from a few people calling for rideshares, it looked as if the majority of guests were planning to stay. The prospect of a scandalous murder was too good to give up. As Heathcliff carried me through the crowd, I caught snatches of rumor flying madly about.

"I heard he was stabbed through the heart with his very own sword—"

"Well, *I* heard that his head had been nearly severed from his shoulders."

"...he clutched a bloody handkerchief in his hand."

"—according to this search I just did on my phone, in order to deliver that thrust, you would need exceptional skill with a sword..."

We pushed our way through the throngs of guests and made our way down the hall to our room. The individual bedrooms in our suite each had a doorway into the main hall, and we'd stopped in front of the guys' door. Morrie fished around in the pockets of his topcoat for the room key, but kept coming up with nothing.

"Hurry up," Heathcliff muttered, bracing himself against the wall. "Mina's been eating too much duck confit. She's not exactly light."

"Hey!" I pretended to slap him on the cheek. "That's no way to address a lady!"

"Croak!" Quoth added.

Morrie recovered the key from his breeches (what it was doing there, I couldn't guess) and shoved the door open. Heathcliff dumped me on the bed, slumping down beside me and pulling me into his arms.

I sank against him. Now that we were alone, the full horror of what I'd seen came at me in a rush. I sobbed into Heathcliff's shoulder, snotting all over his beautiful coat.

"That's it," he muttered in a conciliatory manner, rubbing circles on my back. "Keep weeping on this coat, ruining it forever."

"Want to hear my theory?" Morrie bounced around the room. "If the missing jewels and window escape are anything to go by, it appears tonight's handiwork was the purview of the Argleton Jewel Thief. But it's interesting that he's changed his pattern. He hasn't murdered before. From the angle of the window, he might not have noticed Professor Hathaway sitting in the chair."

"Stop thinking about it," Heathcliff snapped. "This isn't our business. We're all keeping our noses out of it, else Mina will end up in trouble again—"

BANG BANG BANG!

I jumped, clinging to Morrie. Something hammered against the door so hard it rattled the antique dresser. Lydia's voice pierced the wall.

"Mina, Mina. You must help me!"

Morrie rolled his eyes. "Go away. No one's home."

"I can hear you talking, Lord Moriarty."

"Who is Moriarty? We're just three field mice hunting for cheese."

I sniffled back a laugh. "Let her in. She's probably scared out of her wits."

Sighing, Heathcliff opened the door. Lydia fell into the room and leaped on the bed, clinging to my body in desperation.

"Ow!" I cried, as my head slammed into the headboard. I sat up, rubbing the sore patch. "Lydia, I thought I told you not to disturb—"

"This is a matter of life and death!" She flung herself on top of me, her hand to her forehead as though she might faint at any moment. "More precisely, my life and impending death!"

"Professor Hathaway's death has nothing to do with you—ow, what are you doing?"

Lydia grabbed my hand and dragged me off the bed, yanking me so hard she wrenched my shoulder. I followed her into the hall, terrified that if I didn't she'd separate my arm from my body. She pointed with a trembling finger to the door of our bedroom. My heart plunged into my chest.

Across the door, in black paint, someone had written, "YOU'RE NEXT."

CHAPTER TWENTY-TWO

*Y*OU'RE NEXT.

My head spun. What were these words doing on the door to our bedroom? Why would someone leave such a horrible message, unless... unless they meant to scare Lydia?

Or me. My blood turned cold as I realized the message could have been for either of us.

"When... when was this done?" I croaked out.

Morrie touched his finger to the edge of the paint. A smudge came away on his fingers. "It's not completely dry. I'd say it's a few hours old, at least."

"So, around the time someone was murdering Professor Hathaway?" Heathcliff demanded. "That doesn't seem like a coincidence."

"No." Morrie frowned at me. "It doesn't. Mina, did you piss off any Janeites this weekend? Any high school sweethearts or bitter fashion school rivals amongst the guests?"

"You *have* crushed a lot of people's toes with your boots," Heathcliff added.

"Croak!" said the raven.

I held up my hands. "All right, don't pile on. Everyone here is a stranger to me apart from you guys and Cynthia. I think it's much more likely to be about Lydia. She was sitting on Professor Hathaway's lap right before he was murdered—"

"Oh!" Lydia held her hand to her forehead again. "Just the thought of it makes me feel faint."

"—and with that performance she and Morrie gave in the market yesterday and the way she's monopolizing the short supply of eligible young men, I'd say she's made a few enemies."

"I agree that it's much more likely to be Lydia," Morrie added. "That's a relief. I thought I was going to have to care about this."

Lydia threw herself at Morrie's feet, sobbing into his silk stockings. "You must protect me!" she cried. "I appeal to your sense of chivalry."

Morrie glanced around the hallway. "Nope, no chivalry here."

"Of course we'll protect you," I said. "That's why we're going back to the shop, right now. I don't care that it's past midnight. There's a threat to Lydia's life. One of the staff will be able to call us a cab and—"

"No, no." Lydia stood up and fixed me with a determined stare. "I won't go back to that dusty old shop! Not when there is a murderer about."

"You don't really get any choice in the matter," Heathcliff growled.

"Don't I?" Lydia smirked, standing up to her full height. "I had hoped not to do this, but you have given me no choice. If I'm not to stay on here at Baddesley Hall and have my chance at securing a husband of suitable breeding and handsomeness, then I shall blab to that reporter about your magical shop and your pet raven and your real heritage."

"I hardly think she'll believe you," Morrie said, but he exchanged a glance with Heathcliff. I knew what they were thinking. *Even if Alice doesn't write a story about the magical Nevermore Bookshop, some other reporter will.* Lydia could go to any one of the tabloids and they'd eat her tale right up. Hordes would descend upon Argleton to ogle the shop and take pictures with Heathcliff and terrify Quoth and turn our whole existence upside down. And that wasn't even the worst thing that could happen. If anyone saw what Quoth really was, they'd haul him away to some secret lab for tests and I'd never see him again. On my shoulder, his body quivered as the truth of Lydia's statement hit him as well. I held him against my chest, feeling his tiny bird heart patter. *I'm not going to let anything bad happen to you,* I thought with ferocity.

"Your expression suggests you think otherwise," Lydia folded her arms.

"Threatening us is a mistake," Heathcliff growled.

"Perhaps, but I don't know any other way of getting what I want. When I wanted to go to Brighton as Mrs. Forster's most special companion, all I had to do was remind Daddy of what a terror I'd be if he refused, and he folded like a deck of cards. Besides, it's true that you have some skill at solving crimes. I trust you more than those officers downstairs, and here in this house you have a better chance of it than back at the shop." Lydia twirled a strand of hair around her finger. "Therefore, I urge you most earnestly to get to work upon protecting my person."

"Very well," Morrie gathered Heathcliff, Quoth and me into a huddle. "She's got us over a barrel, and she knows it. I can't believe after all the fictional characters who've come through the shop, it would be Lydia Bennet who'd try to destroy us."

"Really?" Noting the ease with which Lydia had trapped them, I found it hard to believe none of the other fictional characters had tried something similar.

"I'm sure others have considered it. But knowing Morrie's reputation has been enough to stop any potential plots," Heathcliff said. "That girl is special."

"I guess we're going to have to try and solve this case," I said, the corner of my lip twitching at Morrie.

"You don't have to sound so glad of it," Heathcliff growled. "I'm trying to keep you safe."

"I know, and Lydia is trying to get us all killed. Let's stop this guy before that happens. Where do we start?"

Morrie glanced over at the door. A small crowd had already gathered, drawn by Lydia's screams. One of the men was dispatched downstairs to send for the detectives. "If we don't know to whom the message was addressed, our next course of action is to consider who might have motive for killing Professor Hathaway. It seems unlikely this message came from the jewel thief, which means it's possible the murderer used the story of the Argleton Jewel Thief to pin the blame elsewhere."

"Hathaway has a long list of enemies," I said. "I've barely known the man a day and already I'd happily watch him get eaten by sharks."

Possibly don't say that out loud during a murder investigation, Quoth said inside my head, as Hayes and Wilson rounded the corner of the hall and saw the message. They immediately started clearing people from the area. We shuffled back with the rest of the crowd.

"Gerald has to be our top suspect," Heathcliff said. "That display over breakfast this morning proves he has a reason to hate Hathaway."

"There's even more to it than that," I said, relating what Gerald told me at the bar. "And he had a red stain on his jacket and a torn sleeve."

"It could match the fabric found on the windowsill," Heathcliff said.

"And I saw Gerald go outside," Lydia explained. "After the first dance, I was... I have learned the new word. Ah, yes, I was *snogging* in the servants' hallway with Mr. Jonathan Grimsby, and I happened to notice Gerald out of the corner of my eye. He came from the ballroom, down the hall and headed through the door outside."

My delight at hearing Lydia Bennet use the word snogging was superseded by my desire to fit this new information into our theory. "Did you see him come back in that way?" I asked her.

"I did not. However, I didn't think much of it at the time, and Mr. Grimsby and I were very much occupied. It's possible Gerald slipped by without my notice."

"Or perhaps he didn't climb back out the window," Morrie said. "If he needed to go back to the ballroom as quickly as possible in order to establish his alibi, and if he knew Lydia and her paramour were in the hallway, he may have decided to simply head straight across the antechamber and into the ballroom without going around the building."

"That makes sense, but how did he look so clean? There were no bloody footprints on the floor around the crime scene, and apart from that one speck on Gerald's coat, he wasn't bloody, either. Wouldn't the person who stabbed him have been covered with blood?"

"He must have cleaned himself up before he went back to the room," Morrie mused. "But where did he stash whatever he used to clean himself? Hmmmm…"

"He's not the only suspect to consider," Heathcliff added. "We have Professor Carmichael, his bitter academic rival."

"I can't believe her capable of killing anyone," I said. "Besides, she was sitting at our table all night."

"Was she?" Morrie inquired. "We spent a great deal of the evening dancing, and Heathcliff was hiding from his future wives. Can you honestly say you watched that table through the entire evening?"

"No." I frowned. "That means Alice Yo must be a suspect, too. She was writing that article about Hathaway that would expose his secrets. Perhaps he confronted her about it and she lost it. Jo said she was desperate for something to sell, and she said something odd to me before. She asked me not to tell the police she was investigating him. 'Someone else's life is on the line', she said."

"It's possible, but unlikely," Morrie said. "I think we need to look into this Gerald more carefully. And this goes without saying, but no one mention to the police that would make them suspect we're doing their work for them. We can't have them investigating Lydia too closely. I'll get some records made up for her as quickly as I can. She's your French cousin, yes? Can I make her a milkmaid—"

"Mina Wilde," Inspector Hayes interrupted, flipping his pad open again and darting his inquisitive eyes around the members of our group. "I guess you and I aren't done talking. If you and your suitemate could follow me."

I grabbed Lydia's arm and dragged her with me.

~

*B*y the time Lydia and I had finished talking with Inspector Hayes and Lydia had given me seven heart attacks with all the embellishments she made to our cousin-visiting-from-France cover story (which checked out in their records, thanks to some fast hacking by Morrie), the crime scene team had photographed the door, scoured the area for fingerprints and forensic evidence, and Cynthia had her staff attempt to remove the paint with a stripper, taking half the door with it. It was now past two in the morning, and I was too tired to take a cab back to the shop, even if Lydia hadn't refused to leave. I crawled into the bed in the guys' room, nestling into Heathcliff's shoulder. Behind him, Quoth lay down and touched my arm, his fingers featherlight as they moved over my skin. Morrie lay down on the opposite side of me, kissing my neck. Immediately, my body reacted, sizzling with heat. I thought about telling him to stop, that he hadn't yet responded to my ultimatum, but I hadn't the strength to deny him. I longed to drive out the horror I'd witnessed tonight with kisses and caresses. Morrie's lips found mine, tipping my head back, exposing my neck to Heathcliff's lips. Quoth's hand trailed across my chest and brushed my erect nipple—

Lydia bounded through the connecting door and leaped on the bed. "Move over. You need to make room."

"Ow!" Morrie leaped up, clutching his jaw. "Ah bit mah tongue!"

"What are you doing?" I murmured. Searing pain arced behind my eyes, even though I'd already taken two of Dr. Clements' painkillers. "You're the one who insisted on staying at the Hall. Now get back to the murder bed."

"I cannot possibly sleep alone in there tonight, especially when you insist upon calling it 'the murder bed'. You shall have to accommodate me in here."

I glared at Morrie, who was too busy rubbing his tongue with ice from the Champagne bucket. *You're no bloody use.* "Fine," I sighed.

Lydia settled herself in the middle of the bed, spreading out her petticoats around her. "I feel so much better to know I have all these big, strong men around to protect me. Mina, you sleep on that edge. That way, any killer will have to stab you first in order to reach me."

"It's nice to know you care." I crawled under the blanket on the other side of Quoth and pressed a pillow over my head to block out the sound of Lydia giggling.

Cock-blocked by Lydia Bennet. I cannot believe my life.

CHAPTER TWENTY-THREE

I stood in the middle of an empty ballroom. Fairy lights twinkled, pinpricks of light piercing the gloom. From somewhere in front of me, a band struck up the first notes of a jaunty Regency dance tune. It took me a moment to recognize the riff from The Clash's 'Guns of Brixton'.

I knew I was supposed to be dancing, but if I took a step in any direction, I'd be flailing blindly. I glanced around, hoping someone would bring the lights up. My hands grabbed at thin air.

"Hello?" I called. "I need a partner. I can't see a thing, and I don't know the moves."

DRIP.

Something splashed on my shoulder. Raindrops? But I was inside. How could it be raining? I lifted my hand to wipe away the water.

DRIP DRIP DRIP.

More raindrops fell on my bare skin. I held my fingers up to my face. In the dim light, I could just discern the reddish liquid on their tips. A harsh, metallic smell hit my nostrils. Not water.

Blood.

Panic rose in my chest. The room spun, the band playing faster and faster until the notes blurred into one continuous cacophony. I looked up, my heart leaping in my throat. Instead of fairy lights, bloody swords hovered in the air above me, their blades hanging over my head. With each thump of the bass, they dropped closer, closer...

"Mina... Mina?"

I woke with a start. Bright sunlight pierced the curtains. A soft hand touched my shoulder. Quoth's anxious face hovered in front of me. There were no swords, no sinister music, no droplets of blood.

"You were shaking," he whispered. "I was so worried."

"I'm fine." I rubbed my eyes. "It was just a nightmare."

I sat up. A neon-green light flashed in my eyes. As it faded and I could make out the room, I realized I was in the guys' room at Baddesley Hall, but no longer in the bed. Instead, I lay on the chaise lounge under the window, my back pressed against Quoth's chest. Lydia sprawled across the bed like a starfish between Heathcliff and Morrie. Even in slumber, a self-satisfied smile played across her face.

"Lydia rolled over in the night and pushed you off the bed," Quoth explained. "I believe it was on purpose, but of course I could not confirm. I carried you here. You've been whimpering and tossing and turning all night."

I squeezed his hand. "Thank you for staying with me."

"Always." Quoth's lips brushed mine, his kiss sweet and searching. I pulled him on top of me, my hands exploring his body, searching for comfort in his embrace.

"Do you want to talk about the dream? Edgar Allan Poe placed a lot of emphasis on the prophetic nature of dreams, and so must I."

"I'm afraid this one is needlessly simple. I was alone in a dark ballroom. I wanted to dance, but if I moved from the spot, it would be too dark and I couldn't see. There was blood dripping from the ceiling all over me."

"I think that means you're afraid of stepping into the unknown, but you know you can't stay where you are," Quoth said, his face serious. "It means you should talk to your mother. And look at those pamphlets Dr. Clements gave you. And tell the guys about the fireworks."

"I think it's about the fact I saw a man stabbed through the heart with a sword," I declared.

"Well, *I* think it's about you running around solving murders so you don't have to think about your eyesight," Quoth observed.

I bristled. "That's not it. What *I* think is that I want to stop talking about it. And it's my dream, so I make the rules. What are our plans today?"

"I'm going back to open the shop so we can still pay the mortgage this month. You're going to stick your nose in where it doesn't belong."

"Yes, I know that, but in order to do that to the best of my ability, I need to continue to pretend to be interested in the Jane Austen Experience."

Quoth picked up the brochure. "As Cynthia said, most of the morning's events have been canceled. But there's a pre-breakfast poetry reading organized by some of Professor Hathaway's graduate students. I thought you might like to attend with me before I head back."

"I'd love to." I'd never much been into poetry, but after Morrie had read aloud the erotic work of John Donne the first time we slept together, I discovered a hidden affinity for it. "Should I wake the others and ask them to join us?"

"I told Heathcliff last night and he said, 'poetry is tough to stomach at any time of day, let alone before I've had my kippers'." Quoth ran a hand through his sleek black hair. "Plus, I thought maybe this was something you and I could enjoy together."

I smiled. I hated that Quoth had been left out of the weekend's events, *again*. It made me think of my dream, how much I'd wanted to dance but wasn't able to because of my disability. Quoth's disability always stopped him from doing things he enjoyed, and it wasn't fair.

Not this morning. Not with me.

I threw on my now-very wrinkled muslin dress, Docs, and a pair of socks featuring titles of banned books (in honor of Mrs. Scarlett, may she rest in peace). Quoth pulled on Morrie's tights, breeches, and topcoat, and hung his lanyard around his neck. As I predicted, he looked stunning. His black hair spilled down his back like a silken waterfall, and the shiny buttons reflected the flecks of orange fire in his eyes. He held out my arm and I took it.

"To Mansfield Park!" I exclaimed.

Quoth and I descended the staircase together. Our footsteps echoed around the silent Hall. Hardly anyone else was awake yet, although Cynthia's staff darted across the entrance hall, carrying dishes and trays of food into the breakfast area. If not for the police tape roped across the entrance to the antechamber, there was no sign that anything terrible had happened last night.

Unless you counted the horrible image of Professor Hathaway's slain body that had etched itself permanently into my brain, that is.

When we arrived at Mansfield Park – a pretty yellow drawing room opposite the marketplace – we found a few other morning birds flittering around. David shuffled back and forth from the front of the room, stopping every few moments to dab at his eyes with a handkerchief. Alice sat in the front row. Her notebook rested open on her knees, and she snapped candid pictures around the room, her right index finger mashing the shutter.

To my surprise, Christina Hathaway sat primly in a chair by herself in the far corner of the room, her eyes fixed on the lectern. I nudged Quoth, and we shuffled down the aisle to sit next to her.

"Hi, Christina. I'm Mina Wilde. We met on Friday. I'm so sorry about your father," I whispered.

She blinked. It took her a few moments to turn her head. "I just can't believe it," she breathed, her voice hoarse from crying. "What monster would do such a thing? Daddy was so beloved, so popular in the community."

"Do you need anything? Can we get you a glass of water or... or..." I stumbled, not sure what to say to someone when their parent had been brutally murdered.

"I'm afraid all food and drink taste like cardboard to me now." Her fingers gripped the edge of her chair. "I'm only staying on at Baddesley because the police want me to remain nearby while they hunt for Daddy's killer. Plus, Daddy would want me to attend the memorial service today."

"If you need anything, please let us know." I slid away to leave her in peace, but she reached out with a cold hand to grip my arm.

"You were the one who found his body," she replied in her soft voice.

"That's right." At that moment, I was glad I'd found him first and Christina might be spared seeing her beloved father with that horrid expression.

"And you had those ugly words scrawled across your door?"

"Yes, but I believe they were meant for my roommate, not me. She was..." *draping herself all over your father like a common strumpet, in the Jane Austen vernacular, and he lapped it up like the creep he was.* But that wasn't something I should say to his grieving daughter, so I settled for, "...friendlier with your father than I was."

"And she is okay?" Christina dabbed at her eyes. "I'd hate to think this foul person is threatening others."

"She's fine. Cynthia had one of her security team guarding the bedroom door all night. No one else will get hurt, and the police are doing everything they can to bring the killer to justice."

"I don't know what I shall do now," Christina said, her eyes glazing over. "I know Daddy would want me to continue his legacy in Austen scholarship, but I don't know how I should manage when every bonnet and book reminds me of him. If only I had someone to help me, but I'm all alone."

I thought of Christina and Alice kissing in the darkened courtyard. "I hope you have friends who can support you. Someone you love who maybe you haven't been able to spend time with."

Her face blanked. "I don't know what—"

"Christine, are these two bothering you?" David dropped into the seat next to her. He collected her hands in his and shot me a frown. "Please don't speak about the incident. Christina has had enough trauma to last a lifetime. She doesn't need to keep reliving it."

"I swear I didn't say anything—" I protested, not wanting him to think I was delighting in recounting the gory details.

"I'm fine, David. Really."

"Come with me. I've saved you a comfortable seat at the front of the room." Christina's eyes flicked to Alice, but she allowed David to help her to her feet. I hoped that in time, she'd be able to fully embrace who she was and be open about her relationship, but I guessed the day after her father's murder was not the day.

"Poor girl," I whispered to Quoth. "She looks to be in shock. I cannot even imagine what she must be going through."

"Me neither. Even if the man was horrible, she loved him dearly, and my heart goes out to her."

The poetry reading began. I couldn't help but notice that David looked to our corner every few moments, a disapproving expression on his face. He really didn't like us speaking with Christina. I assumed it was just his protectiveness, but during one of the breaks between performers, Cynthia and two of her friends leaned over and asked Christina about her father, and he didn't stop them.

Is he worried that I'll reveal details about the murder? And that Christina might figure out who actually did it?

No, that's insane. He's just an insecure boy trying to look out for his friend.

Or is he?

When David's turn came, he read an ardent and passionate love poem, his voice rising with the meter as he locked eyes with Christina. Every word in the poem he spoke to her.

Well, that's obvious. He's clearly smitten with her, and he must've planned this poem as a way to declare his love. But considering what just happened, his efforts are a bit crass! I had the feeling his annoyance at us had more to do with his wanting to keep Christina's mind on the poetry.

When the reading was finished, Christina wandered to the back of the room for another cup of tea. "Did you enjoy the poems?" I asked her. David was already running down the aisle, his face expectant like a puppy.

"I'm afraid I didn't hear a word of it," she said. Behind her, David's shoulders sagged. "I'm so upset by Daddy's death, it all went in one ear and other the other."

I smiled despite myself. *Probably for the best. She probably doesn't need to be forced into coming out to David on today of all days.* "That's to be expected. It really was brave of you to come to the reading today after everything that happened."

David plastered on a brave face and joined our group. "Come with me, Christina, I'll escort you to the memorial. Cynthia will want to speak to you before it begins—"

"No, thank you," she said. "I think I'll freshen up in my room."

"I'll walk you there," he said. She looked ready to protest, but held out her hand and allowed David to take it.

"If you must."

David fell over himself tripping over the chairs as he went around to take her arm and escort her out of the room. I leaned into Quoth. "It must be strange to act like that all the time."

"Perhaps she enjoys it." Quoth offered his arm. I took it, smiling at Quoth as I conceded his point. It had been an interesting weekend retreating into this feminine persona, where I needed a man's arm in order to get anything done.

I might need a man's arm in mine for the rest of my life, stopping me from banging into things.

It was hard to dwell on my own personal hell when Quoth's calming presence was beside me. We went through to the breakfast room and helped ourselves to what little remained at the buffet. Quoth found us a table for two under a window in the darkest, loneliest corner. We poured tea and ate our food while outside, snow blanketed the lawns and parterres in a fluffy white coat.

"You're doing very well," I said, buttering my croissant like the heathen Englishwoman I was. "No urges to fly away?"

"Strangely, no." Quoth sipped his tea. "I wonder if it's something in the familiarity of the clothing, the speech, the conversation. It's weird to think that so many years in the future, people look back at our books with such a romantic nostalgia."

"I have to admit, you look damn sexy in that cravat," I smiled, sliding my hand up his leg under the table. He did at that. The high, stiff collar framed his perfect face, making his skin appear even paler. It was probably a good thing the Brontë Society ladies hadn't got their claws into him yet.

"Thank you." Quoth set down his fork. I noticed he had no eggs on his plate. I guess eating eggs was weird when you were a bird. He cleared his throat. "Mina, I don't like to tell you what to do, but I think you should tell Morrie and Heathcliff about the fireworks."

"Nope." I stabbed a sausage with more violence than I intended. It skidded across the table. Quoth caught it before it toppled off the edge.

"They're going to figure out that something is wrong, if they haven't already."

"I'm not ready to talk about it yet. I just want more time to enjoy being with all of you, being a normal person, before the world turns dark forever and I become an invalid."

"You're never going to be an invalid to us." Quoth's hand rested on mine. "Ever since I arrived here, I've felt less than Morrie and Heathcliff. I've known there are things in this world that can never belong to me. But you made me realize that isn't true. The only disability is in my own mind, and the only thing holding me back is my fear. And now," he gestured to the spread in front of us, and the smile on his lips melted my heart. "Here I am, eating breakfast in public with the most kind and beautiful woman."

"It's different." It wasn't different. I stared at my plate, struggling to hold back the tears prickling in the corners of my eyes.

Quoth laughed, the sound like tinkling chimes. "It hurts me to see you like this. Just because the lights are fading in your eyes, don't let your own light burn out. Please, promise you'll think about it."

A bell rang, signaling the end of the hour and the time for the memorial garden party to begin. Grateful for a distraction from a conversation that was rapidly descending toward breaking me open and dragging out all my dark thoughts, I leaped to my feet. Quoth helped me into my coat (actually, Heathcliff's coat, but he wasn't going to miss it), and we joined the throng of people waiting for a break in the falling snow to dash out to the orangery.

Morrie ran down the stairs – dressed in a new outfit of pale breeches, a midnight-blue topcoat with gold detail, and a shiny sword – and sidled up to us. "Yo, little birdie, I'm going to need my lanyard. And my girl."

"I thought I might escort Mina to the garden party—" Quoth started.

"Nope." Morrie elbowed Quoth out of the way. "Too many people. Too great a risk. See you later."

"No. Quoth, wait." I tightened my grip on his arm. "Morrie, you're being unbelievably rude. Can't Quoth and I enjoy the morning ourselves? I thought you'd be too busy snooping around for clues about our murder."

Morrie straightened his shoulder. "I didn't want to have to say this, but I need to talk to you about something."

I narrowed my eyes. "Is that true, or are you trying to get away from Lydia?"

"Mina, it's fine, really. He's right. There are too many people out here. I shall return to the shop and see you later." Quoth dropped my arm, sinking into the crowd before I could stop him.

"You're mine again." Morrie placed my arm in his.

"I'm angry at you. I'm only holding onto you because it's freezing, and the ground is slippery and I don't want to fall over."

"Sure, gorgeous, I believe you."

As the crowd swept us along, I glanced over my shoulder. Quoth stood on the top of the stairs, his long hair sweeping down his back, his face serene. He raised his hand and gave me a quick wave.

Morrie just acted like a total dick, and Quoth doesn't care.

A wave of sadness swept over me. *For all his fine words, deep down he still believed he was less than.* Quoth just took all the shit life handed him. But he shouldn't have to take it from his friends.

We stepped out into the bitter cold. My teeth chattered as I fought to get the words out. "What you did just then was cruel."

"If you say so." Morrie shrugged. "Quoth knows I'm right. Besides, if I'm down here with you, Heathcliff has no choice but to escort Lydia."

Anger bubbled in my veins. "I knew that was you sole motivation! You robbed Quoth of this chance to enjoy time with me and to hone his skills at remaining human. He's getting so much better now. He could have managed at the garden party. And if he had trouble he could have slipped into the bushes and shifted without a hassle."

Morrie held up his lanyard. "This badge has my name on it. Quoth doesn't have a ticket. You made your choice. Face it, Mina, you're just as cruel as I am, only I'm the one who'll say it to his face."

I opened my mouth to protest more, but Cynthia swept in, her hair immaculate. She wrapped my freezing hands in hers. "I'm so sorry, Mina, that you had to see what you saw last night. And then to find those horrid words on your door! Why, it's just too much! I thought this weekend would help you forget about gruesome murders, but instead, I've landed you in the middle of one. What a nasty business."

"Yes," I tried to step around her, but her umbrella blocked the path. Cold snow pelted my bare face.

"Have the police caught the killer yet?"

"Just because I f-f-found the body doesn't mean the police h-h-have to let me in on their case."

Cynthia moved her umbrella to the other side. Sensing my opportunity, I surged forward, but Morrie yanked me back to his side.

"I imagine they're still processing the evidence from the scene," Morrie said, tightening his grip on my arm, locking me in place. "I believe they thought it might've been an opportunistic killing?"

"Yes. Christina's stolen jewelry may link this case to that terrible thief." Cynthia shuddered. "The murderer must have been skulking around the grounds when he noticed the jewels, came in the window, and stuck our dear professor right through so he could make his getaway. But I don't understand why he went upstairs and wrote that note on your door. I just hate to think someone might be casing our home! Grey has engaged a security firm from London," she pointed to a row of burly, black-clad security guards barking orders at each other through headsets. "Apparently, they look after rock bands and movie stars, so they shall keep the rest of us safe."

"Yes, well, thank you." I wrenched Morrie around her. "We must go find a seat."

"Where's the fire, gorgeous?" Morrie jogged after me.

"In the orangery." I pointed to a glowing brazier in the large building. "And considering my lips are about to fall off, I need to go and hug it. Why would you keep Cynthia talking? You know she never says anything of substance, and I already can't feel my feet."

"I was trying to find out more information. I thought she might reveal any leads the police were following."

We emerged onto the wider garden path leading down to the orangery. I dragged my frozen feet forward, my body curling in on itself with every step. *Just a little further, Mina, and then you'll get to be next to that nice warm heater, and enjoy a hot cup of tea—*

"Mina, can I talk to you?" Alice appeared in front of me, her lips drawn in a tight line.

Nooooooo. "S-s-sure. We could just go inside and stand by the fire—"

"No," Alice grabbed me under the arm and tugged me away from Morrie. "Not near any people. Come with me."

"I'll save you a seat by the brazier!" Morrie called after me.

Alice dragged me across the lawn and yanked me down behind a parterre. I threw out my hand to break my fall, yelping as I slammed my fingers into the icy snow.

"Sorry." Alice crouched beside me. "I don't want anyone to see us. If someone asks what we're doing here, say you were helping me look for an earring."

"You're good at s-s-subterfuge," I said, rubbing my frozen hands together. "Wh-wh-why are we crouching in the snow instead of inside with the fire and hot chocolate—"

"I don't know who else to trust," Alice's eyes widened as she pulled her earring out of her ear. "But then I saw what was written on your door, and I knew I had to tell you what I know."

"Wh-wh-what's that?"

"I know who killed Professor Hathaway, and it wasn't the Argleton Jewel Thief. It was—"

"Alice, there you are! What are you doing down there?"

Professor Carmichael peered down at us, a black shawl wrapped around her shoulders.

"Mina was helping me search for my earring, but I think it's gone forever." Alice stood up so fast as sent a cascade of snow from the edge of the parterres down on me. I stood up, stuttering out a greeting through my freezing lips.

"That's a shame." Professor Carmichael touched Alice's arm. "Alice, I thought you might like to sit with me. I'll be able to make corrections to any false statements made about Hathaway during the memorial."

"Of course," Alice's eyes darted to me. "Mina? You coming?"

I nodded, falling in step beside them. *What had Alice been about to say? Who was the killer?*

At the entrance of the orangery, Professor Carmichael was pulled aside by a Janeite asking about her book. Alice turned to me and hissed. "We can't talk here, in case someone overhears. Can you sneak out of the party and meet me in the *Sacro Bosco*?" She pointed to a path on the corner of the formal gardens that lead off into the wood.

"Alice, if you know who the killer is, you should talk to the police—"

"I can't." She gulped. "I'll give you all the evidence you need to stop the killer before they hurt anyone else, but I can't go to the police. Please, Mina, promise you'll meet me?"

"Sure. I'll meet you."

"There's a statue of three maenads dancing just off the path to the right. I'll meet you there in thirty minutes. Thank you, Mina, really. I... I need to talk to someone about this." Alice's shoulder slumped. Her beautiful eyes were wide, terrified. Whatever was going on, I had a feeling it wasn't just about getting her scoop anymore.

I followed Alice into the orangery, the hairs on the back of my neck prickling. *What does Alice know? What's she going to tell me?*

CHAPTER TWENTY-FOUR

"*A* garden party on one of the coldest days of the year?" Morrie passed me a steaming cup of hot chocolate and a cream scone with a layer of ice on top. "This is the cleverest idea!"

I nodded, too cold even to voice my agreement with his sarcasm. Luckily, Morrie had scored us a seat near the glowing brazier that did little to heat the cavernous space.

In the days when Baddesley Hall was a working estate, this grand building with its irrigation slits in the floor would have been used to grow fruit trees in pots and protect them during the harsh winter months. It wasn't exactly built with entertaining in mind. Fairy lights spilling from a hanging basket on the ceiling and long tables adorned with centerpieces of winter herbs and vegetables looked spectacular but did little to distract from the biting wind and increasingly heavy snowfall outside. Several of Cynthia's new security detail had already been co-opted to place additional heaters around the room. The band in the corner played carols beside a towering pine tree, reminding me that I hadn't even started my Christmas shopping yet. Outside, the patio area had been cleared of snow, and the braver among the guests were indulging in a game of croquet.

"Ah, Lydia must have forced Sir Grumpsalot downstairs." Morrie pointed. Across the patio, Lydia dragged Heathcliff around the croquet field, explaining the rules in a loud, patronizing tone while her other suitors laughed. I noticed he wore his sword at his side. As Lydia lined up her next shot, Heathcliff met my eye and mimed hitting her over the head. I stifled a giggle.

As I sipped my chocolate, Lydia scored point after point. David came to speak to her. She took his arm and allowed him to lead her away. Heathcliff stared after them for a few minutes, then shrugged and dashed inside to join us.

"Shouldn't you be tailing her every move?" Morrie asked, lifting his teacup to his lips. "What if David is really our murderer?"

I remembered that we'd seen David win match after match during the fencing demonstration, and how the rumor was going around that the killer was a skilled swordsperson. "Yes, maybe we shouldn't let her out of our sight."

"I've been standing outside in the snow for fifteen minutes trying to hit a stupid ball with a mallet. My balls have shriveled up into my body. I say let her be murdered," Heathcliff growled. "It would serve her right for blackmailing us."

"No argument." Morrie placed the teapot in front of him. "Tea? Guaranteed to heal your soul and unshrink your testicles."

"No thanks." Heathcliff pulled his flask out of the top of his breeches and knocked back a deep sip.

"While you've been playing nursemaid, Mina might just be able to unmask our killer," Morrie said. Heathcliff's hand circled my thigh, and as quietly as I could, I relayed the conversation with Alice that I'd whispered to Morrie as soon as I'd entered the orangery.

"You're not going alone," Heathcliff growled. "Take Morrie and Quoth with you."

"What about you?"

"I'm still warming my nuts. Besides, someone has to keep eyes on Lydia. I'm not a complete monster."

I smiled at Heathcliff, warmed by his words. Maybe he was starting to see himself the way I saw him.

I glanced at my phone. Ten minutes until I had to meet Alice. Christina hurried in, adorned with an elegant black gown. She took her seat at a table near the front, staring at her clasped hands. Cynthia took her place beneath the Christmas tree, adjusting her solemn black hat. The band ground to a halt. Cynthia tapped the microphone. "If I could have your attention. Welcome all, to the Julius Hathaway memorial garden party. I thank you for braving the inclement weather to be here to pay your respects to this remarkable man who was taken from us in the height of his prime. He had so many more years of Austen scholarship to teach us, and I know we all hope that his daughter Christina will continue the fine tradition he established."

I watched Christina while Cynthia spoke, admiring her composure. Beside her, David rubbed her shoulder and offered her a tea. Behind him, Lydia made a rude gesture Morrie must've taught her.

"Today we shall have members of our community read from some of the professor's most popular works and relate some of their fondest memories of his antics at various Jane Austen events over the years. But first, we'll show you clips from the recent documentary on the professor's life and work."

A projection screen rolled down in front of the Christmas tree. The camera flashed the name of a documentary director famous for creating sensationalist profiles of 'misunderstood' men. It didn't surprise me Hathaway had been connected with him. The camera zoomed in on a younger Hathaway – his features smug as he spoke to a class filled with cheering students. With his windswept hair and military-style jacket, he looked every bit the romantic hero. Emotional music swelled, and the narrator started to list Hathaway's accomplishments.

"Intriguing," Morrie said, leaning forward on his elbows.

The documentary was sickening in light of what Carmichael, Gerald, and Alice had revealed about Hathaway. It spent scant minutes on Jane Austen's life and work, focusing instead on the scholarly methods that led Hathaway to his various Austen discoveries. Interviews with the professor showed a vain man who was an expert at manipulating the conversation to make himself appear clever and humble and attractive. Gushing interviews from David and various young female students seemed sinister in context.

I glanced over at Christina while her father talked on screen. Although she held her body rigid, tears streamed down her face. David offered her his handkerchief, his face wracked with concern.

Concern, or guilt?

The narrator spoke of Hathaway like some kind of intellectual freedom fighter who was disparaged and outright censored by the 'academic establishment' in an attempt to silence his ideas. In reality, he was clearly a manipulative bully with a lot of fringe theories who loved using Jane's own words to advocate for the same misogynist worldview he'd forced onto Christina, who he held up as a shining example of true womanhood. What a dick. If I'd been indifferent to him before, I was now abhorred.

Press clippings and old photographs flickered on the screen as the narrator explained how Hathaway's reclusive wife was struck down by a hereditary bone disease, leaving him distraught and heartbroken. All around me, Janeites sniffed into their handkerchiefs, touched at the sad story.

Next, the narrator spoke about how Hathaway tried to take down the academic establishment 'at their own game', whatever that meant. Cut to a scene inside a packed lecture hall. Professor Carmichael stood at the lectern, delivering a prestigious lecture series. Surprised, I looked around the orangery for her, but couldn't see her anywhere. Maybe she'd left in disgust? Back on the screen, Carmichael was in the middle of a point about Austen's hidden feminism when Hathaway leaped up and started arguing over one of her points. He wouldn't let her get a word in. When she ordered security to escort him from the building, he accused her of being unable to participate in debate, stopping just short of accusing her of censorship. She yelled, "You'll pay for this, Julius! I swear to you that you will suffer for what you've done."

According to the narrator, that event caused Carmichael to be lampooned by Hathaway's followers online, and memes of her red, flustered expression appeared all over the internet. Apparently, this was all part of Hathaway's 'cause'. Carmichael nearly lost her university position over his outburst, on what was supposed to be *her* platform to shine. *Wow, no wonder she hates him—*

"Mina," Morrie pointed to the time on his phone.

Yikes. Time to go. I skulled the rest of my chocolate, collected my phone and purse, and turned to leave. Morrie rose and offered his hand. "I shall help you back to the Hall so you don't slip in your dainty shoes," he said, slightly too loudly, for he was shushed by several women.

We ducked outside, and I raced down toward the wood, the wind biting at my skin. At my side, Morrie kept his hand on the hilt of his sword, his eyes trained on the trees, searching for a foe. As we moved under the canopy of trees, Quoth soared down and landed on my shoulder.

I plunged into the trees, casting my eyes in all directions. Branches snapped behind me as Morrie followed close behind. "Alice?" I called. Ahead of me, a grey statue rose out of the snow. Scantily-clad, nubile women danced in a circle, clutching tiny harps and amphorae where wine spilled into the mouths of bearded satyrs. I turned right and stumbled over the icy ground.

Morrie's fingers dug into my arm. "Gotcha. Over there. I can see something."

He helped me down the slope. I recognized Alice's coat on the ground. "Alice, we're here. Tell us quickly, please, we've got to get back before Morrie's testicles retract into his body—"

"Shite," Morrie stopped dead, his face grim.

"Croak." Quoth's voice cracked, as though he was in pain.

"What?" But then, I saw it, too. Alice's coat covered something else – a white muslin gown, speckled with blood. Beside the body lay a croquet mallet, the flat end dyed with wet crimson.

"Oh, no."

Morrie slid down the slope and rolled the shape over. Alice Yo stared up at us, her mouth wide with terror, and the side of her skull caved in. The coat slid off her shoulders, revealing four bloody letters scrawled across her chest. They spelled out one word.

LIAR.

CHAPTER TWENTY-FIVE

J staggered back. "No. Oh, no."

The professor was one thing. He was a horrible person, and even with our suspicions, we could still end up chalking his death up to a robbery gone wrong. But I liked Alice. And this... this was cold-blooded murder.

Morrie tugged me out of the trees. "The manner of our courtship leaves something to be desired. We keep meeting over dead bodies."

"No jokes, please." Bile rose in my throat. I fought to keep down my breakfast.

"No jokes," Morrie promised, his voice grave. "We need to raise the alarm. The killer could still be nearby."

"Croak." Quoth launched himself off my shoulder and soared into the air. He'd make a scan of the area faster than we could on the ground. If Alice's killer was making a run for it, Quoth would catch them.

When we emerged from the wood, Lydia was outside playing croquet with her posse. "Mina? James? What are you doing in the forest? Mina, why do you have sauce stains on your dress?"

"It's not sauce," I cried, stumbling over the icy path. "Stop the memorial. Alice Yo has been murdered!"

Lydia screamed, clutching her hand to her forehead. Her cries drew people to the windows of the orangery. Security guards raced to the garden, surrounding us. One of them approached me, hand out, telling me to remain calm.

"I am calm," I said, as people started to spill out of the orangery. "I'm telling you, Alice Yo has been murdered. You'll find her just off the path. Turn right at the statue of the maenads. That's the naked dancing girls. I have to sit down now." I slumped in the snow, the cold no longer penetrating my numb body.

Alice was going to tell me who the murderer was. And then someone bashed her head in with a croquet mallet.

Because someone didn't want her to reveal what she knew.

A crowd gathered at the edge of the wood. Lydia's suitors crowded around her, offering her handkerchiefs and smelling salts. I had one better – Heathcliff raced over and mashed my body against his, crushing my ribs with the force of his embrace.

To Cynthia, Morrie said, "Have your security team guard the woods. Don't let anyone in there, and don't allow anyone to leave the grounds. You'll need to call the police. You have another dead body."

Cynthia sobbed. "How could this be? This will ruin us!"

"I'm sorry, Cynthia, but that should be the last thing on your mind." I stumbled to my feet, aided by Morrie and Heathcliff. "Lydia, we're leaving, now."

"No, we're not," she moaned. "I told so many people last night that I'm staying at the infamous bookshop. The murderer will know to look for me there."

"Bloody hell, Lydia!" I yelled. "This isn't a game."

"Don't yell at me like that," Lydia pouted. "You'll stand a better chance of catching the killer if we remain here. I don't wish to leave until I know this brute is safely in custody. My very life is at stake, in case you've forgotten!"

"She's right. Besides, the police aren't going to let us leave," Morrie pointed out.

Quoth swooped in, folding in his wings and settling on my shoulder. *I didn't see anyone fleeing through the wood. There are a few people walking around by the house, including Gerald. But it's possible the killer returned to the party via the rear of the orangery. There's an open door there for the kitchen staff.*

"You don't think the killer was after you, Mina?" Lydia asked. "You entered the woods and then the next moment a woman in a similar pale dress is murdered. It's just too grotesque to think about." She shuddered.

"No, the killer was after Alice. He wrote the word LIAR on her chest. But there's no telling what he might've done to me if I'd been there a few moments earlier..." I shuddered. Heathcliff's body crushed mine again, as though he could someone squeeze the fear out of me.

"I, for one, don't intend to stand around waiting to be beamed with a croquet mallet. We've got one choice," Morrie declared. "We're going to have to solve this murder ourselves."

CHAPTER TWENTY-SIX

"*I*'m in." I shivered as the memory of Alice's bloody face and Professor Hathaway's silent scream flashed across my mind. "Where do we start?"

Heathcliff sighed. "If Mina insists on putting herself in the path of a murderer again, then I'm going to be at her side."

"Croak," Quoth added from my shoulder.

"And I guess I'll help," Lydia said. "Just as long as it doesn't interfere with my husband-scouting duties. I believe that with liberal application of *snogging*, I can convince Mr. Grimsby to propose by the end of the weekend."

Morrie glanced at Lydia as if he was about to say something, then thought better of it. "Very well. First, we need to establish whether both victims were murdered by the same person. If so, it puts the opportunistic killing of the professor to the test."

Heathcliff pointed to the house. "There's the windows that look in on Uppercross. Which window was open?"

I pointed. "The fourth on the left – it's the one located directly behind Professor Hathaway's chair. Morrie, you have your evil genius face on. What are you thinking?"

Morrie rubbed his chin. "I'm beginning to have an inkling of what's happened here. Lydia, I require a distraction."

She gave him a mock salute. "I shall oblige." She ran off toward the patio.

"Let's go." Morrie grabbed my hand.

"We can't just leave the scene! The police are going to be here at any moment. They'll want—"

"Exactly. Less jabbering, more running. Heathcliff, hold the fort here for us." Morrie dragged me across the lawn. Lydia had faux-fainted on the lawn and was busy being revived by the men. The security officers rushed the scene, but they were distracted by keeping guests from entering the wood and didn't stop us as we raced inside Baddesley Hall.

"This way," Morrie yanked me across the entrance hall. "Oh, my heart is racing a mile a minute. Mina, I have to tell you something."

"Can it wait?"

"Not really. I love you."

My throat tightened. I tried to put the breaks on, but Morrie only ran faster. He didn't look at me. "Hang on. What did you just say?"

"No time to discuss it." Morrie ducked under the police tape and headed straight to the window. "Check by the fireplace. Maybe there's something we missed."

Wait, you just said you loved me and now you're back on the murder case? What even are you?

Unfortunately, as mean as he was, Morrie was also right. We didn't have time to deal with his revelation now. My head filled with clouds and happiness, but I tried to rein it in and focus. I cast a glance over my shoulder. Seeing no one there, I ducked under the police tape, my heart in my throat. I made my way to the gilded fireplace and bent down to inspect the marble. Jo had taken the chair and rug as evidence, and the floor had been scrubbed until it shone. I couldn't see anything that would give us new information.

"As I suspected," Morrie said from behind me.

"What?" I rushed over to look.

"Last night at the ball, you opened the window to let Quoth in. He couldn't open the latch from the outside." Morrie showed me the window. "The same is true here. There's no way an opportunistic killer could have opened this window if it was locked, because it opens outward, and the latch is on the inside."

Oh, shite. "Perhaps he forced it in some way?"

"There are no signs of forced entry." Morrie pointed to the smooth edge of the frame. "We'd see damage here if the killer used a tool to gain access. Now, there's a chance of course that Hathaway himself opened the window, but as a good friend once said, 'when you've eliminated the impossible, what remains, however improbable, must be the truth'. I'm suggesting it's impossible for our killer to have accessed this room from the outside on his or her own."

"How did the police not notice that?" I asked.

"The world is full of obvious things which nobody ever observes," Morrie grinned. "Besides, they were distracted. Cynthia gave them the run of the dessert buffet."

"How soon you've switched to cliches."

"What can I say? We're pressed for time. I'll think of a wittier retort and get back to you," Morrie paced across the floor. "We know from Jo that the professor had been dead for at least two hours before you found him, which meant he was killed near the beginning of the ball. This gave everyone a chance to wander through the antechamber and see him in the chair, very much alive. All the killer had to do was leave the ball, go into the antechamber, drive the sword into his heart, change their clothes or clean their shoes somehow, and return to the ball."

"That could be Gerald... but then why would he go outside?

Lydia and her snogging partner both saw him. Gerald wouldn't have been able to get in the window unless it was already open."

"Exactly." Morrie wagged a finger in the air. "I suppose he could have had an accomplice who opened the window, but that's starting to sound unnecessarily complicated. This puts us back at square one. Anyone at the ball could have killed Hathaway. Our key to solving this is Alice. Whoever killed her did it to shut her up. That much is evident."

"Agreed. But how do we find out who it was? Quoth didn't see anything."

"We need to look at Alice's bedroom," Morrie said. "She'll have files on the story she's working on – notes, maybe a laptop. If I could get access to her phone, so much the better, but it's probably on her body—Oh, shite. Here comes the cavalry."

I followed where he was looking. Through the window, Inspector Hayes strode toward the house. He pointed at me, jerking his thumb to indicate we were to get outside.

"So much for that. We're not going to be able to get to Alice's room before the police," I said.

"We're not, but somebody is." Morrie stuck his head out the window. "Oh, birdie?"

"Croak!" Quoth fluttered down on the windowsill.

"Care to do a little reconnoiter for us?"

CHAPTER TWENTY-SEVEN

I peered past Hayes' face at the imposing hall, shivering even under both Morrie's and Heathcliff's topcoats. *Where's Quoth? He should be gone from the room by now.* Hayes was still yelling at us about disturbing the crime scene and how we weren't cops and we needed to leave them to do their jobs. I nodded in all the right places and Morrie poured on the charm and eventually Hayes calmed his tirade and started to question us about finding Alice's body.

I was describing the conversation Alice and I had behind the parterre when Quoth fluttered down and landed on my shoulder. Hayes regarded the bird with a bemused expression. "Is that the same raven that lives at the shop?"

"No. That's his cousin," Heathcliff said without a smile.

"I see." Hayes shut his pad. "Thank you for speaking with us, Ms. Wilde, Mr. Earnshaw, Mr. Moriarty. Please don't leave the village, as we may need to ask you more questions."

I frowned at Morrie. I knew what Hayes was really saying. We found the body, and then he'd caught us mucking about on the primary scene. And Heathcliff had dark skin, which automatically made him a suspect. We were on Hayes' list – maybe not top of the list, but definitely there.

Jo emerged from the trees just as Hayes dismissed me. She gave instructions to the SOCO team to remove the body and take samples from the snow and surrounding plants. As she peeled off her PPE, I wrapped my arms around her.

"I'm so sorry. I know you were friends with Alice."

Jo shook her head. "Not close friends, but still, it's sad. Alice was a talented writer with a desire to do good in the world. All that's left now is to find out who did this to her and get the justice for her in death she never had in life."

"What did you find out about the first murder? Is this the same killer?"

"It's hard to tell at this stage," Jo said. "Different murder weapons were used, but the attacks are equal in brutality. Plus, the handwriting on Alice appears to match the person who wrote on your door. If what you told Hayes is true and Alice knew the identity of the killer, then it suggests they did this to cover their tracks. What I can say for a fact is that the professor's murder wasn't opportunistic. It was premeditated. We found a large number of sleeping pills in his system."

"Sleeping pills?"

"Yes. Apparently, he'd been taking them for years, along with a litany of other pills for various health issues. Under that dyed hair and expensive dental work, Hathaway *was* rather old. But this was far higher than any prescribed dose. Not high enough to kill him, but they'd have made him drowsy, slowed his reaction time way down, made it so that he stayed in that chair all night. They may also have allowed the killer to take the weapon from him."

"I heard someone say that to make that thrust directly into his heart was difficult to do."

"Correct," Jane said. "This type of sword was very thin. If it had hit bone, the blade would deflect or get stuck. The killer was either exceptionally skilled with a blade or had an excellent knowledge of anatomy to know where to lay that blow."

"What about the stolen jewels and the fabric on the windowsill? Do the police still suspect the Argleton Jewel Thief?"

"Yes, now, that's interesting." Jo leaned in close, lowering her voice. "I shouldn't be telling you any of this, mind, but I'm interested in your take on it. We recovered a scrap of fabric from one of the Argleton Jewel Thief's previous burglaries. It got snagged in the clasp of an antique jewelry box. No DNA – so it was a clean shirt the thief wore that wasn't in contact with his skin. However, the fabric doesn't match that on the windowsill – our jewel thief likes cheap cotton shirts, whereas Hathaway's killer used an expensive silk blend. By itself that might not mean much, but when taken with the other evidence..."

"It suggests the scene was staged." I told Jo what Morrie and I had noticed about the window opening the wrong way.

Her eyes widened. "You're right. I can't believe you figured that out. I'm impressed."

"It was mostly Morrie," I said quickly.

"Nonsense. You're quite good at thinking like a detective, Mina. If you ever have enough of the book business, you should consider a career in law enforcement." She grinned. "Or crime."

"No thanks. I've had enough dead bodies to last my lifetime."

I said goodbye to Jo and returned to the huddled group of people the police had already questioned. Lydia – much recovered from her earlier fainting spell – held court, recounting a tale of such dramatic woe you would think *she* was the one who discovered the body.

Quoth had flown off to see if he might be able to overhear the police divulging other clues. Morrie, Heathcliff, and I stood around shivering until the police finally allowed us to return to our rooms to pack our things. This time there was no question about it – the Jane Austen Experience was over, and all guests would vacate Baddesley Hall immediately, although Inspector

Hayes required them all to remain in the area in case they were needed for further questioning.

As soon as I turned the door in the lock and entered the room, Morrie grabbed Quoth and held him up so they were beak-to-face. "Don't keep us in suspense. What did you find?"

"Croak." Quoth lifted a wing, dropping a small, silver flash drive onto the bed. Morrie snapped it up, his eyes dancing.

While Morrie pulled over his own laptop and started typing furiously, Quoth began his shift, his wings retracting in on themselves to form skinny arms that filled out, his muscles inflating like balloons as his body twisted in on itself. His chest filled out, and his legs bent forward and elongated.

Lydia's eyes widened as she stared at the gorgeous naked man who sat on the edge of the bed, where before there had been a scraggly-looking black bird. "No matter how many times I see him do that, it is still remarkable."

"Yeah, yeah, he knows." Morrie waved a hand. "Spill the beans, bird. Describe the room. What else did you see?"

"You were right about the phone," Quoth said. "I couldn't find it anywhere. Alice must have had it on her. Her room was a real mess, clothing everywhere – her whole suitcase was filled with thermal underwear."

I smiled at that. "I believe it. She seemed like a really sensible woman."

"On her desk was a laptop. It was password protected, so I couldn't get into it. I found that flash drive in the side, so I pulled it out and brought it to you. There were some documents torn up in the rubbish. I pulled a few out and managed to read a bit. The first was a newspaper clipping from Oxford, about the scandal that cost Hathaway his fellowship. The second one was about a hearing at another school – a plagiarism case between Hathaway and Gerald. Then there was the student magazine who printed the winner of an essay competition – the piece was about the unwanted sexual advances of her graduate advisor. Finally, there were lots of forms and documents with graphs on them. I didn't understand all of them, but they looked like medical records."

"Medical records?" I hadn't expected that.

"Yeah. One was an in-patient record for a woman named Hera Hathaway, who I'm guessing from the dates was Hathaway's late wife. Then there were all these other files, but I didn't understand what I was looking at—"

"This?" Morrie turned the computer around, demonstrating a line of wiggly graphs.

"Yeah, that looks like it."

"These are DNA tests. Alice had them in her files, but weirdly, they don't seem to be included in Hera Hathaway's official records." Morrie spun the screen around again. "Did you find anything else?"

"Yes," Quoth said. "I saw Alice's notebook. I only looked at a few pages before the police came and I had to get out of there, but it makes for chilling reading. It seems that Professor Carmichael has been sitting on a secret for a very long time, and after Hathaway humiliated her last year, she's decided that now's the time to come forward. Julius Hathaway's wife was also his sister."

CHAPTER TWENTY-EIGHT

"*W*hat?" *No way. That's... that's not possible.*

"How disgusting!" Lydia shrieked.

"Well, that's delicious," Morrie said, steepling his hands together. "And I'm guessing these medical files are the proof of that?"

"Apparently so. Professor Carmichael was acting as a medical authority on Alice's article. She'd also given Alice a list of names of previous graduate students of Hathaway's who might be willing to come forward and speak to claims of sexual harassment, giving the article a #metoo angle that would see it spread worldwide. Gerald had also given her the contact details of his girlfriend, Hannah, but Alice had lots of question marks beside her, as though she wasn't certain Hannah would talk."

"But how is it even possible? You can't just marry your sister."

"I've found some of Alice's notes in a file here," Morrie said, his eyes darting across the screen. "According to her, it seems to have gone like this. Hathaway and his sister grew up as spoiled children of rich if rather eccentric parents, who were themselves second cousins—"

"Gross!" Lydia sniffed.

"—and Jane Austen obsessives. Everything about their homes and lives was perfect Regency harmony, except their marriage. They went through a bitter divorce when Hathaway was a child. His father raised him, and the mother moved away to Eastern Europe with Hera, changing her name and identity in order to forever sever ties with the Hathaway family. The children were never supposed to meet again and the parents hoped they'd forget each other. But in secret, Hera researched Julius' whereabouts and made contact. They were both in their teens at the time, and their fascination with their parents' divorce and the plot to keep them apart blossomed into a forbidden romance. Hera came to England to attend university, and the two met and continued their relationship, bonding over their shared love of Regency ideals. Because the mother had altered their identity, it never registered as an issue when they went to get married. It only came to light when Hera was diagnosed with her condition and the hospital did DNA tests on Christina to ascertain if she had also inherited the genes. They found that her parental genes had a close family match – too close to be anything but brother and sister. Apparently, it was all hushed up with lots of Julius' money and then the mother died and it was forgotten."

"How does Alice know all this?"

"I don't know," Morrie scrolled through the flash drive. "But she has copies of letters between Julius and Hera that prove the whole thing. The way they read, Julius was the one pulling the strings, playing his charisma against Hera's vulnerability to seduce his sister into deepening their relationship. In light of his other harassment charges, it builds somewhat of a vivid picture."

"Isn't Alice shagging Christina?" Heathcliff piped up. "That's probably where the information came from."

"But would Christina incriminate her own father?" I recalled the way she'd shrank away from him on the stairs. She wanted desperately to please him, but she was also afraid of him. "I can't see her wanting this kind of information made public."

"Perhaps she didn't know Alice had copies of these letters." Morrie rubbed his chin. "She may not even know about her mother's lineage at all. Alice may have gained access to Hathaway's files in some other way."

"However she came about this information, it changes how we view what happened here," Quoth said, running fingers through his long, fine hair. "Alice's killer wanted to stop her from making this story public. Hathaway's killer hated him because of one of his many crimes. And the words on Mina's door still baffle me, but they give me great fear."

"I still think Gerald did it," I said, ticking off boxes on my fingers. "He was pissed at Professor Hathaway for plagiarizing his work and tanking his career. He's a big guy, and a goth – you can't tell me he doesn't know enough about swords to make that kill. He had a tear in his shirt and a stain on his coat the night of the ball, and he was drinking all that booze like he was trying to cover up for something bad he did."

"Okay, but then why kill Alice? Surely if this story came out, it would help him get reinstated at the university?"

"You forget – Alice figured out Gerald was the murderer. She was going to spill his secret, although why she wanted to tell me instead of going to the police is anyone's guess. Maybe she spoke to Hannah and she gave Gerald away – I don't know. He had to get rid of her before she exposed him. Maybe that's why he wrote LIAR on her chest, in case she'd already sent something to her editor or written something in her notes."

Morrie rubbed his chin. "Your explanation fits the facts, except for one small thing – why would Gerald write YOU'RE NEXT on your bedroom door?"

I shrugged. "Yeah, I'm stumped on that, too. Perhaps he meant that Lydia would be Hathaway's next victim, and Gerald was saving her by killing him..."

"That sounds like twisting facts to suit your theory, instead of having a theory to suit the facts." Morrie tapped his fingers against the laptop. "I think Professor Carmichael is our murderer."

"You're crazy if you think that."

"I assure you that any jury would find me perfectly sane. Gerald just doesn't add up. Why go outside if you'd arranged a perfect murder from inside the house? Why write the words on your door? He didn't even know you or Lydia. But Professor Carmichael couldn't stand Hathaway. He humiliated her and she publicly threatened to make him pay. She knew that when the article came out she could destroy his career, but seeing him at this event was just too much. Maybe she didn't trust Alice to write the story. Whatever the reason, she decides he has to die. She was near him in the antechamber, and had ample opportunity to put sleeping pills into his wine. Then she realizes that Alice would figure out she did it. Perhaps she realized that she'd slipped up somewhere during her interviews. So she kills Alice and tries to use the word LIAR to discredit her *own* evidence, should anyone find Alice's files. As for the words on our door, Carmichael heard Cynthia talking about how clever we are at solving murders. She wanted to scare you away before you got too close to the case." Morrie leaned back and cracked his knuckles, a self-satisfied smirk on his face. "James Moriarty – one point. Evil sword-swinging professor – zero points."

"Don't celebrate yet. We haven't caught the killer," Heathcliff reminded him.

"All in good time. It looks like the answer to whoever killed our victims is going to be in Alice's files," Morrie said. "I'll get to work."

Quoth went out to eavesdrop on more police officers. With nothing to do, Heathcliff and I took a stroll around the hall. The place was clearing out. Guests poured down the stairs, snapping instructions to the harried staff. Security guards sauntered by, barking orders into their headsets and getting in the way.

Cynthia stood in the center of the balcony, a bottle of wine in her hand and an expression of utter despair on her face.

"Hey Cynthia," I waved. She started as we came up behind her. "I'm so sorry that the weekend had to end like this."

"Oh, it's a disaster!" Cynthia cried, sloshing the bottle around. I noticed it was over half empty. "All these guests are demanding refunds, and we have to find alternative accommodations, and I have a kitchen filled with Cornish game hens for tonight's meal that are going completely to waste."

"I know it looks bad now, but I'm sure it will all work out for the best." I felt bad for her. She really had tried hard to create a wonderful weekend, and two people had been murdered in her home. "You know how much people love a scandal, especially a gory one. Wait for word to get around the Jane Austen community, and in a year's time The Jane Austen Experience will be sold out again."

"You're a sweet girl," she slurred. "No wonder Gladys and Mabel loved you so. No, I'm afraid the Jane Austen Experience will go the way of the dodo. At least Grey still has his plans, or I fear we wouldn't survive. Would you like some wine?"

We declined and left her to her wallowing. I wanted to ask her what she meant by her husband's 'plans' but she was clearly in no state to give a sensible answer. *Isn't it weird that Grey's not here? Wouldn't he come home after a murder to see if his wife was okay?* I still hadn't met the guy, but I didn't have the best impression of him.

I led Heathcliff across the landing, heading for the private covered balcony through Cynthia's office. I had my head turned, looking for the right door, and I noticed the corner of a black leather trench coat disappear over the velvet rope cordoning off Cynthia's private wing.

"That's Gerald," I whispered.

Heathcliff leaned his head near mine. "Pretend I said something hilarious," he growled.

Understanding immediately what he intended me to do, I threw my head back and laughed. From the angle, I could peer further around the corner, and the area was well-lit enough I had a clear view. Gerald leaned against the wall, his eyes darting across the landing. He cast one final look around, then disappeared down the darkened hallway. Heathcliff and I exchanged a heated look. Heathcliff's smoldering eyes demanded that we not get involved.

We followed him, of course. Luckily, I'd eschewed my muslin dress for my 'Jane Austen is my Homegirl' t shirt and jeans, so I could easily step over the rope. The hallway turned a corner. We crept to the end and peered around to see Gerald slipping inside a door.

We scooted across the rug and pressed ourselves up against the wall. I peered around the door into an opulent bedroom – Cynthia and Grey's suite, guessing by the clothing strewn across the bed and the tray of tea things on the armoire. Gerald stood in front of a large dressing table, dropping handfuls of gold jewelry from a large case into the deep pockets of his black trench coat.

I yanked my head back. My elbow hit the vase on the table behind me. It wobbled in mid-air. Heathcliff lunged for it. His fingers grazed the edge and sent the vase sprawling off the table, where it crashed on the marble floor.

SMASH!

Gerald launched himself at the door. Light caught a knife in his hand as his coat flapped around him like an overweight Neo. He lunged at me. Heathcliff shoved me across the hall, shouting, "Don't argue. Just run!"

I sprinted down the hallway. Gerald followed, crashing into the walls as Heathcliff struggled to subdue him. My chest burned. *He's crazy and dangerous. Find one of the security guards and—*

CRASH.

I tripped over the velvet rope and hit the ground, hard. Pain shot up my leg. I gasped for breath and rolled onto my side, just in time to see Gerald tower over me, the knife raised in his hand.

"I don't want to hurt you, Mina," he said. "If you promise not to tell anyone what you saw, then I won't have to—"

He didn't get a chance to finish his sentence. Heathcliff leaped on his back, driving the knife in Gerald's hand into his side. Gerald bellowed, stumbling forward and trying to throw Heathcliff off. In response, Heathcliff sank his teeth into Gerald's neck. Guests screamed and scattered as they staggered across the landing.

"Heathcliff, watch out!" I gasped.

But Heathcliff didn't hear. He was a wild animal lashing out at the predator who threatened his mate. He tore at Gerald, his eyes wild, his features twisted with feral rage. Gerald thrashed back, and the pair of them crashed into the balustrade. With a sickening *CRACK*, the wood cracked, and the two of them toppled over the edge.

CHAPTER TWENTY-NINE

" *H* eathcliff!" I screamed.

The world narrowed. In slow motion I watched, frozen and helpless, as the pair tumbled over the side of the balcony and disappeared. As he fell, Heathcliff's wild eyes met mine, and in them I saw only jubilation. He didn't even *care* that he was about to crack his head open on the floor below.

All he wanted to do was save my life, and it cost him his own.

CRASH.

Screams and shouts echoed from downstairs. The world came back into focus, raw and fast and terrifying. Still gasping for air, I forced myself to my feet. Flares of green and pink neon light danced in front of my vision, blinding me. I gripped the wall and fought my way to the stairs.

Heathcliff, no no no no...

I forced my legs to move, to run to the stairs. I gripped the railing and lurched myself downward, averting my eyes from the center of the room. I had to see, but I didn't want to see.

Don't leave me in this abyss where I cannot find you.

On the last step, my shaking legs gave way. I collapsed in a heap, barely feeling my knees crack against the marble floor. Warm, strong arms went around me sweeping me into an embrace. A smell like grapefruit and vanilla wafted over my nostrils, the effect dragging me back into myself.

Morrie.

"Are you hurt?" he asked, his voice wracked with concern.

"Is Heathcliff…" I choked.

Morrie laughed, his breath tickling my face. "He's fine, gorgeous. Look for yourself."

I dared a look. Gerald lay sprawled in the middle of the floor, moaning with pain. A bloodstain spread outward from his side, where Heathcliff had stuck in the knife. Heathcliff knelt on Gerald's back, but his predator eyes still searched the room. He lifted a huge fist and pounded it into the back of Gerald's skull.

"Don't you… ever… raise a knife… to Mina… again," Heathcliff panted, punctuating each phrase with a slam of his fist.

"Young man, stop that!" Hayes rushed in. It took him and two of his officers to drag Heathcliff off Gerald. "What are you doing to this man? This is assault!"

"I think my ribs are broken," Gerald moaned, trying to roll on his side.

"What I'm doing is your job," Heathcliff boomed. "That man is the Argleton Jewel Thief, and the murderer of Professor Hathaway and Alice Yo."

A collective gasp rose through the gathered crowd.

"What?" Gerald's face crumpled. "That's not true."

"So it's not true that I just saw him stealing Mrs. Lachlan's jewelry, and it's also not true that I had to stop him before he stabbed Mina with that knife?" Heathcliff struggled against the cops. "If you don't believe me, check his pockets."

Gerald moaned, his head dropping onto the marble. Hayes bent down and dug around in his pocket, pulling out a handful of gold and diamond-encrusted necklaces and earrings. "What the—?"

"My jewelry!" Cynthia rushed forward, pawing through the jewels. The gasps turned to murmurs as she pulled more and more pieces from Gerald's pocket. "This was Grey's grandmother's necklace. He gave it to me when he proposed."

Cynthia's face twisted in rage, and she bent down and slapped Gerald across the face. "How dare you? You rotten, despicable little man—" she bent down to slap him again, but Hayes grabbed her wrist.

"Ma'am, you need to step back, or I'll have my officers restrain you, too."

Reluctantly, Cynthia stepped back, clutching fistfuls of her own jewels and staring daggers into Gerald.

"Listen, I can explain," he pleaded.

"No, you can't," Heathcliff shouted. "We know you're guilty. You overhead Christina looking for her jewelry before the ball. You spiked Professor Hathaway's drink with sleeping pills so you could steal the jewels, and then staged the scene to look as though the thief had escaped out the window. When you did that, you accidentally tore your shirt. We know you hated Hathaway because you claimed he plagiarized you and he hurt your girlfriend—"

"Alright, I stole the jewels!" Gerald cried. "I'm the Argleton Jewel Thief. I was *desperate*. I was hoping to pay to finish my post-graduate degree in another country, somewhere where my name wasn't ruined by Hathaway's lies. I hated him, sure, but I never killed him!"

"Then why was your shirt torn?" I cried. "And you had blood on your trench coat. I saw it."

"I told you, it wasn't blood, it was red wine jus," Gerald's eyes blazed as they met mine. "Besides, how could I have done it when I was outside until after the first dance finished?"

"Outside?"

"Yes, I'd just received some distressing news, and I went out to have a smoke and collect my thoughts." Gerald frowned at Lydia.

"She was hanging around in the hallway snogging some bloke and I couldn't deal with that right now, because it made me think of the other thing, so I went back inside for a drink."

"Gerald's telling the truth," Hannah stepped forward. "I told him I was pregnant, and that I decided to keep the baby."

"That's why I was so upset at the bar. How was I going to support a baby? My consulting role barely pays my bills. That's why I was trying to get the jewels today. It was a risk, but I figured that in the chaos no one would think to miss them for several hours."

"But Gerald, I told you that it wasn't your responsibility," Hannah cooed. "I found someone else I wanted to be my baby's daddy." She fluttered her eyelashes at Heathcliff.

"Keep her away from me!" Heathcliff resumed struggling in earnest.

"We'll see how the rest of your story checks out," Hayes said. "Gerald Bromley, you're under arrest. You do not have to say anything, but it may harm your defense if you do not mention when questioned something which you later rely on in court…" The police dropped Heathcliff and swept in to surround Gerald.

I rushed to Heathcliff's side. "I can't believe you did that. Are you hurt?"

He shook his head. "Luckily, Gerald's sizable girth broke my fall."

"Morrie, call an ambulance. I'm going to get you checked over." I hugged Heathcliff tight. "Please don't ever do that again. Leave the flying to Quoth, okay?"

"Careful," he winced. "You're jabbing ribs into soft places."

There were no soft places on Heathcliff, except for his heart. I pulled away. Heathcliff tried to get to his feet, but I pushed him back down. "At least you managed to catch the jewel thief," he muttered. "Now maybe we can leave the rest of the detective work to the real detectives."

"Not likely," I said. "We've still got a murderer on the loose. If Gerald the rotund Matrix cosplayer didn't kill Professor Hathaway and Alice Yo, then who did?"

CHAPTER THIRTY

"*J*'m bored," Lydia moaned, tossing her shoe at the wall. "Can you throw someone over the balustrade again?"

We were holed up in our suite, trying to stall for time while Morrie picked his way through Alice's files, looking for a clue as to who killed her.

"The more you distract Morrie with your incessant prattling, the longer we remain holed up here," Heathcliff growled. "I'd like to remind you that this is entirely your doing. If you weren't blackmailing us into solving this murder, we could be back at the shop."

"That's it. I've had enough." Lydia stood up, pointing a finger at Quoth. "I can't stand it in this room a moment longer with that uncouth gypsy! You there, with the enviable hair. We shall take a turn about the gardens."

"Don't use the word *gypsy*," I hissed.

"I'm not sure—" Quoth began.

"That was not a request, but an order!" Lydia's face reddened.

Quoth shot me a helpless look, but Lydia was already dragging him away. *Morrie will probably work faster without her distracting us. I just hope Lydia doesn't break my poor Quoth.* The door slammed, and they were gone from sight.

"Ah, blessed silence," Heathcliff grinned, leaning against the chaise lounge and raising a tiny bottle of whisky to his lips. We'd had him checked out by the paramedics, who determined that nothing was broken, but he had some bruising around his ribs. He was warned not to undertake any strenuous physical activity for the next few weeks, and was given a handful of painkillers he'd promptly washed down with whisky in true Heathcliff fashion.

Heathcliff and I snuggled up together, drinking and talking quietly while Morrie worked. After some time, Morrie pulled off his headphones.

"Hmmmm," Morrie purred. "That changes things."

"Did you find anything more about Alice's article?" I asked.

"No." Morrie spun his computer around. "But I did find *this.*"

He turned the computer toward me and hit a button. On the screen, a video played, showing a view of the top of a chair, a white wall, and an arched window that looked identical to the one in our room. *This is shot at Baddesley Hall.* In the corner of the screen, the timestamp read 1:03 AM on the night of Professor Hathaway's murder. Outside the window was pitch black, and there was a starkness in the inside light that lit Alice's face as she came into view, leaning down to adjust the camera. Satisfied that it was set correctly and recording, she sat in the chair facing the screen. Tears streaked down her cheeks.

"If you find this tape," Alice sniffed. "It's because I am dead. It was I, Alice Yo, who killed Professor Hathaway."

CHAPTER THIRTY-ONE

"*W**hat?*"

"Shhhh," Morrie raised a finger to his lips. "Keep watching."

I leaned over Morrie's shoulder to peer closer at the screen.

"I did it," Alice paused, then nodded. "I did it because I'm in love with his daughter, Christina. He wouldn't accept that she was gay. He wouldn't allow us to be together and I... I didn't want her to be hurt anymore. I had enough. I intended to write an article to discredit him, but my editor wouldn't publish it because it was all lies I invented. That's why I took the sword and I plunged it through... through his chest."

Tears rolled down her cheeks. She did nothing to wipe them away. "I'm recording this confession in the hope that my dying wish is obeyed. Please, if you find anything, do not publish any of my evidence about Professor Hathaway. Destroy all my research. Tear up my notes and delete all the files from my computer. It's all lies, anyway, and I don't want anything else to hurt my dear Christina. Please, if you're watching this, please..." her voice cracked. The camera clicked off, and the screen went black.

I can't believe it. Something about the confession niggled at me, but I couldn't place my finger on it. Morrie hit replay and we watched it again. Chills ran down my spine.

"Shite," Morrie breathed.

"That's what Alice meant when she said she couldn't go to the police," I said. "She didn't want to turn herself in, but she wanted me to know the truth in case something happened to her."

"Something did happen to her. She had her head bashed in. But why?"

CHAPTER THIRTY-TWO

I glanced out the window, at the crowds of people milling about on the steps. One of them killed Alice Yo, but why? If it wasn't to cover up Hathaway's murder, then it must have been to prevent her article for going public. But who knew about the article, and why would they...

Suddenly, I realized what was wrong with Alice's video confession.

"Give me that." I tried to yank the computer out of Morrie's hand, but he clutched it to his body.

"Careful with my precious," he pouted. "I've seen you on the dance floor. I don't trust you with this computer."

"Stop playing around and listen to me – the video's fake." Morrie and Heathcliff looked up in surprise. "I mean, it's really Alice talking, but she's not filming it herself. There's someone else in the room, behind the camera, making her say what she said. I don't think she killed Hathaway at all."

"Interesting." Morrie rested his head on his hands. "What makes you think that?"

"Show me the video from the start," I said, bracing myself for the horror of watching Alice's tear-stained face again. Morrie hit play.

"If you find this tape, it's because I'm dead…"

"No, back further. Go right to the beginning, where she's fiddling with the camera."

Morrie flicked back a few frames. There was Alice, standing up and leaning over to the left to adjust something on the camera.

I jabbed my finger at the screen. "I watched Ashley do vlogging in our flat all the time, so I've seen a person adjust their camera before a shoot. They always lean into the side where the buttons are. Only I saw Alice use her camera the other day – it's the exact same camera Ashley used. The buttons are on the opposite side."

"So she mirrored the screen," Heathcliff growled. "Isn't that simple to do on those fancy app thingies?"

I pointed to the timestamp in the corner of the screen. "Those little app thingies wouldn't keep the timestamp. Morrie, can you confirm this is raw footage?"

Morrie tapped a few buttons. "Yes, this video was uploaded directly from the camera, nothing altered."

"I don't know," Heathcliff said. "It seems a little flimsy."

"I agree, but I can't think of another explanation to fit all the facts," I said. "There are all those pauses through the video, and the way she kept looking off to the left, as though she were deferring to someone sitting there. Maybe reading prompts?"

Morrie rubbed his cheek. "Okay, okay, say you're right. What are we going to do with this? Taking it to the police is an option, although we'll get in trouble for having the memory stick."

"We should just hand it in, say we found it on the grounds. But it wouldn't matter, anyway. They're going to say it's not enough evidence." My head fell into my hands. "I don't know what to do."

"We solve the murder," Heathcliff growled. "It's the only thing to do."

"My, haven't we changed our tune?" Morrie grinned.

"More like I don't want some sadistic bastard who makes innocent women make their own confession videos anywhere near Mina or my shop. Don't forget the murderer left the message on her door. YOU'RE NEXT. Over my dead fucking body."

"Agreed. But if we're going to figure this out, we need more time," Morrie cried. "All our suspects are leaving."

"I know." I held out my hand. "Hand me your mobile."

Morrie looked horrified. He clutched the tiny rectangle to his chest like it was his firstborn. "Why do you need *my* phone?"

"Because you've got that fancy tech on there that means calls can't be traced. And that app you showed me that distorts your voice."

"Oh, you're going to do something illegal," Morrie grinned. He tossed the phone to me. "Don't let me stand in your way."

Please, don't make me regret this. Heart pounding, I dialed Inspector Hayes' private number (which Morrie had on his phone because of course he did) and clicked on the app. He picked up on the second ring. "Hayes," he snapped in his businesslike manner, just as Quoth and Lydia walked back into the room. Heathcliff shushed them as he ushered them to sit on the bed.

"Good afternoon, Inspector Hayes," I intoned, frantically gesturing for them to be silent and shut the door. My voice came out sounding like a deep, sexy robot. "I understand you have your hands full with another murder investigation. I hate to take up your time, but I fear this matter is of vital importance."

"What are you talking about?" he demanded. "Who is this?"

"You can call me a concerned friend. I'm concerned, you see, because I have planted a bomb in one of the cows in the field behind Baddesley Hall. I can detonate it at any time from my vantage point here. I don't want to do that, but I'll be forced to if you don't comply with my demands."

Quoth's eyes bugged out of his head. Heathcliff regarded me with an intense stare that made my whole body want to shrivel up into a ball. Morrie leaned back and placed his hands behind his head. His smug smile said to all the room, 'I created this monster'.

Yes, you did, you wanker.

"What are your demands?" he asked, sounding tired.

I thought fast. "Everyone in the Baddesley Hall is to remain there. I don't want to see a single car leave the premises, or I'll detonate the bomb. I also want a package containing a first edition of Jane Austen's *Mansfield Park* and a bottle of whisky from the Baddesley cellars to be left for me. Once I see the package has been dropped, I shall disarm the bomb, and on my word everyone will be able to leave."

"Oh, oh," Lydia jumped up and down. "Can I have a pony? I've always wanted a pony, but Father said they were frightfully expensive to keep when they could barely pull a carriage."

I rolled my eyes. *Fine, while we're being ridiculous...* "And I should like a purebred pony to be left with the book and the whisky."

"I'll see that it's done," Hayes said, his voice tight. "How will I reach you—"

"You don't." I yelped and hung up, tossing the phone onto the bed like it was made of molten lead.

Tears rolled down Morrie's face. "A pony?" he sputtered, clutching his stomach as laughter rumbled through his body. "I hope you're proud, gorgeous. That was the bravest, ballsiest thing you've ever done."

"I don't feel proud. I feel *awful*. Everyone out there will be panicking, and the police are going to waste precious resources dealing with this hoax, and all so we can have a shot at finding the killer." I slumped down next to Heathcliff. "You were right. Why are we doing this? We should leave it to the experts."

Morrie snorted. He sat up and planted a tender kiss on my cheek. "You really would make a terrible crook. Your pesky conscience keeps getting in your way."

"I thought it was great fun!" Lydia piped up from the window. "Look, the coppers are scurrying about everywhere like little ants. They're forcing everyone back inside the Hall."

"Yes, well." I shrugged. "I've bought us some time. Now, let's find this killer."

"How are we going to do that?"

"Easy, Mr. 173 IQ. We are going to puzzle it out, the way real detectives do it on TV."

CHAPTER THIRTY-THREE

e didn't have a whiteboard, the way cops in films always did, but we did have a giant impressionist painting across from the bed, and I discovered a pad of Post-it notes at the bottom of my purse. It would do.

Heathcliff, Morrie, Quoth, and Lydia sat along the bed. "Oh, are we playing charades?" Lydia cried. "What fun! I'll go first, shall I?"

"No." I stuck two Post-it notes in the middle of the board, one each for Professor Hathaway and Alice. Then, underneath, I added two more for the message written on our door, and for the faked suicide tape.

"These are the four crimes we need to focus on," I pointed at them. "They're all connected in some way. We're assuming the same person did all four, but we know from Mrs. Scarlett's murder that we can't always assume that. What connects them?"

"Hathaway," Morrie answered immediately. "He's at the center of all of this. And the Jane Austen Experience, because we know that the killer was someone in the Hall."

"We do?"

"I've run several mathematical models, and given the placement of staff and guests at the time, it's impossible that it was someone from outside the house."

"Right." I stuck up another note. "And assuming we're correct and Alice didn't do it herself, and assuming Gerald wasn't the killer either, we've got one main suspect. Professor Carmichael."

"What's our evidence?" Morrie asked, rubbing his chin.

I ticked off on my fingers. "She hated Hathaway. She publicly vowed to ruin him. She gave Alice the information about Hathaway's late wife, so we know they were in contact. She had medical training, so she would have known how to dose him with the pills, *and* how to push the blade in correctly. *And* she had motive for murdering Alice, in order to cover her tracks. If Alice revealed how she'd come by the information, the police would immediately suspect Carmichael."

"And the message on your door?" Heathcliff pointed at the board. "Do you still think she considers you a threat?"

"That's still a possibility, but perhaps we've misinterpreted what the message was about," I said. "We thought it meant, 'you're next' as in 'you're next to be stabbed'. What if it meant, 'you're next to be a victim of Hathaway's wandering hands?' While we were waiting for the ballroom to open, Professor Carmichael noticed Lydia on Hathaway's lap. She made a disgusted face and strode away. Perhaps she went upstairs, wrote the message on our door to warn Lydia off, and then came back down and killed Hathaway—"

"Mina's right. Maybe we're looking at this all wrong," Quoth said. "What if this murder isn't an act of revenge, but one of love?"

"What do you mean?"

"On the video, Alice begs that her files are to be destroyed. If the killer added that, perhaps it's not to cover their tracks but to prevent that information from going public and hurting someone they cared about. It's like you said, Alice's death is about is stopping her article. That's why the killer wrote LIAR on her chest."

I leaned over and kissed Quoth on the lips. "You're a genius."

"Hey, where's my kiss?" Morrie protested.

"And mine," growled Heathcliff.

"No kisses for me, thank you." Lydia waved her hand. "I'm not so awfully keen on this feminism you speak of."

"I'm still in the dark here," Morrie said. "Why is Quoth a genius? I'm the genius."

"Quoth figured out who the murderer is. You can't see it because you're still learning what it means to love," I said. "Heathcliff understands."

"Damn right," Heathcliff growled.

Morrie's crestfallen face made my chest flutter, especially when I remembered the words he'd blurted out to me only a few hours ago. *He's trying.* "Think about it. Who is so besotted with Christina that he plays along perfectly with this farce of Regency manners? Who is in the professor's confidence and likely knew what pills he took? Who's an expert swordsperson who would have no trouble landing a killer blow?"

"Who declares his love through terrible poetry?" Quoth added.

"I think you're onto something, little birdie," Morrie breathed. "Remember Hathaway's documentary?"

Morrie slid across his laptop and brought up the documentary video about Hathaway's life that had been shown at the memorial, freezing it on a scene where David helped Christina out of a car. Her hand gripped his as he helped her to adjust her parasol. She thanked him with her usual breathless air, and his entire face lit up with the rapture of love. He adored her. *Too bad she's gay...*

Oh no...

With Alice out of the way, not only would Christina be saved from humiliation if the article were published, but she'd be a single woman again.

Morrie skipped ahead to a scene where David was talking to

the camera about his role as Hathaway's assistant. "I do everything for him. I arrange his schedule, collate his files, conduct research, answer his phone, look after him at appearances, make his tea. I even manage his medicines."

Lydia gasped, raising her hand to her face, as if she was about to faint. "I can't believe it. The killer is David Winter."

CHAPTER THIRTY-FOUR

"Of course," Morrie breathed. "It makes perfect sense. David is in love with Christina and intimately acquainted with her father. He would do anything to save Christina from humiliation. That waif of a girl could barely deal with a chipped nail, let alone finding out her parents were in an incestuous marriage. David probably hopes that by getting rid of Alice, Christina will be free to marry him and they'll be the perfect Regency couple. That's why he couldn't just kill Alice, he had to make sure her credibility was shot so the story of Hathaway and his sister could never come out."

"Is he's still in the building?" Heathcliff rose to his feet, reaching for his sword.

"We saw him speaking with Professor Carmichael during our walk," Lydia said, her eyes wide. "What is going on? You're not going to hurt David, are you? He collects coins, for pity's sake. He's no danger to anybody."

"How can you say that?" I said. "You saw David in the fencing demonstration the other day. He was *brutal*. Just because someone has good manners and boring hobbies doesn't mean they're not capable of cruelty, in the same way that people who might look a bit different or act gruff or uncaring can be kind and loving." I said the last bit with a glance between Heathcliff and Morrie.

"Where's my sword?" Morrie hunted under the sheets.

"And mine?" Heathcliff peered behind the curtains.

"Perhaps we shouldn't go into this expecting things to get stabby," Quoth said tentatively. "We should speak to the police."

"There's no time!" I cried. "They're tied up with my stupid bomb threat and if we're right, David's still got one more murder to commit. There's only one person left who has information that could hurt Christina." I leaped to my feet. "He's going to kill Professor Carmichael."

~

*T*he police had gathered the majority of the guests and staff into the landing and entrance hall. On the bottom floor, Hayes addressed them in an authoritative tone, telling everyone to remain calm. Cynthia swayed, a second (or third) bottle of wine clutched in her hand. Quoth – who had returned to his raven form - propelled himself off my shoulder and rose up to perch on the chandelier. He glanced around the room, and returned a moment later.

Carmichael's not here, and nor is David or Christina. We should try her bedroom.

Professor Carmichael's suite was down the opposite hall. I pushed my way into the crowd, deliberately stomping on every toe and kicking every shin I came into contact with. "Excuse me," I murmured. "Pardon me. Terribly sorry." With tuts and dirty looks, the crowd parted like the red sea before me, closing up around Heathcliff and Morrie.

"Mina, wait!" Heathcliff called.

"Heathcliff, there you are. I've been looking all over for you." I glanced over my shoulder in time to see Hannah throw herself at him with such force, she sent him sailing backward into Morrie, knocking all three of them to the ground.

No time to stop. Quoth dug his talons into my shoulder. I marched down the hall to Professor Carmichael's suite. Her door was shut, and I couldn't hear anything inside above the din in the hall. I turned the handle, and the door slid open.

He's already here.

Taking a deep breath, I flattened myself against the door and pushed it open. Quoth leaned forward and craned his neck around the tiny gap in the door.

Most of the lights are off, except the for one in the hallway and a lamp beside the bed. There are two figures in shadows, and they're arguing. Mina, I don't think you should—

Too late, I thought back. *We have to stop him.*

Quoth threw a wing into my face in an attempt to stop me, but I shoved him off my shoulder and darted forward, slipping into the room and pulling the door shut behind me. Unlike our suite, where the door opened directly into our room, the professor had a short hallway with doorways into her bathroom and a small sitting area. I pressed my back against the wall and crept toward the bedroom at the end.

"Please, don't kill me," Professor Carmichael begged. "I promise I won't tell anyone."

No. I'm not going to let this happen.

"David, you have to stop," I yelled, lunging forward and reaching for the shadowed figure. "We know what you did—"

The words died in my throat as the killer stepped into the pool of light. A sharpened sword hung in the air, the blade glittering. Behind it, I recognized the smug, perfect features of Christina Hathaway.

CHAPTER THIRTY-FIVE

"Christina?" I gasped. "But what..."

"You thought sweet David was behind this?" she sneered. "As if such a creature were capable of this chaos. It is I, twisted mad by Jane Austen, by a constant adherence to fictional manners while my father behaved abominably to every person in his life, most especially my mother."

"You... did all this? You killed your own father?" Her words made no sense.

"She's crazy!" Professor Carmichael yelled, leaping over the bed. "Get help! Get the police!"

In a flash, Christina shot across the room, positioning herself between the bed and the door. The blade pointed directly at Professor Carmichael's throat. The professor staggered backward, falling onto the bed.

"It would be unwise for you to move," Christina called in her singsong voice. "Mina, sweetie, I think I'd like you to stand over there, against the wall. If you make any move or call for help, I will gut you like a fish, and not feel one whit of remorse for it. Quickly, if you please."

Heart in my throat, I did as she asked, pressing my back into the wall. *Heathcliff, Morrie, I could use a daring rescue right about now.*

From the bed, Professor Carmichael moaned. I scanned the room for Quoth, but so much of it was in shadow, I had no hope of seeing him. I hoped he'd find Hayes and Wilson, but even then, what could he do as a raven? And if a naked guy ran at the detectives, they'd probably assume he was the bomber and shoot him dead.

Quoth, if you can hear me, please don't run at Hayes. Get Morrie's clothes from our room. Or find Lydia. Get her to scream outside. That'll send them all running. Please, there's only one of her, but I think she could kill us all if she desired to.

Fear rippled through me. I couldn't tear my eyes from the sharpened point of Christina's sword pointing directly at Professor Carmichael's heart.

Christina said she took fencing classes. She knows exactly what she's doing. Under the light, I caught her gleeful smile. *She's mad. Completely bonkers.*

"You've got my undivided attention," I said, trying to stall for time. "Can you tell me what's going on, because I'm really confused."

"Nice try," she said, not taking her eyes off Carmichael. "You and I are not enemies of equal intelligence playing at cat and mouse. I'm not going to sit down and outline my moves *tête-à-tête* like a chess game. This isn't chess, it's solitaire. You are merely a speck of dust on the table."

"Very well. I accede to your superior intellect."

"As well you should."

"Before you dispatch with the rest of your plan, could you enlighten me on one point?" *Please, Quoth, Heathcliff, Morrie, anyone...* "Why kill your father?"

"All my life, I've been living in my father's fantasy world. It didn't matter what *I* wanted, I was his perfect Regency princess, the only woman who could heal his heart after Mother died. He took me out of school and taught me from home, so that he could ensure I never learned about things that weren't bright and gay. He had me master a list of accomplishments – the piano, needle-point, calligraphy... the sort of vapid pursuits that occupied the mind of a Regency lady. I wanted to learn the violin, but he forbade it, lest I become too 'emotional' from the power of the music. I was not allowed to talk to other men, save himself and David. All the tutors he procured for me were women. Is it any wonder that I grew to crave their touch, their caress?"

Christina's voice hardened. "When I was sixteen, I told Daddy I was gay. Do you know what he said? 'No'. Not, 'I support you, my daughter' or even, 'I don't understand, but I'll love you anyway'. Just 'no'. I wasn't allowed to be gay, because there are no homosexuals in darling Jane's books. Can you even understand how that might feel?"

"No," I whispered. "I can't."

"Daddy truly believes that he is Mr. Darcy, and that any young woman he encounters is his Elizabeth, and that all he has to do is wear them down until they agree to accept his love. That's what he did to my mother. He wore her down and wed her in an unholy ceremony because he couldn't bear to be without her. His selfish passion and his desire to return to the innocent love of his childhood poisoned her bones as surely as if he'd murdered her himself. I will never forgive him for that, nor for any of his more recent crimes. But it is of no consequence, for he is dead, and I am almost free."

"How long have you known that your parents were... were siblings?" I whispered.

"I suspected something was wrong after Mummy died and Daddy had all these meetings at the hospital and then we didn't have a lot of money for a few years. But I only knew the facts when I saw the records Professor Carmichael sent Alice a few weeks ago. Alice thought she was being so secretive, but when she suddenly started asking all these questions about Daddy, I hacked into her computer and found them. I knew she was going to write the article and ruin Daddy, and I had to kill him before that happened."

"So you could be free?" I asked, starting to understand. By Isis, this is awful. What a sad, horrible story.

"Daddy hasn't written a paper in years," Christina said calmly. "I do the research. I write his keynotes. All day, every day, nothing but Jane, Jane, Jane, while he took the accolades and used *my* words to lure young women into his bed. The situation was intolerable. So I decided to improve my circumstances. Since he requires me to set out his pills every night, I stole away with some of his sleeping pills. One pill, once a week, so he would never notice. Then, I fed him the pills crushed in his tea before the ball, leaving him insensate in the chair. This done, I waited until almost all of the guests had entered the ballroom, and then David and I entered and took our seats.

"This done, I enjoyed the first course and a glass of wine before asking David to accompany me to the bathroom. Of course, he is so completely besotted and clueless that he didn't realize where I had him wait was not in front of a bathroom at all, but a door to a servants' passage that led between the kitchens and the anteroom. I stole along the passage, entered the ante-room, stabbed my father, opened the window, placed the scrap of fabric on the nail, and took away my jewelry." She tugged up the gloves on her hands. "It was nothing to dispose of my gloves and dress into a recycling bin behind the kitchens and replace them with a matching set I'd hidden there earlier, before I returned to David and we resumed our place in the set."

"A most ingenious plan," I said. "But why did you write the note on our door? Were you trying to stop Lydia from becoming your father's next victim?"

She laughed, the sound like broken glass tinkling. "Heavens, no. I was too far into my plan to be concerned with his next conquest. The note was not for Lydia, it was for you."

"Why me?"

"Cynthia boasted of your intellect and your skill at solving mysteries the police could not solve. I realized that my crime scene wouldn't just need to fool the police, it would have to fool you as well. I thought if you were frightened away, it might be to my advantage. It appears you're either too stubborn or too stupid to take the hint."

"It's the first one, the stubborn one," I said, my voice quivering. "But why kill Alice, your own girlfriend? Why create a video where she confesses to Hathaway's murder?"

"She was going to write the story about my father!" Christine screamed. "I begged her not to, but she said it had to be done. When she saw my father's body, she guessed I might have done it, and then she found the jewels in my bag that night as she snuck into my room. So I told her I would kill her if she revealed the truth, and I made her film that video as assurance. But then I saw her lead Mina away from the orangery and I knew she was going to tell you the truth, so I killed her before she could do it. Don't you understand, I had to kill her. She gave me no choice. The story would've been in all the papers, and they would come for me. I'd be hounded by the press and I would never, ever be free of my father's evil and bloody Jane Austen. That's all I want, and as soon as I deal with *her*—" she jabbed the tip of her sword at Professor Carmichael, who whimpered "—I will finally, truly be free."

"What about me?" I asked weakly, my heart clattering against my chest.

"You? You are something I didn't count on." Christina tapped her finger against her chin, in a gesture that reminded me a little of Morrie. "It's your own fault, really. I did give you a warning, which you chose not to heed. I'm afraid that I won't be able to allow you to live."

CHAPTER THIRTY-SIX

"*C*hristina, you don't have to do this," I pleaded. "If you tell your story, everyone will be on your side. You father was a horrible man, and what he did to you and your mother was wrong. You're the victim here. Please, don't become the villain."

"Silly girl," Christina grinned. "There are no villains in Jane Austen." She swung around toward me, lunging forward, the blade of her sword pointing at my heart—

This is it. This is how I die.

Time slowed. Neon fireworks flashed in front of my eyes, and memories flickered through my mind; Heathcliff slamming me against the wall in the bathroom, his eyes looking at me with such wild need; Quoth lying beside me on my bed, our hearts beating in unison; Morrie saying the words, "I love you."

The window shattered. Glass tinkled across the floor. A giant black bird flew at Christina, slamming into her chest and sending her reeling.

Quoth!

Christina staggered back, her mouth open in surprise. Quoth flapped her wings in her face, trying to get her to drop the sword.

Quoth's entrance bought Professor Carmichael precious

moments to dodge around Christina and flee to the door. Unfortunately, her fear overcame her, and she sank to her knees, frozen in place on the bed.

I lunged forward to help Quoth, but I was too late. Christina recovered her balance, grabbed Quoth by the neck, and hauled him off her face. Her face twisted in rage as she slammed him against the wall.

"Crooooo—" Quoth's blood splattered against the wall. He bounced against the floor, shuddering to a stop and lying still and silent. My heart pounded in my ears. *No, no, please. Not my precious Quoth.*

Christina's eyes darted from me to Carmichael. She leapt up on the bed and thrust her sword at the professor. The blade sliced through Carmichael's shoulder, sliding into her flesh with ease. Christina whipped out the blade and Professor Carmichael screamed, clutching at the wound. Blood leaked through her fingers, splattering across the front of her muslin dress. An acrid scent stained the air.

Quoth cooed, dragging his limp wing along the floor. I rushed toward him, but Christina was faster.

"If you love that bird so much, watch me gut him!" she yelled.

"No. Quoth!" I flung myself to the floor, spreading my body over him.

Christina raised her sword. "Fine. You'll die, too—"

There was a flash of skin, a curtain of hair, and a wild cry. I blinked, and Christina was on the floor. Her head bounced as it cracked against the wooden floor. A naked body pinned her down and slammed his foot into her forearm, twisting the blade from her grasp.

"You…" she gasped. "You were a bird! How did you…"

Her eyes rolled back in her head.

"What happened?" Heathcliff demanded, swinging his sword around the room. "Where's David?"

"It wasn't David," I breathed. "It was Christina."

Quoth moved aside, his expression sheepish. He leaned against me, clutching his arm. Heathcliff bent down to examine Christina. Her head lolled to the side, blood trickling down her face. I waited, my heart in my throat.

Christina didn't move.

"No fair!" Morrie wailed, throwing down his sword in frustration. "We were supposed to beat her in a clash of blades. It's been years since I got to skewer someone with a sword. I was really looking forward to it!"

"She's not dead, but she is out cold. Are you hurt?" Heathcliff stood up and scooped me into his arms, his touch gentle as his hands swept over my body. "Did she cut you?"

"I... I'm fine, but Quoth... he saved me, but she slammed him into the wall pretty hard." I reached for his body, but he was no longer there. *Where did he go? Is he...?*

"Croak?"

Morrie cradled a grinning raven to his chest. "Poor, poor birdie. I'm so sorry we doubted you. What did she do to you?"

"Crooooooooo—" Quoth's faint cry tore at my heart.

"Yooooo hooooooo, Mina? Morrie? The surly one?" Lydia cooed from the hallway. "That stupid bird led me up here, and I brought the nice detective with me, just in case there was an incendiary device, whatever that is—"

Hayes started as he stepped into the suite. He flicked the rest of the lights on, revealing Carmichael on the bed, clutching her bloody shoulder, Christina slumped, unmoving, on the floor, swords scattered everywhere, and Morrie hugging a raven. "What happened here?"

"What does it look like? Christina stabbed me, you idiot!" Carmichael yelled.

"We're fine," I croaked out, clutching Heathcliff. "We're just shaken up. Christina and Professor Carmichael need an ambulance."

"Christina will need an undertaker when I'm done with her."

Morrie nuzzled his face into Quoth's feathers. "No one hurts my Mina or my birdie."

Hayes scratched his head. He tore a walkie talkie from his belt and relayed a message to Wilson. "We've got paramedics here, but we can't get you to a hospital right now. The whole building is still in lockdown—"

"Just get someone up here with medical supplies and some drugs, stat. I fear I might be about to go into shock." Professor Carmichael balled up a section of the duvet and pressed it against her wound. "Why are you hugging that raven?"

"Croak?"

"Because," Morrie said. "Because he's family, and I love him. I can say that now, because I'm in touch with my feelings. I love this strange little bird, and I love Heathcliff, and I love Mina, and I even love you, Detective Hayes. Would you like a hug, too?"

Even with the horror of the situation, Morrie's words made my heart swell with love. I sank against Heathcliff, wrapping my arm around Morrie so that I could stroke Quoth's neck and feel his tiny heart beating furiously beneath his feathers. *My family. We are all safe.*

Morrie's admission of love to me, and the way he held Quoth, healed something inside me. It was the final puzzle piece falling into place, revealing an image more radiant and real than I ever thought possible. I knew that all three of my guys cared about each other in the same way they cared about me.

A corner of my father's letter scraped against my chest. In all the excitement, I'd hardly thought of him or it the entire weekend. Which was exactly what I'd wanted, but also... it didn't matter anymore. Whatever his reason for doing it, the reality was that my father abandoned me. But Quoth, Heathcliff and Morrie – they were here for me. They were my family now.

CHAPTER THIRTY-SEVEN

"*A*nother day, another murder solved." Morrie leaned against the side of the building, tapping away on his phone. "If I wasn't still trying to run a criminal empire, I might consider hanging our shingle out as consulting detectives."

Heathcliff shoved the shop door open. A ball of fur launched itself from the blackened depths and wound around Heathcliff's face. "Meeerrrroooww!" Grimalkin howled, letting every resident of Argleton know just how abominably treated she'd been, locked up in the shop for a night and a day.

"All right, all right." Heathcliff tore her off his face. "I'll get you some food."

Grimalkin's ears pricked up. She immediately jumped down and trotted off in the direction of her food bowl. *Cats really are nature's master manipulators.*

I went through the shop, flicking on lights and lamps as I went. Outside, the sun had already sunk below the horizon, and I could barely see a foot in front of my face. We'd been such a long time at Baddesley Hall, filling Hayes and Wilson in on what we'd uncovered. They found David tied up and stuffed inside Christina's closet, his own silk stocking shoved in his mouth as a gag. It

271

appeared she cared enough for him not to kill him. He confirmed our story – he knew Christina was seeing Alice in secret, and he'd been escorting Christina through the garden before the memorial when she had him stop to eavesdrop on Alice and my conversation.

Murder thus solved, we then had to wait for the police to figure out the bomb threat was a hoax and let us all go. I felt terrible about that, but if I hadn't done it, we wouldn't have caught Christina in time, and Professor Carmichael would've been her next victim. Lydia didn't get a pony, which was at least one upside. I couldn't imagine how we'd keep the thing at Nevermore.

"Stop lighting this place up like the Blackpool Illuminations," Heathcliff muttered as he slumped behind his desk. In retaliation, I flicked the Snoopy lamp above his head. He waved a hand in front of his face. "Gross. This place smells like customers. How many people did you let in this weekend, Quoth?"

In response, Quoth flicked the ledger open and pointed to his total for the weekend. Heathcliff glowered at the number. "You put the decimal point in the wrong place."

"I didn't. That's how many books you can sell at Christmas time if you're not the Grinch." His point made, Quoth transformed into his bird form and perched on the chandelier to stare down at Heathcliff, as if daring him to do better.

While Heathcliff stared at the number in disbelief, I collected my nerve. "Guys, I have something to tell you."

Quoth immediately fluttered down from the chandelier and settled on my shoulder. *Now?* He asked inside my head.

I nodded.

"What?" Heathcliff demanded.

"Don't tell me," Morrie added. "You've decided that next week we're going to a Jane Austen dance-a-thon. I'll go out and buy some shin-guards."

As quickly as I could, I explained about the lights I'd been seeing, and what Dr. Clements said at my appointment. "I'm sorry I didn't tell you before. I wanted to, but I was afraid. Talking about it makes it real. I just wanted more time with you all, having fun, solving murders and shelving books, before the lights went out."

"You told Quoth," Morrie said. He looked hurt.

"I did. Because I needed the comfort only he could give." I looked at all three of them in turn. "This weekend has shown us why this crazy thing we're doing actually seems to work. We all have strengths. Morrie's brain works in incredible ways. Heathcliff's loyalty and passion protect us all. Quoth's kindness makes us want to be better people. I love you all. I do." Tears pricked in my eyes. "I know that's crazy, but I can't help it. You've bloody wormed your way into my heart and you won't leave."

"We'll never leave," Heathcliff growled. "But you can't keep stuff like this from us."

"Agreed. I won't do that anymore. I promise." I held my hand over my heart. "If it's any consolation, I fucking hated every minute of it."

Heathcliff crushed me against his body. "I hate that I can't fix this," his voice rumbled against my ear. "Just take my eyes. I'm only wasting them reading books and labels on whisky bottles."

"Reading books is never a waste," I sniffed. "That's how I fell in love with you the first time."

"Hey, if she's having anyone's eyes, it's gonna be mine," Morrie piped up. "Yours are too dark. Blue with her complexion would be *magnificent.*"

"She should have mine," Quoth said quietly. "They work better than your human eyes."

"I'm not taking anyone's eyes," I laughed, even as fresh tears spilled down my face. "But you guys might have to be my eyes sometimes, if you're okay with that? Things could change quite quickly for me, and I don't want any of you to be in this if you're not comfortable with how it's going to end."

"Don't say shit like that," Heathcliff snarled. "I could no sooner forget you than my own existence." He pressed his lips to mine, crushing out my final doubts in a kiss that sizzled from my lips right through my veins. *There he goes, taking my breath away again.*

As if to prove his point, Heathcliff reached behind his desk and turned on a red Japanese lantern light I'd left there. "You brighten the place up," he muttered.

Quoth nuzzled my cheek. *I'm always here for you,* he promised. I broke from Morrie's kiss to press my lips against Quoth's soft feathers.

Morrie stepped up to our little group, his arrogant smirk wavering at the edges. "Don't make me say it again," he muttered.

I tapped my foot.

Morrie sighed. "Fine. I love you, Mina Wilde. And I love Sir Grumplestein and that stupid bird, too. Happy?"

"Ecstatic." I wrapped them all against me, holding them close. My men made of flesh and blood and complications, better in every way than their fictional counterparts. I didn't ever, ever want to let them go.

"Will you stay the night?" Morrie asked, his voice hopeful.

"I'd love to. You have no idea how much. But not tonight," I sighed. Lydia was kipping on Morrie's bed, which meant we couldn't do anything R-rated anyway. In my pocket, my phone vibrated. *Again.* "There's something I have to do."

CHAPTER THIRTY-EIGHT

J stepped out of the rideshare, my heart in my throat. Even though I faced down a crazed murderer earlier today, it was this meeting that made my whole body shake with fear.

In front of me stood the flat I grew up in. The broken screen hung on rusty hinges. From the depths of the neighbor's house, someone yelled obscenities. The other neighbor's kitchen windows were blacked out with newspaper – a sure sign that inside they were cooking drugs. Old car parts and overflowing bins littered the pavement.

It had been my home once, but it wasn't anymore.

I took a deep breath, climbed the steps, and shoved my key in the lock. Pushing the door open a crack with my boot, I checked she wasn't waiting in the hall to murder me. If she did, I honestly wouldn't blame her. Seeing and hearing nothing, I pushed the door open the rest of the way and stepped inside.

"Hey, Mum."

She glanced up from the kitchen table. The red rings around her eyes made her look older. When she registered my presence, her whole face collapsed with pent-up emotion. "Mina? Where have you been? I was so worried when you didn't reply to my messages. I was about to call the police!"

A wave of defensiveness welled up inside me, but I bit it back. My lower lip quivered. "I know, Mum. I'm sorry."

"You're—"

"I'm *sorry*. I've been acting like a real cow lately." I set my bag down in the hallway. "Can I make some tea? I'd really like to talk."

Mum nodded toward the kitchen. Her whole body sagged in her seat, and she wrung her hands together. I studied her as I filled the kettle and set it on the stove. Why didn't she run at me to hug me and touch me, the way she always did? Something kept her in her seat, staring at me with wary eyes. I hated myself for hurting her so deeply.

"Where have you been?" she said, her voice hoarse. "Why didn't you answer my calls? I called the shop, but Allan told me you were at Baddesley Hall. Then I heard there was a murder and a bomb scare. A bomb scare, Mina! You should have told me you were okay."

As I collected our two favorite cups and some biscuits from the tin, I noticed the kitchen had been thoroughly cleaned. There was still a faint smattering of glitter everywhere, but that was only because glitter was the herpes of the craft world – no matter how carefully you wash, you can't stop it spreading.

"I know. I really am sorry. I wanted to call, but the police wouldn't let us make calls out while the Hall was in lockdown. It really wasn't as exciting as they made out – just some dumb local kids playing a hoax." *Minimize it as much as possible, or she's not going to accept what you say next.*

"What were you even doing up there, anyway? Is this your life now that you're dating Morrie, swanning around in grand houses and being too good to talk to your mother?"

"Please don't think that! First of all, I'm not dating Morrie. Cynthia Lachlan invited me to their fancy Jane Austen weekend because I helped clear her husband's name in Mrs. Scarlett's murder. I wish you'd been able to see Baddesley Hall, Mum. It was insane. The room I stayed in was four times the size of this entire flat. There was a gilded fireplace!"

"It sounds special," Mum said, her voice closing up.

I found the sugar bowl hidden behind a stack of soap-making instruction sheets that still bore the scars of the Great Glitter Unicorn Poop Attack. "If I'm ever invited again, I'll take you with me. I think you'd really enjoy it."

The kettle boiled. I poured our tea to our individual tastes, and set hers down in front of her. Mum didn't touch it, her eyes following me as I moved around the table and sat down opposite her.

I sipped my tea, the hot liquid giving me the courage to say what I needed to say. "I'm sorry. I know I've said that a hundred times, but I need to say it again. I've been ignoring you because I was angry, and that was wrong. I promise I won't do that anymore."

"I don't understand you anymore!" Mum shot back. "I'm trying to look after you and keep you safe! I thought that's why you came home, because with your eyesight you're going to need so much help. But ever since Ashley was killed and you started working at the bookshop, you've been pushing me away. You snap at me whenever I try to help. You don't listen to me. You're acting like a spoiled teenager, and that's not like you at all!"

"You're right, I have been acting horribly. That's on me, too. I resented having to come back to England. I wanted to be in New York, working in fashion. I didn't want things to change, and I took that resentment out on you." I set down my cup. "It stops right now, all of it. From now on, I promise I'm going to tell you what's going on in my life and to let you know what I need so you can help. I'd better start by letting you know that I went to see an ophthalmologist in Barchester last week. I went because I've been seeing strange lights blowing up in front of my eyes – flickers of neon colors."

Mum gasped, covering her mouth with her hands. "Mina, no. Why didn't you tell me?"

"It's okay, Mum. I was scared. I kept it a secret because talking about it made it real, and if it was real it meant I was going blind. But the important thing was that I *did* tell someone – my friend Allan. He convinced me to make the appointment, and I'm glad I did. I like my new specialist, Dr. Clements. I'm glad she's going to be looking after me. I'll take you to meet her next time I have an appointment."

"What did she say about the lights?"

I sucked in a breath. "She told me that the degeneration in my retina is occurring at a faster rate than my New York doctor initially thought. She believes I have around eighteen months left before I lose my sight completely."

Mum wailed. Tears rolled down her cheeks, dropping onto the 'Soapgasm' posters spread across the table. I rested my hand on hers, making a mental note to tease her about that horrible name at a later point.

"It's okay. It truly is. When I was trapped in the house this weekend, it made me realize that everything I've been so afraid of was going to happen, and I could handle it. All the stuff I thought was important isn't what really matters in life. I might not be able to be a fashion designer anymore, but that doesn't mean I'm going to curl up into a corner and die. That's not me, and I'm sick of acting like it is. So please don't cry. Because I'm done crying about it."

"Oh, Mina." Mum's tears dripped on my arm. "You're handling this so well."

"I'm not really, but I'm trying to get better." I gave her a weak smile. "With that said, I've decided that I'm moving out."

What?

I am?

The words just fell out of my mouth. I hadn't intended to say them, but as soon as they hung in the air between us I knew they were right.

"You're... what?" Mum's mouth twisted in confusion.

"I'm moving out. I can't live here anymore. I'm twenty-three years old. I lived on my own for four years in a foreign country. I can't expect to move back into *your* space and be happy. I need to be independent."

"But who's going to look after you?"

"*I* am," I said. "I realized that ever since I got the news, I've been so busy moping and mourning that I haven't done any thinking about how I'm going to live after I lose my sight. I don't have that luxury anymore. And you know what? People have been living without their eyesight for thousands of years *and* doing awesome things. James Holman circumnavigated the globe on foot. Helen Keller was a political activist. Stevie Wonder captivates millions with his music. I've been reading about this bloke called Homer, who wrote the most famous story in the world."

Mum's brow furrowed. "Some blind bloke wrote *Wonky Donkey*? Did he draw the pictures, too?"

"Um... yes. Sure he did. My *point* is, if they can deal, so can I." I pushed a pamphlet across the table to her. "Dr. Clements gave me this. These are programs that will teach me how to use a cane and go shopping and even put my makeup on when I can't see. And I could have a guide dog. I've always wanted a puppy!"

Mum picked up one of Dr. Clements' glossy brochures. "These look so expensive, Mina."

"There's funding available to help get the equipment I need, and anything else I'll just have to save up for. Luckily, I've learned some pretty neat tricks if I ever need an additional income stream," I grinned at her. "It's time that I stopped moping about what I can't change and start embracing the good things in my life."

"But moving out is such a big step... are you sure about this?"

"I've never been more sure about anything in my life," I picked up one of her posters. "Except that 'Soapgasm' is a terrible name. What were you thinking? Can I redraw these for you? Seriously, they're terrible."

She threw her arms around me. "Oh, Mina. I'm so glad you're back."

"Me too."

"Let's never fight again." Mum planted a kiss on my forehead. "What about your father?"

I reached into my pocket and touched the note. "I don't know. I'm not sure I'm ready to reach out to him just yet. But I need to count on your support if I decide to. Just because you don't want a relationship with him, doesn't mean I don't."

"Fair enough."

I grinned. "If I do, you'll be the first to know."

Mum's smile lit up our dingy kitchen. "Now that I've got you back, can I just ask one important question?"

"Sure."

"Are you going to marry James Moriarty? Because it would be much easier to get all the equipment if you had a rich husband to pay for it all. And maybe he could get me a new car while he was at it. Oh, and one of those tubs that massage your feet while you watch the telly, and a mink coat, and a Tiffany necklace..."

CHAPTER THIRTY-NINE

"*E*xcuse me." A customer approached the desk and set down a children's paperback adventure book. "I purchased this book about a month ago."

"Yes, I remember you." I smiled. I'd sold the woman a racy reverse harem romance by KT Strange for her beach holiday, and the adventure story for her niece. "Did your niece enjoy her present?"

"Oh, she hasn't taken her head out of that book I gave her," the woman smiled. "That's not what I came about. I'm not happy with the choice you made for me. I wanted to get lost in a whirlwind romance, but I finished this book in a matter of minutes and let me tell you, the plot was rather juvenile and I didn't feel the love interest *at all*. Next time, you need to listen to what a customer is asking for and—"

"Um..." I stared at the cover, struggling to contain my laughter. "Ma'am, this is the book we chose for your niece. The book you gave her was supposed to be for you."

"Oh." The woman raised her hand to her mouth. "Oh, no."

She dropped the book on the counter and dashed off. Unable

to contain myself any longer, I collapsed into giggles. Heathcliff looked over the top of his book.

"Don't mind me." I wiped the tears from my eyes. "It feels good to be back in the shop."

It *was* good. Hayes had already stopped in to let us know that Christina would be going to a psychiatric facility, which seemed like the best solution. I hoped they'd let her keep her bonnets. The tear in Gerald's shirt cuff matched a scrap of fabric found at one of the previous Argleton Jewel Thief scenes, and a search of his house revealed a stash of jewels nicked from the homes of his British Heritage clients. Hannah dumped him and had started frequenting the shop, much to Heathcliff's dismay and my delight. Morrie hadn't called Quoth 'little birdie' once, and the boys were bickering less than usual. Lydia was as annoying as ever, but she'd spent most of her time exploring the village and sorting out her newest scheme, so we'd hardly had to worry about her. The only thing that could have improved life was if Heathcliff would hang some Christmas decorations.

BANG. BANG. BANG. Lydia dragged an oversized suitcase down the stairs. Morrie had made the mistake of lending her his credit card so she could buy an appropriate wardrobe. Although considering where she was going, perhaps it was good she got some practice lifting heavy things.

"I still can't believe you joined the army," I admonished her.

"Oh, Mina, stop fussing. It will be such good fun!" Lydia clapped her hands. "If I'm to find a soldier to marry me, I must go where the soldiers are. Besides, I thought you'd be pleased that I am throwing off the patriarchal yoke and taking the King's shilling—"

"It's actually the Queen's shilling now," I pointed out.

"Don't vex me with your feminism on today of all days!" Lydia spun around, revealing the tailored scarlet military jacket with gold braid and epaulets she'd purchased from Mrs. Maitland.

"Don't I look absolutely stunning? Don't you think I shall land myself a wonderful soldier to marry?"

I didn't have the heart to tell her that she'd be in fatigues as soon as she arrived on the base. Some problems were not mine to solve. "Sure, Lydia. You look amazing."

"Well, won't you all see me off, then?" She thrust her hands on her hips.

"Goodbye," Heathcliff muttered, without looking up from his book. From his perch on top of the chandelier, Quoth shook his head vehemently.

Excellent self-preservation skills, I said inside my head. *You're much safer up there.*

Morrie slumped over and wrapped his arms around her. "Good luck, Lydia," he said. "We're going to miss your annoying face around here."

"Does that mean you wish I could stay?" Lydia batted her eyelashes at Morrie.

"No!" yelled Heathcliff, Morrie, and I in unison.

"Croak!" seconded Quoth.

"Meow!" added Grimalkin, for good measure.

Lydia laughed. She threw her arms around me. "I shall miss you most of all, Mina. You remind me a little of my older sister Lizzie, although not as bossy or plain. I still can't believe she marries that Mr. Darcy."

I laughed. "I'll miss you too, Lydia. You come visit if you're ever back in Argleton."

"I shan't think so. Not for a very long time!" She blew kisses as she hurried into the street to place her bags in the back of a waiting rideshare. I watched her go, half of me terrified she wouldn't last an hour, the other half certain she'd be a general in no time.

As soon as her car backed away from the curb and took off down the street, Morrie slumped into a chair. "Thank the gods."

I smiled. "Hey, we all liked Lydia in the end."

"I've run the most successful criminal empire in the developed world, but that woman tries my every nerve." He lifted a limp hand to me. "Fetch me a cup of tea, would you?"

"Fetch it yourself." I punched him in the arm. "I have some boxes to unpack."

"How can you have more stuff for Jo's apartment?" Morrie had helped me move into the spare room at Jo's house last night. It was a tiny room, barely big enough for the single bed I'd found on Gumtree and a rack of clothing. But it was a palace compared to my last room, which wasn't a room at all, but a conservatory with the windows taped over with cardboard. Jo's place was amazing – she had a rain shower and heating and an espresso machine in the kitchen (and an anatomical skeleton in the bathroom, but we won't talk about *that*), and absolutely no mother in sight.

"I told her, she should have just moved in here," Heathcliff muttered, turning the page.

I'd been sorely tempted when he made the offer, but in my heart, I knew I wasn't ready to accept. We may have all said the three scary words, but everything with me and the guys was still so complicated. I needed time to be on my own in the world before I took that step. But at least Jo lived nearby, so I could come and see them any time I wanted, without forking out a fortune for rideshares or walking through my old, scary neighborhood.

"Nope, not more clothes." I dragged a box from behind the desk. "Christmas decorations."

"No." Heathcliff's book clattered to the floor.

"Yes!" I threw open the box, revealing strings of bright, glittering tinsel. Instantly, my eyes were drawn to the iridescent colors, and the rest of the room fell into shadow. "It's my mum's newest scheme. Apparently, Sylvia's shop's been shut down by a hazmat team after one of their make-your-own-soap kits exploded. So now she's selling these 'designer' Christmas decorations at a two hundred percent markup." I held up a string of tinsel hung with miniature books. "Take the other end of this. We're going to hang it along the front of Heathcliff's desk."

"No, we're not." Heathcliff folded his arms.

"Yes. We are. No arguments. No more Ms. Nice Mina. If I'm going to stay working here, you're going to let me try my creative ideas. I need this shop to turn a profit so I can earn some more money, because I'm in need of adaptive equipment and a guide dog. And also a new pair of Docs."

"Meow?" Grimalkin's head popped up from behind the armadillo, her whiskers twitching with concern.

"Don't worry, kitty," I patted Grimalkin's head. "I promise my doggo won't chase you."

"Meow!" Grimalkin swiped at the tinsel, attacking one of the tiny books with her teeth, as if trying to demonstrate what would happen to any guide dog that dared cross the threshold of the shop.

"Where's all this sass coming from?" Morrie asked as he shoved Heathcliff aside to hold up the tinsel. "Don't get me wrong, it excites me. It's just not like you to lay down the law."

"It's coming from me. I've decided I don't want to end up like Christina."

"You mean, locked away in an institution tal?" Heathcliff ventured with a twinkle in his eye. "Telling some cock'n'bull story about how a raven transformed into a man?"

"Croak!" added Quoth proudly.

"Or do you mean a sword-wielding maniac? I think we can all agree that isn't the ideal outcome for any situation." Morrie rubbed his chin. "You're way too uncoordinated for a sword."

I kicked out my leg and pretended to swing at him. Unfortunately, I misjudged the angle and ended up swinging so far forward that I lost my balance and fell over.

"Fine. I concede your point." I held up my hand, and Morrie

helped me up. "There are only two sword-wielding maniacs around here, and it's you two. I'm just sorry I didn't get to see you in action."

"Next time," Heathcliff promised.

"I blame the bird," Morrie added. "If it wasn't for him saving the day, I'd have been able to show off my double *riposte* with spinning jump kick."

"Croak!"

I laughed. "What I meant was, Christina was so consumed by inaction. She couldn't face up to her father and the things he'd done, so she continued to exist in the box he stuffed her into, until one day she just snapped. I realized I'd been doing that with my eyes, putting myself into this box where I couldn't enjoy the things I loved without vision. And I've been ignoring things I didn't want to think about, like the time-travelling room and meeting Victoria and my father's letter and this whole 'covered in blood' thing. Now I see how limiting it is to put yourself in a box and hide away, how Christina couldn't see a world where she just told her father, 'I'm gay, and I hate Jane Austen', and lived her own life. And now, she'll never get that chance."

"In an odd way, I admire her," Morrie said, holding up a little shepherd figurine. "She created a little welcome chaos around here. Oooh, a nativity scene. Can we put this over on that table?"

"Yes. I actually had an idea that we could make a stable out of books." I stacked two hardcovers on their sides and placed a third on top to make a roof. Morrie arranged the porcelain figures inside.

And the armadillo could be God. Quoth shoved him into place with his beak.

"No," Heathcliff growled.

I ignored him. "And then we just need the baby Jesus and... Morrie! You can't have Joseph and the first wise man snogging!"

"Why not? I thought that was the sort of thing that went on in barns," Morrie grinned wickedly.

"Not this one." I moved the figures back into place, and grinned at Heathcliff. "You haven't said much about Christina. I remember you feeling empathy for her when you saw how much she feared her father."

Heathcliff shifted in his chair. "Don't remind me. I just wish that fear hadn't turned her ugly."

I thought I knew what he was alluding to, but I wanted him to talk about it. "Care to elaborate?"

"Hindley," Heathcliff breathed. The word seethed against my skin, carrying all Heathcliff's malice with it. "All my life he treated me with cruelty. He said I was a monster and I believed it. How could I not, when I was so different from all of them at *Wuthering Heights*? When I heard Cathy say that she could never marry me, of course I knew it was because of this," he rubbed his cheek, indicating his dark skin. "Christina's father treated her in a different but no less destructive way. He made her into a monster. She deserved to be free of him."

"But did she have to kill Alice?"

"Of course not. She was desperate. I could understand that. I can't forgive it, but I can understand."

The shop bell tinkled, interrupting our conversation. Quoth shrunk into a corner. Heathcliff picked up his book and indicated I should deal with the customer.

A man entered the room, wearing a sharp suit and pressed white shirt. He was handsome in a real-estate agent kind of way – slick hair and boyish features. He marched straight up to the counter and extended his hand to Heathcliff.

"Biographies are up the stairs and to the left," Heathcliff muttered without even looking up. He knew the sort.

"Ah, but what if I don't want a biography?"

"Then get out." Heathcliff turned the page.

The man laughed, extending out a hand. "Mr. Heathcliff, sir. Allow me to introduce myself. My name is Grey Lachlan. Let me guess, that tall fellow is James Moriarty. And you must be the indomitable Miss Mina Wilde."

He turned to me with his slick smile, and a strange wobbly feeling settled in my stomach. Instantly, I wanted to curl up into a ball and hide from this man, but I couldn't say why.

If Grey Lachlan sensed my unease, he didn't acknowledge it. His grin spread wide across his earnest face. "My wife has told me how you all solved the murder of her friend Gladys and saved the Jane Austen Experience. We're incredibly grateful."

"Yes, well." Heathcliff sat down and folded his hands across his chest. "Biographies are up the stairs and to the left."

"No, no. I've come for something even better than books." Grey Lachlan set his briefcase on the counter and plunged his hands into the depths. He pulled out an envelope and set it on the table in front of Heathcliff. I started when I noticed the envelope was sealed with wax. "I would like to buy your bookshop. And I'm willing to make you an offer you cannot refuse."

"Think again," Heathcliff growled. "I refuse."

Grey waved the envelope in front of his face. "You should look inside, Mr. Heathcliff."

"No."

Grey sighed. He dropped the envelope on the desk. "Let me be clear. I'm a powerful man, more powerful than you could ever imagine. You do not want me as an enemy. If you do not cooperate with me, I have other means at my disposal. I suggest you give this offer due consideration, because I *will* have Nevermore Bookshop, even if I have to step over your dead bodies to get it."

TO BE CONTINUED

A murdered writer threatens to derail Mina's author event, and a biblical plague threatens her sanity in book 4, *Memoirs of a Garroter.*

Can't get enough of Mina and her boys? Read a free alternative scene from Quoth's point-of-view along with other bonus scenes and extra stories when you sign up for the Steffanie Holmes newsletter.

FROM THE AUTHOR

As I was writing this book, my country was hit with one of the greatest tragedies we've ever faced. 50 citizens going about their daily prayers at two mosques in Christchurch were gunned down by a terrorist. The attacks left the whole country in shock – this was more innocent people dead than are usually murdered in New Zealand in a *year*. Is this who we are? Are we no longer safe? Were we ever really safe?

In the days that followed, I struggled to put words on the page. In the face of such an overwhelming act of hate, I couldn't see the point. What good did my silly stories about love and acceptance do against such a world?

It turns out, everything.

Because this crime was only possible because there wasn't enough love. Because the community that was attacked had said for some time that they didn't feel safe. Because small acts of love, just like small acts of hate, can add up to a lot. With love, attacks like Christchurch wouldn't happen. With love, everyone would be allowed to feel safe.

Over the days and weeks following the attack, a nation came together to mourn. A government took swift action. And in my little home library, through a haze of tears and with love in my heart, I wrote THE END on this book.

Pride & Premeditation has become my favourite book in the whole series. While my country did its soul-searching and came out strong and mighty and filled with *aroha* (love), Mina dug deep and found her strength. In this book, she accepts what's happening to her for the first time and starts to look forward, instead of grasping for the past.

She sees the love she has – not just from the guys, but from her mother and her friends and herself – and in the safety of that love, she can free herself of fear. She finds her strength. She feels safe. She is free.

What makes us different – our race, our religion, our wonky eyes – isn't as important as what unites us – our love, our humanity, our strength.

I hope, I wish, I believe… that with more love in the world, we can all be free.

Kia kaha, aroha nui.

(Stand strong, with love).

Steffanie

NEVERMORE BOOKSHOP 4

MEMOIRS OF A GARROTER

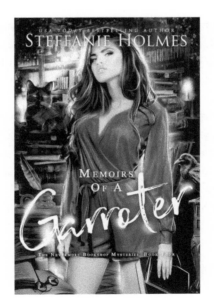

READ NOW

Murder is bad for business, especially when the hot local crime writer is garrotted between the shelves!

With grudging permission from Heathcliff, Mina Wilde has transformed Nevermore Bookshop. She's running author events, hosting Quoth's art show, and using her creative flair to attract more customers. But when crime writer Danny Sledge is murdered moments before his writing workshop, the bookshop goes from bustling to broke.

No one in the village will set foot inside Nevermore. What if the murderer is targeting the bookshop? What if it's connected to Mina's father and the mysterious room? All Mina knows is that if she doesn't solve the crime soon, she can kiss her livelihood goodbye.

Add in a plague of locusts, an emotional school visit, and a magical visitor from the past, and poor Mina has her work cut out for her. Luckily, she has Heathcliff, Morrie, and Quoth to help... that is – if they can keep their hands off her, or each other...

The Nevermore Bookshop Mysteries are what you get when all your book boyfriends come to life. Join a brooding antihero, a master criminal, a cheeky raven, and a heroine with a big heart (and an even bigger book collection) in this brand new steamy reverse harem paranormal mystery series by *USA Today* best-selling author Steffanie Holmes.

READ NOW

Dear Fae,

Don't even THINK about attacking my castle.

This science geek witch and her four magic-wielding men are about to get medieval on your ass.

I'm Maeve Crawford. For years I've had my future mathematically calculated down to the last detail; Leave my podunk Arizona town, graduate MIT, get into the space program, be the first woman on Mars, get a cat (not necessarily in this order).

Then fairies killed my parents and shot the whole plan to hell.

I've inherited a real, honest-to-goodness English castle – complete with turrets, ramparts, and four gorgeous male tenants, who I'm totally *not* in love with.

Not at all.

It would be crazy to fall for four guys at once, even though they're totally gorgeous and amazing and wonderful and kind.

But not as crazy as finding out I'm a witch. A week ago, I didn't even believe magic existed, and now I'm up to my ears in spells and prophetic dreams and messages from the dead.

When we're together – and I'm talking in the Biblical sense – the five of us wield a powerful magic that can banish the fae forever. They intend to stop us by killing us all.

I can't science my way out of this mess.

Forget NASA, it's going to take all my smarts just to survive Briarwood Castle.

The Castle of Earth and Embers is the first in a brand new steamy reverse harem romance by *USA Today* bestselling author, Steffanie Holmes. This full-length book glitters with love, heartache, hope, grief, dark magic, fairy trickery, steamy scenes, British slang, meat pies, second chances, and the healing powers of a good cup of tea. Read on only if you believe one just isn't enough.

Available from Amazon and in KU.

OTHER BOOKS BY STEFFANIE HOLMES

This list is in recommended reading order, although each couple's story can be enjoyed as a standalone.

Nevermore Bookshop Mysteries

A Dead and Stormy Night

Of Mice and Murder

Pride and Premeditation

Memoirs of a Garroter

Prose and Cons

A Novel Way to Die

How Heathcliff Stole Christmas

Kings of Miskatonic Prep

Shunned

Initiated

Possessed

Ignited

Broken Muses of Manderley Academy

Ghosted

Haunted

Briarwood Reverse Harem series

The Castle of Earth and Embers

The Castle of Fire and Fable

The Castle of Water and Woe

The Castle of Wind and Whispers

The Castle of Spirit and Sorrow

Crookshollow Gothic Romance series

Art of Cunning (Alex & Ryan)

Art of the Hunt (Alex & Ryan)

Art of Temptation (Alex & Ryan)

The Man in Black (Elinor & Eric)

Watcher (Belinda & Cole)

Reaper (Belinda & Cole)

Wolves of Crookshollow series

Digging the Wolf (Anna & Luke)

Writing the Wolf (Rosa & Caleb)

Inking the Wolf (Bianca & Robbie)

Wedding the Wolf (Willow & Irvine)

Want to be informed when the next Steffanie Holmes paranormal romance story goes live? Sign up for the newsletter at www.steffanieholmes.com/newsletter to get the scoop, and score a free collection of bonus scenes and stories to enjoy!

ABOUT THE AUTHOR

Steffanie Holmes is the author of steamy historical and paranormal romance. Her books feature clever, witty heroines, wild shifters, cunning witches and alpha males who *always* get what they want.

Before becoming a writer, Steffanie worked as an archaeologist and museum curator. She loves to explore historical settings and ancient conceptions of love and possession. From Dark Age Europe to crumbling gothic estates, Steffanie is fascinated with how love can blossom between the most unlikely characters. She also writes dark fantasy / science fiction under S. C. Green.

Steffanie lives in New Zealand with her husband and a horde of cantankerous cats.

STEFFANIE HOLMES NEWSLETTER

Can't get enough of Mina and her boys? Read a free alternative scene from Quoth's point-of-view along with other bonus scenes and extra stories when you sign up for the Steffanie Holmes newsletter.

Come hang with Steffanie
www.steffanieholmes.com
hello@steffanieholmes.com

Milton Keynes UK
Ingram Content Group UK Ltd.
UKHW011304281023
431503UK00001B/25